Not The One

Deirdre Savoy

BET Publications, LLC
http://www.bet.com
http://www.arabesquebooks.com

ARABESQUE BOOKS are published by

BET Publishing, LLC
c/o BET BOOKS
One BET Plaza
1900 W Place NE
Washington, DC 20018-1211

All Kensington Titles, Imprints, and Distributed Lines are available at special quantity discounts for bulk purchases for sales promotions, premiums, fund-raising, and educational or institutional use. Special book excerpts or customized printings can also be created to fit specific needs. For details, write or phone the office of the Kensington special sales manager: Kensington Publishing Corp., 850 Third Avenue, New York, NY 10022, attn: Special Sales Department, Phone: 1-800-221-2647.

First Printing: November 2003
10 9 8 7 6 5 4 3 2 1

Printed in the United States of America

For my grandmother Ethelind Farr Reid. I talk to you all the time, Grandma. I miss having you answer back.

And for my grandmother Gertrude Reid. We are blessed that you chose to join our family. I love you.

ACKNOWLEDGMENTS

Thanks to my agent, James B. Finn, whose guidance, expertise and patience keep me sane.

Thanks to my writer friends—you know who you are—who encourage me and inspire me with their own work.

Thanks to my son and daughter, Nicholas and Francesca, who make me so proud. Now I've used both your names in books, so quit bugging me. You can read them when you're older.

One

She was a tigress.

That much was clear. You could see it in the way her cat's eyes ensnared you in their hazel-green gaze, as if measuring how tasty a morsel you might be. You saw it in the slender graceful lines of her body, a predator's ease of motion. It was as if the song "Man-eater" should automatically begin to play the moment she stepped into the room, as a warning to unsuspecting and susceptible men. Even though she held a crying child in each arm and one more clutched at her leg, the impression remained.

Matthew Peterson swallowed. For although she looked at him with an expression of relief and yearning, it wasn't his skill as a man that she wanted. He'd been on his way out the door for a late-night run when she'd called him twenty minutes ago to tell him one of her charges was sick. For not entirely unselfish reasons, he'd volunteered to make the only house call of his medical career.

Her delicious red mouth stretched into a smile. "Thank God you're here."

She stepped back, allowing him to enter. He stepped inside, shutting the door behind him. "Which one is the culprit?"

"This one." She nodded to the lone boy of the group. "Justin. He started crying an hour ago. The others chimed in out of sympathy. I took his temperature with the ear thingie. It's 104."

She'd told him as much on the phone. He set down his bag and took the infant from her. As he did so, the back of his hand grazed the curve of her breast. "Excuse me," he said with little contrition.

She stepped away from him, clutching the other baby more tightly to her chest. A sardonic smile tilted one corner of her mouth. "Not a problem."

He couldn't gauge if she'd felt the electrical jolt of that simple contact between them, but he knew she knew he had. Well, he wasn't here to play footsie, anyway, much as he wished that was the purpose of his visit. "Is there somewhere I can examine him?"

"Oh, of course. How about the changing table in the bedroom?"

"That's fine." She led the way down a long hall that had offshoots for a living room and kitchen. He knew that at one time, her brother had lived in this apartment, but once he'd married the woman who owned the building, they'd converted it to a family play area. The large bedroom still held two cribs, a toddler bed, a dresser, and a large changing table.

Matthew laid the boy down on the table. After checking the infant's eyes, nose, and throat and retaking his temperature, he made his diagnosis. "He's got a cold."

She blinked and her brow furrowed. "A cold with that high a fever?"

"It's not uncommon in infants this young. How old is he? Three months?"

"Two and a half."

"Their internal temperature regulation systems aren't fully developed yet. But we do need to get his fever down. Can you bring me a large bowl of luke-warm water and a washcloth?"

"Sure. Let me put Arianna down." The baby in her arms had fretted herself to sleep. She laid her in the crib and covered her with a blanket.

The toddler, Emily, tugged at her skirt. "Justie be okay?"

"Justin will be fine, sweetheart." She took the little girl's hand. "Dr. Peterson is going to make Justin all better, but he needs us to help him. Can you do that?"

Emily nodded.

"Come on, then."

As she led the little girl toward the bathroom, Nina glanced back at him. He saw concern in her hazel eyes, but also the faith that he would make things right. He offered her a smile of encouragement. She gave back a wan one before turning and leaving the room with Emily in tow.

When she'd gone, he stripped the baby down to his diaper. Justin Thorne fought him all the way, balling his little fists and stiffening his body. He hadn't cared much for Matthew's examination and sought to preserve himself from further indignities.

Matthew cradled the baby in the crook of his arm. "Relax, slugger," he crooned to the baby, not quite baby talk but not adult-speak either. "We'll have you feeling better in no time."

The baby's response was to sneeze right in his face.

Matthew took his handkerchief from his back pocket and wiped his face. "Thanks a lot, buddy. See if I make another house call for you."

"Making threats to babies? Isn't that against the Hippocratic oath?"

"Not if they've sneezed on you."

"I see." She lifted the basin she carried a fraction of an inch. "What do you want me to do with this?"

He motioned for her to set the water down on one end of the table. He laid the baby at the other end. Deprived of his source of comfort, the baby began to cry again.

"You're going to like this even less," Matthew warned the infant. He took the washcloth from Nina and dipped it into the water with one hand, then squeezed off the excess. The instant the cool water touched his skin, the infant's cries intensified and his body stiffened. His little body shook in anger and from the shock of the cool water on his heated skin.

"You're not kidding, he doesn't like it."

His gaze slid to Nina, who hovered next to him. He noted the expression on her face, a mixture of concern for the baby and outrage on his behalf. She was a second away from asking him if this was truly necessary or perhaps from snatching the baby from the table herself. To forestall a mutiny, he said,

"He's cold, mad, and wet, but other than that, he'll be fine."

She cast him a look full of skepticism. "If you say so."

"I do. He'll need a change of clothes." He added the last to give her something to do. In the few minutes it took her to find a new diaper and new stretchie outfit, his ministrations with the washcloth had worked. The baby's temperature was noticeably cooler. His heartbeat was a little rapid due to the crying and the cold, but once he was dry and warm and once the liquid Tylenol Matthew managed to get the baby to swallow started to work, that would settle down, too.

When she came back, he asked her, "Do you want to do the honors?"

"Why?"

"He's a little too free in sharing his bodily fluids with me. If you don't mind, I'd rather tuck Emily in bed." While the adults were busy, Emily sat on her bed sucking her index and middle fingers.

She nodded toward the bed. "Be my guest."

He went over to the little girl and squatted down beside her. At one time, he had been her pediatrician. The first time he'd met Nina was in the hospital after Emily had contracted a case of viral meningitis. But the girl clearly didn't remember him. "Hi, sweetheart."

She popped her fingers out of her mouth long enough to ask, "Justie be okay?"

"Justin will be fine. Now it's time for you to go to bed."

She nodded sleepily. He helped her settle under

the covers. Instinctively he placed a kiss on her fore-head. "Good night, sweetheart."

She grabbed his face with her wet-saliva fingers and kissed his most prominent feature, his nose. "G'night."

Smiling, Matthew stood. Her affectionate gesture was the mark of a child who was well loved and who loved others in return. He turned to Nina. She had her back to him, still changing the baby. Now that his attention focused on her, he realized she sang to the baby in a low, off-key voice. That surprised him, considering that her brother was Nathan Ward, an internationally known singer. It also charmed him, as she wasn't inhibited about displaying her lack of talent in order to soothe the baby.

She stopped singing abruptly and picked up the baby, cradling him in her arms. "There now, isn't that better?"

"How is our guy doing?"

She turned to face him. "Much better. Thank *youch!*" She stared down at the baby, a surprised expression on her face. "The little cannibal bit me."

"He's hungry." Matthew understood the feeling, though it wasn't nutritional sustenance that he lacked. "Jenny breast-feeds, doesn't she?"

"Well, cut that out. There's nothing in there for you." She lifted the baby to her shoulder. "Let's get you something to eat."

Matthew turned out the light and followed her to the kitchen. As he walked behind her, he noticed a slight hitch in her walk, as if she favored one leg. It was nearly midnight. Maybe she was just tired, but he wanted to make sure she was all right before he left.

She shook her head. "You don't have to do that."

"I know, but I want to. I want to make sure my patient is well fed and sound asleep before I go."

She looked as if she might protest, but she sat down in one of the kitchen chairs. He warmed a bottle from the refrigerator in the microwave and shook it. Otherwise, pockets of hot milk could burn the baby's sensitive mouth. All the while, he watched Nina lavish her affection on the baby. She ran her hand over his delicate scalp, tickled his tummy, and cooed to him in a soothing voice. He suspected that one of these days, this tigress would be one hell of a mother to her own children.

He couldn't stand there forever, watching her. He came to stand beside her and extended the bottle toward her. "Here you go."

"Thank you." She offered the bottle to the baby, who sucked greedily.

Although he hadn't been invited, he slid into the seat next to her. "If you don't mind me asking, how did you get roped into watching three kids at once?"

"Actually, I've got four. Andrew fell asleep watching TV in the other room and hasn't been heard from since. My cousin Yasmin punked out on me at the last minute. Something about a party for some firemen who have this calendar out."

"So she left you in the lurch."

"In a toss-up between gorgeous hunks and me with a bunch of crying babies, the gorgeous hunks won." She shrugged. "To be honest, I only invited Yasmin along for companionship. Well babies I can handle. Sick babies freak me out."

"That's understandable." He could tell her horror stories of parents who telephoned him in the dead of night, hysterical over complaints more minor than hers. "I'm glad you called."

"I think our friend here is asleep." She placed the bottle on the table. "I'll be right back," she said, but when she tried to rise, she winced in pain.

He remembered the stiffness he'd noticed in her gait. "Why didn't you tell me you'd hurt yourself? What happened?"

"It's nothing. I banged my hip on the doorway earlier."

"Do you want me to have a look at it?"

She fastened a green-eyed glare on him. "Why, Doctor, are you trying to play doctor with me?"

Her voice held a note of arrogance. She knew he was attracted to her. She *expected* him to be attracted to her. She wasn't wrong, but he wasn't so needy that he had to trick unsuspecting women into showing him their goodies, either. "You're a beautiful woman, Nina."

"Thank you."

"But there are enough beautiful women in the world that I don't have to waste my time on one who isn't interested."

The skepticism disappeared from her gaze, replaced by a look that said she wasn't sure if she should be insulted or not.

"Funny thing about us doctors," he continued.

"We like to examine injured people to make sure they haven't done permanent damage to themselves."

"All right."

He took the baby from her. "I'll put him in bed, and then you can show me what happened."

When he returned to the kitchen he helped her to her feet. Both of them recognized the problem at once: panty hose.

"Close your eyes. I'd go in the other room, but it hurts too much to walk."

He sat and did as she asked, but all the while he imagined her sliding those stockings over smooth, shapely legs. He doubted reality could be much better than what his imagination conjured up.

"Okay," she said finally.

He didn't know where she'd hidden the panty hose and he didn't care. "Show me where you injured yourself."

She took a sideways step toward him, then lifted her skirt enough to show him a reddened patch of skin at her hip.

"Ouch."

"Exactly."

"Tell me if this hurts." He probed the edge of the area with his fingertips.

"Ouch."

He circled inward. The skin at the center was swollen and had already darkened somewhat from the rupturing of capillaries just under her skin.

"Ouch," she said more forcefully. "I thought you wanted me to tell you if it hurt?"

"I do. I never said I was going to stop." He moved upward about a half inch to press against her hip-bone. "How about here?"

"No."

So it was only muscle that was affected. While bone injury could be painful for months, a muscle bruise might be ugly but it would only be a nuisance for a few days. He went back to the spot, that had purpled even more just from his inspection. "You're probably going to have one hell of a bruise tomorrow."

She stepped away from him but made no move toward her seat. "I kinda figured out that part for myself."

"If you can, I want you to lie down and get something warm on that hip, a compress or a heating pad if you have one."

"We'll see what the babies have to say about that. Anything else?"

"Keep Justin away from the other children if possible. No sense in all three of them getting sick."

She nodded.

"I'd better go." Since she didn't protest, he stood and picked up his medical bag.

"I really do thank you for coming."

"You haven't seen my bill yet." Since she didn't so much as crack a smile, he had to assume she thought he'd actually do such a thing. He'd stuck his own neck out purely out of a desire to see her. He certainly wouldn't charge her for that.

He headed toward the door. He paused to let her open it for him. She leaned against the door frame with her hand on the knob. "Thanks again."

Matthew swallowed. He wondered if she knew how provocative she looked with her hair tussled, her shirt in disarray, and bare-legged. He guessed she didn't. She'd already shown him her disinterest and she wasn't trying to tempt him. Temptation pulled at him anyway—the desire to pull her into his arms, not only in a sexual way, but to comfort her. Coping with a sick child was hairy for veteran parents. Although she'd been concerned for the baby's health, she hadn't gotten hysterical on him as some of his patients' mothers would have.

After bidding her good night, he went down to his car and started the engine. Nina Ward was both a tigress in need of taming and, he believed after watching her with the children, a woman of strong maternal instincts. With a twinge of regret that he wouldn't be the one to help her out on either level, he pulled away from the curb and headed for home.

The following Monday, Nina Ward walked into her office building off Bleeker Street in Lower Manhattan just after eight o'clock in the morning. Or more appropriately, their office. She shared space and a receptionist/secretary with two other women, one an accountant, the other a book publicist. Aside from the savings on the exorbitant Manhattan rent, the arrangement afforded them the opportunity to refer their clients to one another, as the need for their services often overlapped.

Kim, the receptionist, wouldn't be in until almost nine o'clock. Nina headed straight for her office.

Monday mornings were reserved for sending rejection letters to those writers whom she would not take on as clients, the part of her job she liked the least. Ninety percent of the manuscripts she received were either unpublishable or were not quite right for her vision of the Nina Ward Literary Agency.

She preferred to handle contemporary mystery, romantic suspense, and mainstream fiction that dealt with realistic issues. That's what she read and felt comfortable with representing to editors. Yet folks insisted on sending her science fiction, which she didn't begin to understand or appreciate; so-called erotica that read like a string of letters from the front of *Penthouse* magazine; long historical sagas on the order of *Gone With the Wind* without the charm, southern or otherwise. Worst of all were the unabashedly autobiographical novels. Apparently most people thought their own lives were much more fascinating than anyone else did.

Yet writers, especially those just starting out, had delicate egos. It took courage for writers, even veterans, to send their work to an agent or editor they didn't know. Unlike most other agents, Nina didn't use form rejection letters. To her mind, that was like salting a fresh wound. She answered each writer personally.

The only letter she looked forward to writing was to a young woman whose story line, imagery, and characterizations had intrigued her. Yet the woman's prose was rife with grammatical errors and misspellings. Nina suggested she take a course in basic grammar, reedit her manuscript, and resubmit. If the woman took her advice, Nina wouldn't have any problem representing her.

Nina wrapped up her letter writing a little before noon. Her phone rang. She answered it herself, as she usually did unless she was with a client. "Nina Ward."

"Hello, Nina. It's me. I'm in New York."

A mixture of surprise, warmth, and relief flooded through her at hearing Ronald Carter's voice on the line. Her long-distance lover had been particularly distant of late. "Ron! You bastard. I don't hear from you for six months and you just show up?"

"I need to see you."

She ignored the dispassionate quality of his voice. "I need to see you, too. The usual place? Two o'clock?"

She thought she detected a slight hesitation before he said, "That's fine. I'll see you then."

Nina smiled as she hung up the phone. There were advantages to being your own boss, like being able to pack it in for the day whenever you wanted. She hadn't scheduled much for the afternoon, anyway, besides curling up in bed and reading a few manuscripts. She still intended to curl up in bed, but with a man, not a book.

She packed her things in her briefcase and headed for the door. She stopped briefly at the receptionist's desk. "I'll be out for the rest of the day. I won't be home until later, so if anything urgent comes up, call my cell."

The receptionist winked. "Have a good time."

Shaking her head, Nina snorted. Kim had worked

for her long enough to know that Nina never high-tailed it out of the office without an appointment or an explanation of where she was going—not unless Ron called. He called and she came running. Something about that arrangement had always disturbed her, but she pushed it out of her mind as she turned and headed out of the office. She still had time to pick up a bottle of champagne and a quick stop at Victoria's Secret on Fifty-seventh. She'd pick up some pricey confection that would last all of five minutes before Ron divested her of it. A thrill ran up her spine in anticipation of the lovemaking to follow.

The only chink in her otherwise perfect setup was the fact that Ron wanted more. In the last year or so, he'd begun to press her to marry him. She didn't doubt he'd ask her again this time. Part of her suspected the reason for his long absence was to prove to her that she missed him. She had, but that didn't change anything. A continent still separated his home in California from hers in New York, her agency was just taking off, and she didn't want to sidetrack her career with marriage and babies just yet. And most of all, she simply didn't love him, not the way a woman expects to love the man she plans to marry.

She didn't know if she was even capable of that kind of affection. Having grown up watching her mother, her grandmother, and her aunts, she almost hoped she wasn't. Maybe some sort of curse hung over the women of the Ward family, but every one of them had married young, only to have their man disappear, a victim of one of the three Ds:

death, divorce, or desertion. Her own father had flown the coop when she was only two months old. She didn't intend to end up one of them, a woman left alone to pine for a man who couldn't go the long haul. She'd rather be alone than go through that.

The only problem was, she wanted children. Her role as frequent baby-sitter for the Ward clan wasn't entirely without selfish motives. Having none of her own to pamper, she craved the occasional kid fix with her brother's children. She imagined she could always go the sperm-in-a-can route, but when it came to children she wanted them the old-fashioned way: with a husband. Kids needed a father, someone to look up to, to be there for them, to share their lives. Having felt the lack of one in her own life, she would never bring a child into the world without at least the prospect of a father. But if she couldn't find a man she loved or trusted enough to stick around . . .

The circle went round and round without any resolution.

Nina arrived at the Plaza Hotel forty-five minutes after she'd left her office. She paid for a suite on the fourth floor and made arrangements for Ron to be able to pick up a key at the desk. Once inside the suite, she took a brief shower, dabbed on a little bit of the perfume she kept in her handbag for just such an emergency, donned her new black teddy, and waited beneath the covers. She hadn't heard from him in six months, but it had been even longer since she'd seen him. She wasn't ashamed to admit her need to be with him.

After a few moments, she checked her watch. T minus two minutes and counting. The sound of the outer door opening reached her. Anticipation stirred in her belly and every feminine part of her body. She fluffed her hair, then took a sip of the champagne she'd set out in glasses on the table beside the bed. When she looked back, Ron leaned against the jamb, filling the doorway to her room.

"Hello, Nina," he said.

Immediately, she knew something was wrong. Usually, by the time he got to the bedroom, he was down to his trousers and perhaps his socks. This time, he still had on his trench coat. Nina swallowed, despite the sudden tension in her throat. "What's wrong?"

He sighed, looking down at his shoes a moment. "Now that I'm here, I don't know how to tell you this."

He looked back at her with a beseeching expression on his handsome face. What did he want her to do? Understand? Forgive? Make it easy on him? "Just spit it out."

"I got married last month." He held up his hand to display a simple gold wedding ring.

For a moment she simply stared at the band of gold around his finger. Ron was *married!* It hadn't even occurred to her that he might be seeing someone else. She couldn't even be angry with him for that since she'd never demanded exclusivity from him. It seemed impractical given the distance between them and the infrequency of their times together. It had never occurred to her that he would want to see anyone else, given his constant pleas for her to reconsider her view on marriage.

Nor had it occurred to her that, faced with losing him, such a pervasive feeling of emptiness would sweep through her, swamping her. Tears stung her eyes, but she blinked to banish them. She'd never cried in front of any man and she wouldn't start now. She drew her knees up to her chest and wrapped her arms around them. "I see."

"You have to believe I didn't intend for this to happen." His lips curved in a rueful smile and his gaze became pensive. "I had resigned myself to waiting you out. I figured sooner or later you'd realize you needed me."

Nina bit her lip, considering his choice of words. He expected her to realize she needed him, not loved him or wanted to be with him. That said something about their relationship, about her, but she wasn't sure what. "What changed your mind?"

"I met my wife at Bouchercon, the mystery conference. She's a mystery writer also. Something with us just clicked right away."

Did he intend to tell her all the gory details? She didn't think she could handle that. "Are you happy?"

With a sigh he pushed off the door frame and came to sit beside her on the bed. She drew herself in tighter, feeling naked and vulnerable in her skimpy outfit while he remained fully clothed. He stroked her cheek with the back of his knuckles. She turned her head away from him, not wanting the contact or the tenderness in the caress. She wanted him to leave so she could assess the internal damage his revelation had caused, and maybe down three-quarters of the contents of the champagne bottle.

He withdrew his hand and placed it on the mattress beside her. "I'm sorry, Nina. I'm sorry things didn't work out between us. I didn't realize it before, but I was being unfair to both of us. You made it clear to me that you didn't want marriage, but I was determined to change your mind. You were content to spend weekends at the Plaza when I needed more than that. I needed a life."

She knew he was right. They had both been stringing each other along, he waiting for things to change, she hoping they'd remain the same. "Why did you wait so long to tell me?"

"I know I should have told you sooner. I honestly don't know why I didn't, except maybe I figured I wouldn't be able to break free." He laced his fingers with hers. "You have this hold on me, Nina, a stranglehold on my heart. I could imagine myself ninety years old, still coming here and you still refusing to settle down. I couldn't go on like that."

He released her fingers. "It's different with us, my wife and I. I don't love her the way I love you. I don't think I could ever feel about another woman the way I feel about you. But it's enough."

With a finger under her chin, he tilted her face up to his. "Good-bye, Nina."

When his lips touched hers, she fought the urge to wrap her arms around him and draw him to her. She didn't doubt she could still get him to succumb to her, but this was another woman's husband and she was nobody's whore. She allowed the kiss to be what it was, a brief, bittersweet moment of connection before separating forever.

He pulled back, sifting a strand of her hair through his fingers. "I hope you find what you're looking for." Then he was gone, closing the bedroom door behind him.

Nina covered her face with her hands. Never had she imagined the day would come when Ron would walk out on her. He'd told her she had a hold on his heart. She'd always known that, but she'd thought it was strong enough to keep him coming back.

She didn't know whether she wanted to laugh at her own foolhardiness or cry over it. She reached for her champagne glass. Maybe she'd solve her quandary by getting good and drunk over it. She brought the glass to her lips, then changed her mind. Losing herself in alcohol wouldn't change anything. More angry than hurt, she hurled the glass at the closed bedroom door, shattering it and spraying champagne against the walls. Even that didn't make her feel any better.

She slumped onto her side and curled up into a little ball. What the hell was she going to do now?

Two

"How are you holding up there?"

Nina fastened a green-eyed glare on her cousin Yasmin. Ever since she'd made the disastrous mistake of mentioning her breakup with Ron, Yasmin had been her constant shadow. If Yas was expecting her to fall apart over the loss of any man, she'd have a long time to wait, like forever. "Believe me, I'm fine."

Nina glanced away from her cousin's skeptical look to survey the crowded room around them. How Yasmin had talked her into attending some society party at the posh Metropolitan Club on Twenty-ninth Street, Nina would never know, except that when Yasmin wanted something she didn't give up until she got it. Which was probably why at the age of twenty-two she owned one of the fastest-growing couture businesses in New York. In truth, the only thing Nina relished about this evening was wearing one of her cousin's creations, a black satin sheath that dipped daringly between her breasts and rode low on her hips. There was nothing like looking fabulous to lift any woman's spirits.

But here among the Jack and Jill set, the upper crust who sent their offspring to Horace Mann or the Fieldston School or Whoever's Even More Exclusive Academy, she felt edgy and out of place. She wished she could lock herself in the library down the hall and lose herself in one of the ancient leather-bound volumes housed there.

Instead, she hovered at the edge of the room, to Yasmin's chagrin, nursing her second glass of champagne. It wasn't that she was unused to society functions, or that she lacked the decorum to be comfortable in such a crowd. She'd much prefer not to be around anyone, particularly this stiff crowd, at the moment. Although she'd never admit it to Yasmin, she still smarted from Ron's defection, and like a wounded animal she'd rather crawl off somewhere alone to lick her wounds.

"See anything you like?" Yasmin asked. "Or should that be anyone?"

Nina shot her cousin an aggrieved look. Yasmin was of the opinion that when the horse throws you, you are supposed to get back on. Nina was still at the point of lying in the road assessing her injuries. "I wasn't looking."

Yasmin canted one hip to the side and fastened an assessing look on her. "Tell me you're not letting what that jerk did sour you on men."

"I'm not. I've never been too hot on men in the first place, at least not in the sense of let's fall in love and get married kind of thing. Face it, kiddo, not everyone can be as big a fan of the male half of the species as you are."

"I'm not complaining. Leaves more of them for me."

Nina shook her head at her man-crazy cousin. "You can have them." Nina sipped from her champagne flute. If she was going to be completely objective about it, she had to admit she'd always been partial to a man in formal wear. Nina's gaze snagged on an elegantly dressed man across the room. A tall graceful man. He had his back to her, talking with a group of women that seemed to be glued to his words. Nina blinked and looked away.

"Come on," Yasmin urged. "I want to introduce you to our hostess for the evening."

Nina gritted her teeth. She no more wanted to meet another society matron than she wanted to set her hair on fire. But whoever this woman was, she had arranged the evening as a fund-raiser for some childhood illness Nina couldn't begin to pronounce. From what Yasmin had told her, their hostess was active in supporting medical charities. For that, she owed the woman the respect of at least meeting her.

Mrs. Peter Hairston, as she liked to be called, was nothing like what Nina would have expected. First, the woman didn't look anywhere near her reported seventy-three years. Petite, with a trim figure displayed in a gown that Nina knew had come from Yasmin's shop, she greeted the two women warmly.

"I have to tell you, Yasmin," Mrs. Hairston continued after the introductions were made, "I have gotten so many compliments on this gown. Don't be surprised if you hear from half the women here."

Yasmin beamed. "Thank you, Mrs. Hairston. I'm so pleased you are enjoying the gown."

When Mrs. Hairston's gaze swung to her, Nina had the uncomfortable feeling she was being sized up in the same way a butcher eyes a side of beef.

"You're very lovely in an exotic sort of way. Have you met my son, Miss Ward?"

"I haven't had the pleasure."

"That's a pity." She glanced around the room, apparently in search of her missing offspring. After a moment, she fastened a shrewd look on Nina. "Just like a man, never around when you need him." Mrs. Hairston's expression grew determined. "I'll be right back."

Nina's eyebrows lifted as she watched Mrs. Hairston retreat from the room. Her first thought was, what was wrong with this man that his mother had to snag introductions for him? And the woman thought she'd actually wait around for that? She took Yasmin's arm, steering her back the way they'd come. "What do you think of my chances of avoiding our hostess and her son?"

"Not much. Mrs. Hairston can be as persistent as I can."

"I was afraid of that."

"By the way, did I mention Dr. Frumpy is here?"

No, Yasmin had certainly not mentioned that. If she had, Nina probably would have stayed home. She'd inadvertently given that name to Matthew Peterson when Emily had been in the hospital. Someone had asked which doctor was Emily's. Nina had seen him, but hadn't known his name. She'd pointed him out, saying, "the kind of frumpy one over there." Yasmin had referred to him as Dr. Frumpy ever since.

In truth, he was a perfectly ordinary-looking man, whose best features were his dark coloring and misty brown eyes. But she'd known from the first time she laid eyes on him that he had to be single. No woman in her right mind would let her man out of the house in such a disheveled state day after day. Even on the night he'd come to her rescue, he'd had on old sweats and a pair of running shoes that looked like the *Hesperus* after the wreck. Then again, having a man with no care about his appearance could be a good thing given the rampant vanity running through the male half of the species lately.

Even if that were true, she didn't want to see him. She had the feeling that although he might be attracted to her, he didn't like her or didn't approve of her in some way. He'd made that clear after she'd made that comment about him wanting to play doctor. Not that his like or dislike of her mattered, but she still remembered the feel of his hands on her skin, soft, gentle, and strong. He hadn't really hurt her, but she'd told him he had, because she wanted his hands off her. Never would she have expected a few impersonal touches from a man to rouse her so thoroughly. She'd found herself wanting to turn a few inches and let him explore someplace that really mattered.

Heat rose in her cheeks and she felt Yasmin's

eyes on her during her long silence. As nonchalantly as she could, she said, "Matthew is here?"

Yasmin arched a brow. "So it's Matthew now, is it?"

Nina had made the equally disastrous mistake of telling Yasmin about Matthew's house call, in an attempt to guilt her for not showing up. All Yasmin had heard was that Nina had a man at the house.

"Don't start."

"I'm not starting anything," Yasmin said, "just making observations."

"Right. How did you know he was here, anyway?"

"Whose tux do you think he's wearing tonight?"

"Yours, by any chance?"

"Of course. A double-breasted number in a black silk blend." Yasmin sipped from her champagne glass.

Nina raised her glass in salute to her cousin. "My compliments to the designer." Having one of the men here wear one of her creations would be a great advertisement in this crowd. She scanned the room again, looking for a man wearing the tuxedo Yasmin described. Her gaze settled on the man she'd seen before, only now his profile was visible. His features seemed vaguely familiar, but at this distance and with the dim lighting he could be anybody.

Turning back to her cousin, Nina said, "You don't have to baby-sit me, you know. This is your scene, not mine. I'm sure you have some friends you'd rather hook up with or some clients to shmooze."

"Are you sure?"

"I'm sure."

"I tell you what, let's meet by the punch bowl in half an hour and compare notes."

"It's a deal."

After Yasmin left, Nina downed the last sip from her glass. For some reason, her gaze went unerringly to the man she'd seen before. Something about him called to her, intrigued her. She didn't know why. She was about to look away when he turned to greet someone who'd come up to him. Good Lord, no. It couldn't be. It could not be Dr. Matthew Peterson she'd been panting over all night. She shook her head and blinked, but he was still there, looking handsome in her cousin's tuxedo.

She'd seen him, what, four times in her life, and three of those times she'd been completely unfazed by him. Well, except for those few moments when he'd inspected her injury. And in retrospect she wondered if her reaction to his touch was due more to the fact that she'd been celibate so long, she would have felt the same if her doctor had been Herman Munster. She hoped she wasn't so shallow that seeing the man looking fine for once could turn her head.

That decided it. She was heading for the library for the duration. On the way out of the room, she substituted her empty glass for a fresh one, but she'd downed half of that by the time she made it inside the library door.

Matthew's gaze followed Nina as she exited the room, envying her easy escape. He'd been snagged early in the evening by Mrs. Patterson Foster, a woman nearly as wide as she was tall. He found nothing wrong with her Rubenesque figure, except that at her size she had the uncanny ability to latch on to a man and enough strength to make sure he stayed latched.

Truthfully, he didn't mind her so much. As she made a point of reminding him, she was a friend of his mother's, a very dear friend, so ditching her and tying one on at the bar was not a viable option. It was the young butterflies that fluttered around him, hoping to catch his attention. Not one of them truly saw him, or would have cared if he had a humpback or a prehensile tail. All they saw was the male heir to the Hairston family fortune, and the opportunity to hitch their wagon to a star.

Such nonsense didn't bother him as much as it had as a young man, but it still rankled. A wicked smile curved his mouth as he wondered what these beauties would say if they knew every cent of his trust fund's payout went to charities like the one they supported tonight, if they knew that since the age of twenty-one, he hadn't accepted one cent from his family that he hadn't personally earned. They'd probably disappear faster than a canary at a cat convention. He was almost tempted to tell them.

But such a revelation would embarrass his mother, who had worked hard to put this event together once she found out he'd become interested in the disease. Later, there would be a silent auction, the proceeds of which would go to a foundation study-ing the disease. That was Margaret Hairston's concept of mother-son bonding: spending money on the same thing. He couldn't complain, since the foundation could use the money, but he didn't intend to waste his time talking to her cronies now that Nina had left the room.

He'd watched her surreptitiously since she'd come in the door. Nina Ward, dressed in a black halter gown that dipped low between her breasts and her hair pinned in an elaborate coiffure, took his breath away. Yet he had to admit there was something different about her tonight, aside from the killer dress she wore. She'd always struck him as aloof and untouchable, but her gaze had also held a brittle quality he'd never noticed before. Not that he was any expert on the workings of Nina Ward's psyche. He'd been in the same room with her precisely four times, twice when Emily was in the hospital, once in her brother's apartment, and now.

After those first meetings in the hospital, he'd been attracted to her, but he'd put her out of his mind, never expecting to see her again. He hadn't really thought of her again until the night little Justin got sick. But the moment he'd seen her, those initial feelings of attraction had rebounded through him with the force of a tidal wave.

And now? He didn't know what to make of her now. But he intended to find out. He excused himself and followed her. He paused in the hallway, assessing his options. If she'd gone to the left, she could be anywhere, even downstairs in the garden. There were only two rooms to the right on this floor, a bathroom and the library. He chose the latter, figuring that as a literary agent she'd be interested in books.

He opened the door softly. She stood with her back to him, holding her nearly empty champagne glass in one hand, a slim volume in the other. He stepped into the room and closed the door behind him. "Nina."

She spun around, her eyes wide, her mouth an O of surprise. Her chest heaved against the fabric of her gown. "Matthew."

"I'm sorry I startled you."

A faint smile turned up her lips. "That's all right. I just love having my heart leap into my throat. What are you doing in here?"

"Same as you, I guess. I wanted a few minutes to myself." That was an out-and-out lie, but he told his conscience it didn't matter. Better a fib than to tell her the truth, that he wanted a few moments with her, alone. "How's your hip?"

Her cheeks reddened becomingly, but she turned her back to him. "All better. Thank you." She replaced the volume on the shelf. She turned to face him again, but didn't quite look at him. "I'll go now and let you have that alone time."

She took a step forward, but he blocked her path. "Please don't. I really just wanted to escape from one particular woman who seemed to think I was her personal sounding board."

"Look, Matthew, I'm not feeling well. I'm going to find Yasmin and tell her I'm going home. I'll catch a cab."

He didn't doubt she might feel ill. Although he'd

seen her drink at least two glasses of champagne, she hadn't touched the hors d'oeuvres. Even if she wasn't tipsy, as he suspected, he didn't want her going home alone. "I have a car here. I'll take you."

She shook her head. "That isn't necessary."

"I know, but I'll feel better if I know you got home safely." She looked as if she might protest, but he was ready to dig in his heels. No way would he allow her to leave by herself.

She huffed out a breath. "All right. I have to find Yasmin. I'll meet you downstairs in five minutes."

He nodded. That gave him enough time to find his mother and tell her he was going. He didn't expect her to be disappointed by his leaving, but she was.

"What do you mean you're going? I did this for you."

"I appreciate it, really, but I've got an emergency." A white lie at the worst, and the one thing he could say that he knew she wouldn't challenge.

"Nothing too serious, I hope."

"I'll call you tomorrow." He bent and kissed her forehead.

"You'd better."

He made it downstairs in time to see Nina gathering her cloak from the coat-check girl. He tipped the woman, then helped Nina on with her wrap.

She turned to face him. "This is the last call to back out of taking me home. You can stay if you like. I'll be fine, really."

Back out now, when he got what he wanted—time alone with her? No way. He offered her his arm. "Let's go."

* * *

Matthew had a car waiting outside, all right. A stretch Mercedes with every conceivable appointment save for a bed concealed beneath the floorboards. Or maybe it did have one, but Nina wasn't about to ask.

She stared out the passenger-side window, unable to come up with a single thing to say. Aside from him asking her for her address and her giving it to him, neither one of them had said a word She watched him through the corner of her eye. She didn't understand him. Why should he care if she got home all right? He probably thought she was drunk, which was close enough to the truth to bother her. She usually limited herself to two glasses a night of anything alcoholic; tonight she'd doubled that. It didn't help that she hadn't been in the mood for rich hors d'oeuvres either.

Or maybe he was one of those do-gooders who couldn't leave a bad situation alone without improving it. He was a pediatrician, which meant on some level he'd dedicated himself to helping others.

Nina sighed. Either way, telling a doctor you were feeling ill was probably not the best way to get rid of him.

But she hadn't lied, even though the malady she suffered from was psychic, not physical. She recognized in herself a layer of melancholia shimmering beneath the surface of her emotions, one she lacked the power to dispel. She didn't have to probe her psyche too deeply to figure out why she'd overindulged, or why the presence of the man beside her bothered her. He sat too close, not crowding her, but invading her personal space in a way that disturbed her. Maybe he wasn't a do-gooder at all, but an opportunist, a man who saw a woman at a vulnerable moment and sought to press his advantage.

His next move seemed to confirm her new theory. He shifted in his seat to face her more fully and ran a finger down her bare arm to draw her attention. "How are you feeling?" He laid his palm against her forehead, then her cheek, and finally the pulse point at her throat. Without volition, her eyes drifted closed at the delicacy of his exploration. Those weren't the touches of a doctor examining his patient but of a man seeing to his woman. She inhaled and her breath fluttered out on a sigh. How could this man, a man she didn't even want, affect her so completely?

"Nina?"

She opened her eyes and gazed into his. There she saw concern, but also a hint of self-satisfaction. Anger rose in her, anger at him, but also at herself for letting him get to her so easily. She tilted her head to one side, her eyes narrowing.

"Let me ask you something, Matthew. Why did you really volunteer to bring me home? What do you really want from me?"

Even without him answering, she could see it in his eyes. He wanted her. That's what this car ride was all about. Well, maybe she'd give him what he wanted, but not the way he wanted it.

Cradling his face in her palms, she leaned up and pressed her mouth to his. Her plan was to knock his socks off with a kiss, inform him that that was all he'd ever get out of her, and get out of the car, leaving him to stew in his own juices.

But the minute her lips touched his, something electric leaped between them, something she hadn't felt in a long time, if ever. It sizzled through her like a flash of lightning, heating her, making her wild. Her arms slid around his neck, holding him to her as her tongue searched for and found his. But he held back from her, refusing to yield to her over-ture, which only made her more desperate to make him succumb. Her arms wrapped more tightly around him and she pressed her body against his.

Finally, he pushed her away with his hands at her shoulders. She sat back against the upholstery, looking up at him, her heartbeat rapid, her breath-ing labored, while he seemed completely unfazed by her. If anything, she'd angered him with that kiss, not aroused or embarrassed him as she'd hoped. The car drew to a halt at a red light. Sticking to her plan, she jumped out. Inspiration flashed when she saw the sign for the Fiftieth Street Station for the D train to her right.

With a little luck, she'd be on a train and gone by the time Matthew caught up with her. That is, if he bothered to follow her. For all she knew, he'd consider it good riddance to the crazy lady in the black dress. She felt a little insane at the moment, dashing through a nearly deserted station. A train was pulling in, which didn't give her time to pay the fare. The clerk had opened the metal gate for a woman coming through with a shopping cart, and Nina dashed in after her before the gate had time to close. Then she was on the train, looking back through the window, looking for Matthew. But he hadn't come after her. She didn't know why that realization disappointed her so much.

Matthew arrived at the turnstiles in time to see the tail end of a train pulling out of the station. Undoubtedly Nina was on it. He huffed out an exasperated breath. He'd wanted to see her home safely, but now she was on the subway, worse off than if he'd let her take a cab alone. He probably shouldn't have reacted so strongly to her, but that kiss! It had taken every ounce of his willpower not to return that kiss. It wasn't that he didn't suspect such heat lay below her poised exterior, just not directed at him. That kiss was intended for another man, one who had both angered and aroused her. Matthew had simply gotten caught in the cross fire.

He should probably leave her alone, since aside from that kiss she'd shown no interest in him. He knew he wouldn't do that. He wanted to know what made Nina Ward tick, and he wanted to know that the next time she kissed him, she knew who was kissing her back.

He went back up to the street level to where he had told the driver to wait. He already knew where she was headed. He'd wait outside her apartment building until she turned up.

Nina rode the train to the next stop, got out, and caught a taxi. She huddled in one corner of the backseat, berating herself for her overall foolish behavior that evening. Kissing Matthew had been juvenile and dangerous in the extreme. If he'd been another sort of man, he wouldn't have pushed her away, he'd have taken all she'd offered and probably more than that. The fact that she hadn't managed to arouse him even a little bit more than mortified her. The only saving grace of the evening was that she would never have to see Dr. Matthew Peterson again.

Her spirits plummeted when the cab pulled up in front of her building at the corner of 79th Street and Central Park West. A big black limousine sat at the curb. Matthew. Her only hope was to slip inside the building without him noticing, because she certainly couldn't deal with any more from him tonight. She paid the driver, got out, and walked to the building as rapidly as she could.

She knew her efforts were wasted when she heard the sound of a car door slamming behind her. He called her name, but she didn't stop. He caught up with her and spun her around with a hand on her arm.

She put up a hand to forestall whatever he was about to say. "Matthew, please. I have just been on the subway in an evening gown. I am not in the mood."

She broke away from him and darted into her building just as the doorman swung open the door. She cast him a worried look as she passed. Maybe he could succeed in preventing Matthew from following her, but she doubted it.

She hurried toward the elevators, hoping to be aboard one before Matthew found her. But luck wasn't with her this time. During the day the elevators were slow, but at night they seemed to go to sleep along with everyone else. Seeing Matthew approach, she pressed the button again to no avail. Having no other means of escape, she turned her back to him.

She knew the minute he came up behind her. The heat of his body warmed her and the scent of his cologne reached her nostrils. His hands cupped her shoulders, his fingers moving in a soothing manner. His breath fanned her ear as he spoke to her. "Nina, look at me."

She ignored his entreaty. "What are you, a glutton for punishment? Go home."

"Not until you explain what went on in the car back there."

She turned around then, pressing her back against the wall. "It's simple. I kissed you. I wasn't aware that was a federal crime."

"It isn't. But that kiss didn't have anything to do with me. I doubt you knew I was there."

Now what the hell did that mean? "If I wasn't kissing you, who was I supposedly kissing?"

"You tell me."

"I wouldn't know." That's what she said, but she acknowledged that maybe her experience with Ron had colored her actions, fed her feelings of disillusionment and the desperation in her kiss.

With a swiftness that surprised her, he turned the tables on her. Taking her face in his hands, he touched his mouth to hers. His lips were soft and warm and his touch so gentle that she could easily have melted into that kiss and stayed forever. But she held back, determined not to make a fool of herself twice in one night over the same man.

He pulled away from her, enough for her to see the gray storm going on in his brown eyes. For the first time they held an iciness that sent a chill through her. "I rest my case," he said, his voice as frosty as his eyes. The elevator came and he stepped back from her. "Good-bye, Nina."

"Good-bye," she echoed, not knowing what else to do. Part of her wanted to throw herself in his arms, for no other reason than to prove him wrong. He'd been searching for the truth of her feelings with that kiss. By holding back she'd offered him a lie.

But she got on the elevator and watched the doors close, shutting Matthew out.

Once the elevator had started its ascent, Matthew let out a pent-up breath. So much for Nina seeing him for himself the next time he kissed her. She saw him all right, but what she saw she didn't want. It would be laughable if her rejection of him didn't sting quite so much.

He turned to leave the building and noticed that everything that had happened between them was visible to the doorman at the front of the building. Damn. He didn't know about this one, but the doorman in his own building would have filled every old biddy's ears with the details by morning. He didn't know if Nina cared about her reputation in the building, but he did. As he walked toward the front desk he folded into his palm a bill large enough to ensure the man's silence.

By the time he reached the door, the doorman had it open for him. "I hope we can keep this between friends," he said to the man, extending his hand.

The doorman looked down at his hand, then back again, lifting his free hand as if in surrender. "I'm taken care of. The young lady's brother has me keep an eye on her."

Matthew's eyebrows lifted. He wondered if Nina knew about that arrangement. "I see." He shoved the money into his pocket. He stepped out into the April night that had suddenly grown chilly. Tonight, he'd seen Nina Ward for probably the last time. He'd put her out of his mind twice already, but he figured thoughts of her wouldn't disappear quite so rapidly this time. With his luck, she'd probably haunt him for the rest of his life.

Three

I ought to have my head examined. Not for the first time during the ride from his apartment in Manhattan to Nina's grandmother's house in Queens, that thought sprang into Matthew's mind. When Nina's brother, Nathan, had called two weeks ago to invite him to Emily's second birthday party, he'd initially declined. Although he maintained a friendship with both the Wards and the Thornes, his wife's family, he knew Nina would be there. Considering how they'd ended their last night together, he didn't figure seeing her would be that good an idea.

But in the last month and a half, thoughts of her had tormented him, plagued his dreams, disrupted his daytime hours. When he'd woken in a sweat two nights ago after a dream in which Nina had made incredible love to him, he'd decided not to skip the party after all. If nothing else, he hoped that seeing her could exorcise her from his mind in a way that staying away from her had not.

He turned onto her grandmother's street and maneuvered his bike into a spot between two parked cars. He hung his helmet from the handlebars, then retrieved his present, an oversize teddy bear that he'd fastened onto the chick seat like a passenger, complete with its own helmet. He'd gotten quite a few odd looks from other motorists, but he didn't care. With the bear under his arm he headed up the walkway to the house.

To his chagrin, Yasmin opened the door for him. With her one hand leaning on the doorknob and the other on her hip, a broad grin spread across her face. "What a nice surprise. Nathan told me you weren't coming."

He said nothing to that. Yasmin was the sort of minx likely to get herself or some unsuspecting male in a heap of trouble. No doubt that's what his mother had counted on when she'd recommended he get a new tuxedo from the fabulous new designer she'd discovered. The old girl must really be getting desperate in her bid to marry him off. Yasmin Cole was nearly half his age.

Fortunately, he'd done nothing to focus Yasmin's attention on him thus far and he planned to keep it that way. "Where's the birthday girl?"

"Out back." She motioned him forward. "Come on. I'll show you."

He stepped over the threshold and waited while she closed the door behind him.

Coming up beside him she said, "You know I never got to see you in your tux the other night. I heard you left early."

He fell in step with her as she began to walk toward the back of the house. "I did."

"Funny, Nina left early, too."

He gave a noncommittal look that would have to suffice as his only comment. If Nina hadn't told her cousin about them leaving together, he wouldn't let her fish it out of him, either.

She shot him a disgruntled gaze. "Have it your way. You're only making it harder on yourself."

He doubted that. Despite her threat, he suspected Yasmin knew when to press an advantage and when to let a thing be.

They reached the open back door, which led out to a large backyard, wider than the width of the house. Yasmin pushed open the screen door. "They're all back here somewhere." She reached for the bear. "I'll put this with the rest of the gifts."

"Thanks," he said, most grateful for the fact that she didn't intend to join him. He descended the three steps to the lawn and headed for a group of men clustered around the barbecue. Most of them he knew, either as friends or those he'd met when they'd visited Emily in the hospital. As he approached, Nathan waved him over.

"Hey, buddy. Glad you could make it."

He shook the hand Nathan extended toward him "Glad I could make it, too." Nathan introduced him to the men he didn't know: his cousin Nelson, a former cop who now worked as a PI, a younger cousin, whose name he didn't catch, who'd just turned twenty-one, and Alonzo Clark, whom he knew by voice from the radio but not by face. A young boy, probably Alonzo's son, sat beside him in the grass.

Matthew took the only remaining seat at the edge of the circle of men and surveyed the yard. Children of all ages romped through the backyard between clusters of adults who laughed and talked easily. Although he knew Nina had a large extended family, he was unprepared for the number of people and level of noise they generated. Gatherings at his parents' house were so sedate and boring he usually required the aid of alcoholic fortification just to get through them.

But Nina was nowhere in sight. He doubted she'd skip her own niece's birthday party, but was loath to ask about her whereabouts. He'd have to explain why he wanted to know, and he wasn't prepared to do that.

Someone offered him a beer, which he accepted with great relish. His mother never allowed beer in the house unless it was imported and tasteless. His throat parched from the long ride, he knocked back half of it in one gulp.

"You ride, don't you, Matt?" he heard Garrett Taylor ask him. He and Garrett both had visiting rights at Columbia Presbyterian Hospital and had been friends for years. Once Nathan had married Garrett's sister-in-law, he'd taken over as the family pediatrician.

Matthew looked toward the front of the house, where at that angle the motorcycle was visible. "That's my bike parked at the curb."

"That's not a motorcycle, that's a Popsicle with wheels."

That remark came from Michael Thorne. Matthew recognized a Hog enthusiast when he saw one. "I've also got a custom-built Deuce, the hundredth-anniversary model, but I don't keep it in the city."

"Oh, man, that must be a smooth ride," Michael said, awe replacing the derision in his voice.

"She does all right."

"What we need to do is get these other maroons some wheels," Michael said.

"Don't look at me," Nathan said. "If the bike didn't kill me, Daphne would."

Michael gestured and made a sound like a whip cracking.

Nathan raised his beer bottle in salute. "Not any more so than you, my friend. Just remember that."

"I don't have to. Jenny doesn't let me forget it."

One by one, the women invaded the men's space. The first to come was Daphne, Nathan's wife. She wrapped her arms around her husband from behind. "How's the food coming?"

Nathan circled his arm around her shoulders, bringing her around to his side. "Hot dogs and hamburgers will be ready in two minutes. Then I'll start the chicken."

"Sounds good." She cast her gaze around the circle of men. "How are you guys doing? Can I get you anything?"

"No, thank you," Matthew said, which joined in a chorus of refusals from the men.

"Looks like some of you have already had enough." That came from Daphne's older sister, Elise. She wrapped her arms around her husband, Garrett's, neck.

"I only had two beers," he said, holding up three fingers.

Elise giggled. "I wasn't talking about you. I was talking about him." She nodded in the direction of her younger brother.

"Who, me?" Michael asked. "That's not drunk, that's tired."

Michael's wife, Jenny, slid onto his lap. "Mike was in the studio last night finishing production on a little song some people have been talking about doing for a while now." She cast a mischievous look at Nathan. "If you're nice to us, we'll let you hear it later."

That prospect met with the approval of the group. "As long as I get exclusive rights to first airplay," Alonzo said. He looked up as a petite woman came to stand beside him.

She looked down at the boy in the grass. "Nicholas Johnson, you go play with the other children."

"Aw, Mom," the boy protested.

She pointed in the direction of the other children. "Scoot."

The boy seemed ready to protest until the back door opened and a statuesque girl walked out into the yard. "Can I play with *her*?"

"Nicholas!" his mother chided, but the boy had already scampered off.

"Daria, let him be," Alonzo said, pulling her onto his lap.

"I think your son has a crush on my daughter," Garrett teased.

"He's not my son yet, but he will be," Alonzo said in a determined voice, looking at Daria. He shrugged and cast a smile to the group. "At least the kid's got good taste."

Matthew laughed, as did the others. But he noticed that he, Nelson, and the eighteen-year-old were the only men whose laps or arms were empty. He glanced around the yard, hoping to see Nina headed this way to join the group. He didn't expect her to fling herself on his lap, but he wondered how she reacted to the closeness between the couples in her family.

Matthew blinked as another woman filled his field of vision. Yasmin. She stopped at the edge of the group, next to his chair, and looked around. "Doesn't this look cozy?" Her gaze fastened on him. "Lend a girl a seat?"

He'd have gladly given up his, but that wasn't what she had in mind. Before he had a chance to move, she perched herself on his lap. Several of the men and most of the women shot her disapproving looks, but Yasmin seemed not to care. He was about to extricate himself from the chair when something round and soft hit him on the back of the neck. He turned to see a multicolored children's ball land in the grass behind him.

And in search of that ball came Nina. She wore a tank top and a pair of shorts. Her feet were bare and her hair was wild around her face. Her gaze traveled from the ball to him, then Yasmin, and back to him again, her eyes narrowing at each change of view.

Matthew swallowed, withering in that hazel-cat's gaze of hers. He knew what thoughts must be crossing her mind and he didn't like them any better than she did. He lifted Yasmin from his lap with his hands at her waist and retrieved the ball. Nina stood in the same spot she'd stopped in, watching him with an expression he couldn't read.

When he reached her, he extended the ball toward her. "I believe this is yours."

She lifted one eyebrow, letting him know his feeble attempt at humor had failed. "I thought you weren't coming."

And from the tone of her voice, he assumed she would have preferred it that way. "I had a change in plans." He gestured in the direction of the others. "That wasn't my idea."

"I know. Yasmin follows her own drummer."

That was a nice way of putting it. But he didn't want to talk about Yasmin. "The other night—" he began.

She raised a hand to forestall him. "I know. I owe you an apology. I'd just broken up with someone and wasn't fit for human interaction that night. I should have followed my better judgment and stayed home."

He saw the pain reflected in her eyes. For a crazy moment, he was tempted to hunt down this man who'd hurt her and show him all the places medical school had taught him to inflict harm. He doubted she would appreciate any such gesture anyway. If she were a vindictive woman, she would have found some way to make him pay for the way he'd left her rather than apologizing for being out of sorts.

"I'm sorry, too," he said.

She offered him a smile of entreaty. "Do you think we could forget that ever happened?"

Not if he lived to be a million years would he forget the feel of having her in his arms, the taste of her. "If that's what you want."

She nodded. "Thank you." She held up the ball. "I'd better get back." With one last smile she moved away from him, going back around the side of the house.

He ambled sideways, just enough to catch a glimpse of her. She and some of the little ones were rolling a ball to one another across the grass. When the little boy next to her caught the ball, she scooped him in her arms and tickled him. The other children wanted their share of her affection, and soon all of them had piled on top of her, hugging her. She had her back to him so he couldn't see her face, but her laughter delighted him.

Yes, Nina Ward was a woman ready to be a mother. He wondered if she'd pinned her hopes of that on the man who'd disappointed her. At twenty-nine, her biological clock must be sounding an alarm. Some time soon, she'd settle on the man to be the father of those children. With a sigh, he shoved his hands in his pants pockets. It saddened him to know that when the time came, it wouldn't be him she chose.

Three hours later, after most of the food had been consumed, the cake cut and eaten, and the presents opened, Nina stood at the sink, loading

dishes into the dishwasher. The women had re-
tired to the one area of the house where the men
dared not tread: the kitchen. Crowded into the
small area were two of Nina's four aunts, Nathan's
wife, Daphne, and her sister Elise. Nina's grandmother sat at the kitchen table cooing to little
Arianna, Nathan's youngest, who had cranked up
and refused to sleep.

As Nina moved about her task mechanically, she
eyed her grandmother with envy. Grandmothers,
like mothers, had a special place in a child's life.
Nina was only an aunt, a childless aunt at that. She
wasn't credited with having any knowledge or expertise where babies were concerned. Every time a
child in her care so much as hiccupped, there was
someone to corral that child away from her into
more experienced hands. They thought they were
doing her a favor by relieving her of a recalcitrant
child. Although well intentioned, they made her
feel as useful as a third foot.

She saw the years stretching out in front of her,
years in which she remained childless and alone,
never to be the one any child looked to as the one
person who could make their world right. She
knew she would leave this life unfulfilled if all she
ever was was Aunt Nina to someone else's child.

An almost unbearable ache squeezed her chest,
and tears rushed to fill her eyes. Luckily no one
noticed her distress, as Yasmin chose that minute
to bound into the kitchen, drawing everyone's attention. She carried a tray full of discarded plates
that had been used for serving cake.

"I forgot. Are we saving or throwing out plastic this time?"

"Throw it out," her grandmother said. "Now that we don't recycle plastic anymore I don't have to worry about getting a twenty-five-dollar fine for putting one fork in the wrong bag."

Feeling more composed, Nina helped her cousin empty the plastic dishware into a garbage bag, then went back to her task of loading the dishwasher. Yasmin sidled up to her, leaning her back against the kitchen counter.

"So, surprise, surprise," Yasmin said in a voice only Nina could hear. "Dr. Frumpy showed up after all."

Nina fastened a glare on her cousin. The two of them hadn't spoken two words most of the afternoon, mostly because Yasmin had spent that time practically glued to the man in question. To Matthew's credit, he'd done an admirable job of fending her off. But when Nina had gone in search of the children's ball and seen Yasmin throw herself on his lap, something white-hot and deadly had flashed through her. She couldn't give a name to the emotion, only she was sure it wasn't jealousy. To be jealous, one had to feel one's ownership challenged, and Matthew Peterson definitely was not hers.

"What's your point?"

"He's definitely not looking frumpy today."

Like most of the other men, he wore jeans and a sport shirt that defined a leanness and muscularity she would not have suspected. All right, so he looked good. So what? That didn't change anything. Nina loaded the last dish into the washer and closed the door. "And . . ."

"Face it, cuz, Matt is a catch."

"So it's Matt now, is it?"

"Once you've measured a man's inseam, formalities are meaningless."

It hadn't occurred to her before that Yasmin must have had her hands all over Matthew measuring for the tuxedo. That alien emotion surfaced again with increased fervor, mixed with a dose of anger at herself for succumbing to it. "If you are so fond of *Matt,* why don't you go out with him?"

"Because he didn't spend the entire afternoon staring at me; he was staring at you."

Nina gritted her teeth. She couldn't deny that. Every time she looked up he was there, gazing back at her in an unabashed way. She didn't doubt that everyone had noticed, though no one but Yasmin lacked the tact to leave it alone.

"Besides, I'm not into that whole older man thing. Dating Methuselah is your bag, not mine."

Nina supposed that dig stemmed from the fact that Ron was fifteen years her senior. "You could have fooled me. I'd have sworn you'd have tattooed your phone number on the man's forehead by now."

Yasmin crossed her arms in front of her. "Finally, I get a rise out of you."

"What is that supposed to mean?"

"Oh, please. Most of this afternoon you've been like a Zamboni machine operating full-tilt. Now you're all heated up because you thought I might have been making a move on the dear doctor. The green-eyed monster is a bitch, isn't she?"

"You were trying to make me jealous? Why would it even occur to you to do such a thing?"

"Because, dear cousin, I happen to know you left the auction with Matt. At first, I thought he was simply being nice seeing a friend home, but since neither one of you would own up to the fact that you'd left together, I figured something else must have happened. I decided to test my theory."

Great. Yasmin decided to play games in front of all their friends and family. "In that case, I'll thank you to mind your own business next time."

"If you had any sense you would be thanking me. You forget I've seen the way you look at him, too. As I said, Matt is a catch, more than you know." With those cryptic words, Yasmin sauntered off, pausing long enough to exchange a few words with their grandmother that Nina couldn't hear. She went back to the task of wiping down the counter, only to pause a few moments later at the sound of a familiar male voice.

"Yasmin asked me to bring this in."

Nina turned to see Matthew framed by the archway of the room. He bore the tray containing the remnants of Emily's birthday cake. One of the aunts rushed to relieve him of his burden.

"Can I help with anything else?" Had it been any other male, he would immediately have been expelled. But not only was Matthew a guest in the house, he was the man they all credited with saving Emily's life. They welcomed him into the room as if he were Richard the Lionhearted back from the

Crusades. Rather than accept his desire to be useful, they all but forced him into a chair and got him something to drink and a fresh slice of cake, neither of which he appeared to want. Her gaze met his and all she could do was shrug. If anything, the women in her family were giving to a fault.

Although she understood them, she didn't care to watch them in action. She volunteered to put the now sleeping baby in a crib upstairs, scooped the child from her grandmother's arms, and headed for the second floor.

After she laid Arianna in her crib, Nina watched the slow, steady breathing of the sleeping child. She didn't know what name to give this malaise that claimed her. Part of it, she knew, was that she missed Ron, not in the usual way of missing sex and the other benefits of male companionship. Now she missed the idea of Ron, not so much the man himself.

Although she never would have brought him to a family function like this one, she'd always had the secret knowledge that someone cared for her. Someone loved her enough to wait for her to be as ready as he was. In an odd way, Ron had grounded her, and without that mooring she felt adrift, at sea.

Nina sighed. And worse yet, why did she have to pick now to finally be ready to commit, even if that readiness sprang more from a desire for motherhood than for marriage? Why did she wait until she'd lost the only prospect of a father for her children she'd ever had?

Well, if Yasmin could be believed, she did have

another option. For some unknown reason, he attracted her, but she knew she wouldn't pursue it. He struck her as the kind of man who would only marry for love, probably a great love, or some woman would have managed to snap him up by now. Since Nina didn't think herself capable of returning such love, that made him not the man for her any more than she was the woman for him.

Nina sighed again, running her hand over the sleeping baby's back. So where did that leave her? She honestly didn't know.

Standing behind her in the hallway, Matthew watched the slow descent of Nina's shoulders as she expelled a heavy breath. Shards of waning sunlight peeked in through the slats from the window in front of her, casting a rosy glow across her hair and shoulders. He hadn't intended to sneak up on her, but she watched the baby so intently she hadn't noticed his approach. He spoke to her softly, so as not to startle her. "Nina."

Her head lifted and she twisted to look over her shoulder at him. "I didn't hear you come up."

"Are you all right?"

"I just needed a few minutes alone. My family can be a bit much."

He couldn't argue with that. But twice in the two times he'd seen her recently she'd sought refuge from other people. He wondered if his presence had prompted her need for solitude this time. "I hope I didn't do anything to cause you to run screaming from the room."

A wan smile stretched across her face. "No, of course not."

She turned her back to him to look down at the sleeping child, prompting him to wonder how big a lie she'd just told. He knew he hadn't helped his position any by watching her all day.

But something about her drew his eyes to her. Maybe it was the solitariness he sensed in her, an ability to contain her thoughts, her emotions, her self to herself, and be content with that. It was a trait he didn't possess. He could never be accused of wearing his heart on his sleeve, but he acknowledged in himself a need for connectedness that she apparently didn't share. Not with grown-ups anyway.

He shoved his hands in his pants pockets. "I volunteered to come up and tell you that they are going to play Nathan and Michael's song, if you want to hear it."

"I'll pass. If it's anything like the last one, I'll be hearing it all over the radio soon enough."

He shook his head, though he knew she couldn't see him. He couldn't imagine that she didn't want to share in this happy moment with her brother. She had never struck him as being callous or insensitive to the feelings of others. He took a step toward her. "Nina?"

"Don't let me keep you from hearing it."

Her voice rose enough in pitch to let him know she was in distress. He doubted she'd intended to convey that to him, so he tried to humor her. "Are you trying to get rid of me?"

"Yes."

Too bad. He couldn't leave anyone, especially her, in an agitated state without trying to help. Grasping her shoulders, he turned her so that she faced him. She gazed up at him with troubled eyes. This time he sensed in her, not solitariness, but aloneness, and it tore at him. He pulled her to him, locking his arms around her waist. She didn't exactly melt into his embrace, but she tolerated it. He sensed a restlessness in her body, in the motion of her fingers trapped against his chest.

Suddenly, the sound of a haunting melody reached them from the lower floor. Apparently the others hadn't bothered to wait for them and played the song. He moved with her to the slow beat of the song, stiffly at first, but then their movements became more coordinated, more fluid.

With a sigh, she laid her cheek against his chest, burrowing closer. He tightened his arms around her, absorbing the heat of her through his skin, the scent of her through his nostrils. It was a heady feeling holding this woman in his arms, and it wasn't long before his body betrayed his emotions, hardening in response to her.

She started to pull away from him, but he didn't want to let her go. He wasn't ashamed to admit that holding her in any way, shape, or form turned him on, but he didn't want their dance to end because of it.

But she didn't leave him. She stared up at him and whispered, "Matthew."

That single word and the sloe-eyed expression on her face and the way her lips parted expectantly were an invitation he couldn't ignore. He lowered his head and took her mouth, sliding his tongue past her lips to join with hers. This time she kissed him back with the sort of fervor that could drive a man to the brink of his control in an instant. Her fingers gripped his shoulders and she molded her soft body to his.

But suddenly, as if she just realized what she was doing, or more accurately, whom she was doing it with, she stopped and pulled away from him. She leaned her forehead against his collarbone. "I'm sorry. I don't know why I did that."

Maybe not, but he did. The same need for connectedness that he felt, but she didn't want to acknowledge that need, didn't want to feel it. Cupping her nape in his palm, he brushed the tender skin with his thumb. "It's all right, sweetheart."

She stepped back from him, enough so that he dropped his hands to his sides. "What do you want from me, Matthew?"

Now it was his turn to be honest. He knew what she needed and he knew he couldn't give it to her. "I don't know." He touched his fingertips to her cheek. "Maybe, for the present, we could just be friends, get to know each other a little better."

She smiled in a self-deprecating way. "It sounds so odd hearing a man say that, but I guess in the scheme of things that makes sense."

He didn't know what to make of that comment. "Was that yes or no?"

She laughed, a sound he hadn't heard since she was playing with the children. "That was yes. Give me a call some time. Maybe we can hang out."

Mentally Matthew shook his head, wondering at

how he'd maneuvered himself into the position of being this woman's friend. As his first act of friendship, he'd clue her in on something. "Are you aware your brother pays your doorman to keep an eye on you?"

"Sure. I pay him even more to keep his mouth shut. Between the two of us and his regular salary, the man drives a Mercedes."

Matthew gave a snort of laughter. "I'm going to head out, then. I'll talk to you soon."

"Don't start sounding like a man. Then I'll know you'll never call."

The smile fell away from his face. No, he wouldn't want to start sounding like a man. That was him, the all-purpose eunuch, the guy friend. Or that's what he'd made himself into tonight. "See you around, Nina," he said, then turned and loped down the stairs and out the front door.

"Mijita, que estas haciendo aqui?"

From her spot on the back steps, Nina twisted around to see her grandmother staring down at her from the other side of the screen door. What was she doing out here? After church, Nina had changed into a pair of jeans and a T-shirt and come out here to what she'd dubbed the brooding spot, so named because it had at one time been her brother's place to, as he put it, think. She came out here to do some thinking of her own, but not two minutes had passed before her grandmother found her.

"Just enjoying the afternoon sunshine."

"*Sí,* and I'm Cristina Aguilera. *Compre, Pepsi!*"

Nina shook her head at her grandmother's imitation of the young woman they had seen the night before in a commercial during one of her grandmother's shows on channel 41. Her grandmother pushed through the screen door. Nina scootched over to make room for her on the step and helped her sit. When her grandmother remained silent for more than a moment, Nina went back to shredding blades of grass. Whatever her grandmother wanted to say, she'd get around to soon enough.

With a dramatic sigh, Luz said, "It was so nice of Dr. Peterson to come to Emily's party . . ."

Her grandmother let her words trail off in such a way that they served as neither question nor statement, but as a conversational gauntlet she expected Nina to pick up. "Yes, it was nice to see him."

"According to Yasmin, you've been seeing a lot of him lately."

Nina gritted her teeth. Leave it to Yasmin to call in the big guns. "What else did Yasmin tell you?"

"Don't look like that. She didn't volunteer the information. I asked. It's a grandmother's prerogative to poke around in her grandchildren's lives."

"So I've noticed."

"It's not like the two of you didn't issue an invitation to snoop, the way you were staring at each other all afternoon. None of us is blind, *chica.*"

No, but all of them must have misinterpreted his attention for interest, as she had. Even though he'd kissed her last night, she'd known he'd held back from her. And when she'd asked him what he wanted from her, he'd chosen friendship, not the option to pursue anything romantic between them. That surprised her and bruised her ego, as she usually had to fight men off, not be fought off by them.

She didn't know why she even cared, as moments before she'd made the decision to leave him alone. Maybe it was the way he'd held her, like something precious, even though he had no idea what bothered her and hadn't pressed her to confide in him. In the end, he left her feeling confused and shookup, not her normal emotional state by a long shot.

"*Abuela,* if you are waiting for me to tell you that something is brewing between Matthew and me, you're going to be disappointed."

Her grandmother frowned. "No? My graydar must really be off then."

Nina laughed. "Your what?"

"My graydar. Old people's intuition. I heard some comic talk about it on TV. The one with the frizzy hair."

She had no idea whom her grandmother meant. "When did you start watching English TV?"

Luz ignored her comment. "So what's the problem? You don't like him or he doesn't like you?"

"There isn't any problem. We've decided to be friends."

Luz threw up her hands dramatically. "Men and women being friends. Bah. That's like a lion and a tiger being friends. They get hungry enough, someone's going to get eaten."

"I think Matthew and I are a little more civilized than that."

"Maybe too civilized. Sometimes a man like that needs a woman to take him in hand. I'm sure you know what I'm talking about." She winked and patted Nina's knee.

Nina tilted her head to one side and considered her grandmother, the woman from whom she'd gotten her eye color and the olive cast to her complexion. The woman who had been more mother to her than grandmother, since her own mother had died when she was only six years old. Sometimes she didn't know this woman at all. Between her comment about graydar and her advice about sexual aggressiveness, this was one of those times.

"Are you sure you're feeling all right?"

"Perfectly. Do you know you always ask about my health when we hit on a subject you don't want to talk about?"

"I wasn't aware of that." Nina sighed. "Why are you so concerned with my relationship or lack thereof with Matthew?"

"You know I worry about you. I'm an old lady. I'm not going to live forever. I want to make sure you are settled, like your brother is settled, before I go. I want to play with some more grandbabies. A grandson would be nice."

It was a familiar tune her grandmother sang. She'd been at it since Nina turned twenty-five, the perfect age for marriage in her grandmother's mind. Now, four years later, her grandmother sang it with increasing frequency and duration. If that's all her grandmother planned to say on the subject, she was getting off easy this time.

"Nathan and Daphne are trying for a boy."

Luz shook her head. "It'll be another girl. That's all the men born into this family tend to produce: more girls. The only boys come from outside the family." Luz grinned. "My graydar is sure about that one."

Nina laughed and hugged her grandmother. "I'll make sure to tell Nathan he's wasting his time."

Rather than joining in her humor, Luz held up a hand to cut her levity short. "*Eschuchame, chiquita*, you may think I'm a crazy old woman, but I'm going to tell you something important, so you better listen. I think you've met your match in Dr. Matthew Peterson, so don't mess around and ruin it. He's a good man. When little Emily was sick, he didn't leave that hospital until he was sure she was better. Not every doctor would do that. Most of them would be adding up your bill before you knew whether your child would live or die."

Nina relaxed her hold on her grandmother. "I know he's a good man, *Abuela*." But that didn't change the fact that he didn't want her and that she didn't know what she wanted. In the end, it probably didn't matter. After the expression she'd seen on his face when he'd left last night, he probably wouldn't call her anyway. It was probably best for both of them if he didn't.

Four

He didn't call.

In the six days since she'd seen Matthew, Nina hadn't heard a peep out of him. Not that she really expected to. Not that she was sitting by the phone waiting for it to ring. She'd never been much of a phone watcher, either in a literal or a metaphorical way. If the phone rang she answered it and dealt with whoever was on the line.

Matthew didn't call. And since she figured he wouldn't if he hadn't already done so, she decided to put him out of her mind, the way she'd put Ron out of her mind. Only Matthew didn't seem to want to vanish. What was so compelling about that man that thoughts of him disrupted her waking hours and invaded her sleep? Maybe it was her grandmother's prophetic comment that Matthew was her match. If that was true, Nina was destined to go through life alone, since he clearly wasn't interested.

She reminded herself she wasn't looking for a man now, anyway, one destined for her or not. After Ron, she needed some time alone to sort out what she wanted.

Nina checked her watch. Almost five o'clock. Usually she met Yasmin on Friday evenings, if only for a quick drink, before heading out to whatever plans they might have. Each woman brought whomever they were going out with, which is how Yasmin met Ron. The meeting served a practical purpose as well. If something untoward happened to either of them the family would know whom to look for. But Yasmin had called her earlier from God-knew-where to remind her that she was out of town. Nina was tempted to stop in the bar anyway, as the idea of heading home to be alone held little appeal for her.

She set her briefcase on her desk and began packing it with the work she planned to get done over the weekend: a promising manuscript from a new author, several contracts, and other correspondence. As she inserted the last file into her briefcase she heard a familiar male voice.

"Flower delivery for Ms. Nina Ward."

Matthew! Although she would have figured him more of a Brooks Brothers than a Hugo Boss type, his navy blue suit fit him perfectly. Damn, the man looked good when he had something decent to put on. He carried a bouquet wrapped in pink and white florist's paper, which he extended toward her. Despite everything she'd told herself about not wanting a man right now, she was glad to see him.

"What are you doing here? I thought you were going to call."

"I am. The old-fashioned way—in person."

He came around to her side of the desk and handed her the flowers, a dozen perfect red roses. She took them and brought them to her nose, inhaling the powdery scent of the flowers. She gazed back at him in time to catch him watching her with a heated look in his eyes. This was the man who told her he wanted to be her friend?

"Seriously, what are you doing here?"

"I wanted to see you."

His simple admission sent a thrum of excitement through her, but she was determined not to show him how much he got to her. She cocked her head to one side and said in a droll voice, "Really? How did you know I'd be free?"

"A little birdie told me."

Remembering her conversation with Yasmin, who'd asked her three times if she'd made plans for that night, she figured she knew the songbird in question. "One of these days that little birdie is going to get her neck wrung."

He leaned his hip on her desk. "It's not her fault. I had intended to call her earlier in the week to get your phone number, but I had a crazy week and didn't get in touch with her until yesterday. I asked her to find out if you were busy tonight."

That's what he said, but the whole thing smacked of Yasmin's influence. But she couldn't find the will to be angry about it. She wanted to see Matthew and wasn't too particular about how it was arranged.

"What do you want to do tonight? I'm game for almost anything, but I must be fed."

A grin spread across his face. "I have tickets for the *Chicago* revival. I figured we could have a late dinner after that."

Nina's eyebrows lifted. As far as she knew tickets for the limited run of the show were expensive as hell and completely sold out. If all he wanted from her was her friendship, she wondered about his extravagance. She wondered even more once they got downstairs and she discovered he had a car waiting for them. As he had last time, he seated her on the passenger side, then went around to get in on the driver's side so she wouldn't have to scootch over.

Even with unusually heavy cross-town traffic, the driver pulled up in front of the theater an hour before they would need to find their seats. As Matthew handed her out of the car, she glanced around. She'd always been equally fascinated and repulsed by Broadway's bright lights and huge show posters.

After giving instructions to the driver, Matthew came up beside her. "What do you want to do now? We have time for a drink before the show."

She shook her head. The night was warm but lacked the characteristic New York humidity. "I'd rather take a walk instead."

"Whatever you want, sweetheart."

He guided her forward, along Seventh Avenue, with a hand on her waist, a possessive, not a friendly, gesture. She glanced up at his profile as they walked. She didn't understand him any more now than

she did that first night when he'd kissed her sense-
less. Yet, he'd shown up dressed to kill and brought
her flowers. And there was that endearment that
had slipped so casually from his lips. Talk about
mixed signals. What exactly did this man want from
her?

He should have stayed away from her. Knowing
that he could not give her what she wanted, he
should have left her alone. He tried that for almost
a whole week until his desire to see her outstripped
his common sense. He'd rationalized his actions,
thinking that for all he knew she wouldn't appreciate his unexpected visit and refuse to see him, or
they'd find themselves incompatible after a few
dates and no harm would be done. All he knew for
certain was that he couldn't stay away from her.

"Do you mind if I ask you something?" he said a
few minutes into their walk.

She turned her head to look at him. "No."

"Yasmin told me you are an agent. How did you
get into that?"

"I was an editor at Dalton for five years until the
company was bought up by a publishing conglom-
erate. It seems they were interested in their back-
list, but most of the staff was expendable, including
me. I assessed my options. I probably could have
gotten another job editing, but I couldn't stand
the endless meetings and paperwork most publishing houses are noted for, or the long hours of
work at home, on top of everything else."

They stopped at the corner of Forty-seventh,

waiting for the light to change. "Now, I'm still working with authors, I set my own hours, if I don't feel like coming into the office, I work at home. The best of all possible worlds."

"Sounds like you enjoy what you do."

"I do. And after a couple of years of struggling, it's finally starting to pay off. I just negotiated a couple of major deals for two of my clients, so neither I nor my pocketbook is complaining."

The light changed and they started across the street. "How about you? Did you always want to be a pediatrician?"

"No, I wanted to be a cowboy, but since there aren't too many ranches in Manhattan . . ."

"Or cows, for that matter."

Smiling, he shrugged. "I wanted to be a doctor, I liked kids. It seemed a natural choice."

"What do you like most about it?"

"Kids aren't like grown-ups. They tell everything they know. You wouldn't believe the number of parents that leave my office red-faced because little Johnny spilled the beans about what Mommy and Daddy were doing on the sofa one night. Children are so trusting, too. They don't worry about HMO coverage or listen to news reports that give the medical profession a black eye. They look to you to make everything all right."

"What's the worst thing about it?"

"Sometimes the world isn't a very nice place for children."

She nodded and looked away. Undoubtedly she knew what he meant, and he was grateful she didn't press him to explain further. He'd seen things done to children, sometimes by their own parents, that tore at his heart and, at times, made him hate all of humanity. Things he kept to himself, because they were too painful for him as the speaker and whoever else might be the listener to share.

They stopped at the corner of Forty-sixth Street and Seventh Avenue to wait out another red light. She turned to him, her eyes intense as her gaze met his. "Do you mind if I ask you a question?"

"No."

"What do you want from me, Matthew? I asked you that before, but I don't think you gave me a truthful answer."

His lips curled in a self-deprecating smile. That was the nicest way anyone had ever called him a liar. The warm breeze stirred her hair. He didn't resist the impulse to tuck an errant strand behind her ear.

"An unfortunate choice of words on my part. I felt as if we were rushing along to something, but we didn't really know much about each other. Do you know what I mean?"

She nodded.

"I'd like to take things a little more slowly, if you don't mind." That's what he said, but his fingertips brushed her cheek. In response, she bit her lip and for an instant, an avid look came into her eyes, one that mirrored the hunger he felt inside. He brushed his thumb over her lower lip.

"Matthew."

He didn't know if she intended that one breath-less word to act as a warning or as an encourage-ment. Either way, this wasn't the time or place to take things any further. He laced his fingers with hers and led her across the street.

A Bob Fosse musical was not the thing to see when you had agreed to take things slow with a man, Nina decided after the show. The subtly sexy choreography, as well as the sexy man seated beside her, had gotten to her, giving her an appetite for something other than food. It hadn't helped that he'd held her hand for the duration of the show, weaving erotic patterns on her skin with his thumb, or that when she'd glanced up at him she'd felt the intensity of his gaze even in the darkened theater.

Once they were both seated in the car on their way downtown, Nina asked, "Where are we off to now?"

"I made reservations at a new Spanish restaurant, Seviche in the Village. I figured you could show me how the other half eats."

She grinned. "I'm only one-quarter Puerto Rican."

"Close enough."

Seviche boasted a corner location, the facade of which was entirely made up of tinted glass. A band and a small dance floor occupied the space in front of the windows. Tables and chairs lined the other side of the restaurant and a gallery on the second floor. The tropical motif of the restaurant reflected the fact that the menu incorporated dishes from Puerto Rico and Cuba, as well as South America and Spain. The hostess led them to a small square table in the corner of the room and took their drink orders before departing.

Most of the illumination in the room came from scented candles at the center of each table. After the waitress brought their drinks and took their food order, Nina watched Matthew's face in the candle glow as he sipped from his glass. The gray flecks in his brown eyes danced in tune with the motions of the flame.

He set his glass down. "Are you having a good time?"

She nodded. "You didn't tell me there was a dance floor."

"Actually, I didn't know." He nodded toward it. "Shall we?"

"Want to find out how the other half dances?"

"Something like that."

Out on the dance floor, he pulled her into his arms. Surprisingly, they moved easily together, not like the first time they had danced. She cocked her head to one side, considering him.

"Where did a gringo like you learn to do the merengue?

"My first job was at a clinic in the South Bronx. Most of the nurses were Dominican. When things got slow we used to turn on the radio." He spun her around and pulled her back to him, even closer than before. "That's my second best move."

"What's your first?"

He pulled her closer still, his hand on her waist sliding down to cradle her hip. She inhaled the remnants of his cologne, felt the warmth of his breath on her cheek as he leaned down to whisper in her ear. "It's not on the dance floor."

A tremor shimmered through her, imagining the possibilities.

Undoubtedly, that's the reaction he'd hoped for, as a self-satisfied grin spread across his face. "Just checking," he said.

"Checking what?"

"That I'm not the only one going crazy being close like this."

No, he wasn't the only one. She lowered her head so that her forehead rested against his collarbone, unable to withstand the intensity in his eyes or the husky sound of his voice.

"Nina, look at me."

She complied, gazing up into his gray-brown eyes. But his eyes were on her lips that parted involuntarily in expectation. She knew what he was going to do, merely brush her lips with his. But this time with neither of them holding back, the kiss got out of control. His tongue sought hers and his fingers tensed, clasping her to him. She squeezed her eyes shut, giving herself over to an ardor she wouldn't have expected from him.

When he finally pulled back, she stared up at him, bemused. The more she learned about him, the more he surprised her. She wasn't proud of it, but she'd dismissed him as inconsequential from the beginning. But there was nothing inconsequential about that kiss.

He ran a finger along her cheek. "Come on, sweetheart. Our food is probably getting cold."

* * *

They went back to the table, but Matthew had lost his appetite, for food anyway. Judging from the way Nina picked at her elaborately decorated shrimp dish, she was as distracted as he. After a few minutes of silent noneating, he decided to give up the ghost. He paid the bill and asked the waitress to wrap up their food. The driver awaited them outside. Once they were in the car, he steered the conversation to a neutral subject, inquiring about her family.

After a while, she tilted her head to the side, considering him. "You know, I don't know anything about your family."

"I'm sure you met my mother at the charity auction."

She shrugged. "I met so many people that night, I wouldn't remember."

"Well, consider yourself lucky. Heaven help me, but I agreed to spend next week up at the house."

She laughed. "That bad, huh?"

"You have no idea."

"Then why are you going?"

He shrugged. "My kid sister will be there. I don't see her as often as I would like."

"Were you two always close?"

"Not when we were kids, but we are now. She's a lot younger than I am, and according to my mother, the living example of why women over forty shouldn't have children."

"I take it the two of them don't get along."

"A minor understatement."

He took her hand and caressed her fingers. He'd

tired of talking about his family, and they were nearly to her apartment. She'd asked him for honesty earlier, and he needed the same from her now. Despite the abandoned way she'd kissed him, he needed to hear the answer from her lips.

"Tell me something, Nina. The man you were seeing—are you over him?"

"There wasn't that much to get over. I wasn't in love with him. He bruised my ego more than my heart."

"I'm sorry."

"For what? You didn't do anything."

"Sorry you were hurt."

"Why? Want to kiss it and make it better?"

Her voice was low and sultry and she fastened those cat's eyes on him in a narrow suggestive glare. Her fingers went to his tie and used it to pull him down to her. His mouth met hers, and this time the kiss was slow, gentle, but highly erotic. Her soft hands rose to cradle his face and hold him to her. He could have lost himself in that kiss, but the car drew to a halt and he knew they'd reached her apartment.

When he pulled away from her, she gazed up at him, confused. He ran a finger down her nose. "We're here."

Nina blinked and tried to pull herself together. If the man could zonk her with a single kiss, she wondered what he'd do to her if he really put his hands on her. For a moment, her mind spun with the possibilities. But then he opened her car door and she had to get out and behave with at least a little decorum. She took the hand he offered her and stood.

Once they got to her apartment on the sixth floor, she opened the door, expecting him to follow. She left the flowers on her coffee table and headed to the kitchen for a vase. When she returned she found him still standing at the threshold having deposited her briefcase just inside the door.

She set the vase on the table and went up to him. "Aren't you going to come in? I'll make some coffee."

He shook his head. "If I come in, we're not going to be taking it slow, at least not the way we agreed to earlier."

So she hadn't been the only one affected by that kiss or the sum total of the evening spent together. She wanted him, and though common sense told her it was too soon, at that moment she didn't care. She wrapped her arms around his neck and pressed her body to his. "I know."

His hands stroked her sides. "Behave, Nina. I only have so much willpower."

"I know." But apparently more than she had at the moment. She sighed. "Then kiss me good night and I'll let you go."

He did as she asked, lowering his mouth to hers for a fiery kiss that rocked her to her toes. When he pulled back, he grinned down at her. "Will that do?"

She drew back from him, realizing he'd been

trying to zonk her that time, to leave her all stirred up, just because he could.

"You rat!" she accused, though his humor had infected her, too.

"Come here, baby." He pulled her to him and hugged her, his hands moving on her back in a soothing manner. It was an embrace more potent than any of the kisses they'd shared, because it was filled with simple affection. She laid her cheek against his chest, absorbing his warmth, inhaling the remnants of his cologne and his own natural scent. The effect was both alien and intoxicating, as no man had ever held her before without wanting it to lead to something more. She shut her eyes and enjoyed just being held by him.

He kissed her forehead. "I'd better go."

She nodded and pulled away enough to see his face.

He winked at her. "Pray for me up in the hinterlands of Westchester."

She suspected that despite his complaints about his family, a bond of affection existed there also. "Send up a white flag if you need me to come rescue you."

He laughed. "I just might." He huffed out a breath, obviously as reluctant to go as she was to have him leave. "Good night, Nina. Thanks for tonight." He brushed her lips with his and pulled away from her.

For a moment she watched him walk down the hall toward the elevator. She had to admit that her grandmother was right. At least on a physical level she'd met her match in Matthew. Usually, she had no problem keeping her libido in check, but he'd been the one to slow them down tonight.

And more than that, she liked him, appreciated his deference to her and his impeccable manners. A girl could definitely get spoiled by such treatment. That and the gentle way he'd held her. Nina sighed. Matthew Peterson was definitely not what she'd expected. Her own profession should have taught her the dangers of judging a book by its cover.

As she closed the door she wondered what other surprises Matthew had in store for her. It surprised her how much she was looking forward to finding out.

Five

Nina woke to the sound of the phone ringing. She groped for the cordless phone and brought it to her ear. "Hello?"

"So how did it go with Matthew last night?"

"Yasmin?" Nina blinked and focused on the clock by her bedside. Barely six-thirty. "Don't you ever sleep?"

"Not when I'm dying to know how your date turned out. So spill it."

Nina sat up and brushed the hair out of her eyes. "Actually, Lucy, you're the one with some 'splainin' to do. Why did you stick your nose in where it didn't belong—again? Matthew told me he asked you to find out if I was free, but somehow I doubt that's what happened."

"Come on, Nina, you can't actually be mad at me about that."

"Why not? I distinctly remember telling you to mind your own business."

"I was not meddling."

"No? Then what would you call it?"

"Being helpful. You know how I said once you fall off the horse you should get right back on?"

"Of course."

"I was just trying to supply you with a decent mount."

"Very funny."

"Look, anything to keep you from dating those Pappy Smurfs you're so fond of."

Another dig at her relationship with Ron, but maybe she was right. Nina had never been interested in men her own age. She'd often wondered if she was looking for a father figure in a lover, the parent she lacked from her own youth. Then again, she'd always felt older than her age, more mature. Losing a parent did that to a child, especially when there was no other parent to take up the slack. Even Matthew, though younger than Ron, had to be a good ten years older than she. She wondered briefly what Yasmin would say if she pointed that out, but decided to keep that information to herself.

"Stay out of it. I know you think you did me a favor by trying to surprise me with Matthew, but you needn't have bothered. Unlike some people, we are two grown adults who can handle our own business in our own way."

"So you're not really mad at me?"

Nina sighed. "No, but I will be if you try another stunt like that again."

"Cross my heart. So how did it go last night?"

Nina ground her teeth together. Although Yasmin meant well, Nina didn't plan to tell her one thing.

"Have a nice day," she said in a saccharine voice and hung up. She doubted Yasmin would let her off the hook that easily, but she'd worry about Yasmin later.

Sighing, Nina threw off her covers. Now that she was up, she might as well get her day started. After making herself a breakfast of eggs, toast, and coffee, she tidied the apartment and settled on her sofa to read the first of the manuscripts she'd brought home with her, a mystery.

She'd requested the first hundred pages to see if she wanted to represent the author. By the time she finished reading, she wanted more, and the analytical side of her brain had already started thinking about which editor to send it to. It looked as though the first manuscript of the day was a keeper. She gathered the notes she had made while reading and clipped them to the manuscript.

She stretched and checked her watch. Nearly ten o'clock. She wondered if Matthew had made it to his parents' house yet. She missed him already, but she refused to be one of those silly women who sat around all day mooning over some man. She started on her second manuscript, a romance, but the going was slow. Not only did this author lack the fluidity of language of the first, but in her mind's eye the hero had Matthew Peterson's face.

"Have you given any more thought to your great-aunt's will?"

Matthew checked his watch. He and his father had been alone in the older man's study for an entire six minutes, and already he started in on his favorite subject of late. Matthew had given his great-aunt's will all the consideration it deserved, none. She had been a controlling old biddy when she'd been alive, and he hadn't paid any attention to her then. Why anyone expected him to subject himself to her manipulations now that she was dead, he couldn't imagine.

"You're wasting your time, Dad. I'm not interested in her money or the conditions for receiving it, so forget about it." He started to rise from the wingback chair that faced his father's desk.

Sighing, Peter Hairston waved him back. "Please, sit. I promise not to mention it again."

Matthew gritted his teeth. If his relationship with his mother consisted mostly of spending money on shared projects, his relationship with his father consisted mostly of the older man's lecturing while Matthew listened trying to look interested.

The only person in his family whom he understood and who tried to understand him was his sister, Francesca, and he wished she'd hurry up and get here. He wished he'd known her flight had been delayed before he showed up today, or he would have waited. Then again, better to get the lecture over with early, which would leave him the rest of his time to do as he liked. Although his father was a pretentious man, used to being indulged, Matthew did love him and refused to show him the disrespect he often earned.

Matthew retook his seat. "What do you want to talk about?"

"You, son. How are you doing?"

"I'm fine. Why do you ask?"

"Well, even without this will business, that's more your mother's concern than mine. You'll be forty years old on your next birthday. Shouldn't you at least be thinking of settling down? Most men your age are starting on their second wives already."

For some reason, humor seized him. "Is this your way of telling me you're leaving Mother for a younger woman?"

"Heavens no. Even if I considered it, she'd have that Mirabel put some sort of spell on me." He gave a mock shudder.

Matthew chuckled. His father and his mother's maid did not get along, why he had no idea.

"It's a father's prerogative to worry about his son, isn't it? To wonder if he has brought him up right? To care if he's happy? We don't see you much anymore unless your mother or I seek you out. Your mother tells me you left the charity auction she organized with only the barest of good-byes."

Leave it to his father to lay on the guilt thicker than a Jewish mother. "That had nothing to do with Mother. I had an emergency."

"But when she called the hospital, you weren't there."

It hadn't occured to him that his mother might check up on him. "It wasn't that sort of emergency."

His father's eyebrows lifted. "Oh?"

He huffed out a breath. He supposed he had to tell his father something. "A friend of mine wasn't feeling well. I brought her home."

"A young lady." His father rubbed his hands together. "Anyone I know?"

"No. Her niece used to be one of my patients."

He expected a frown of disdain from his father, as his medical practice didn't boast a particularly wealthy clientele. All his mother cared about was securing a daughter-in-law that she could manage; his father expected him to marry someone of his station. Or he had until now.

"Don't look at me to disapprove. At my age, you discover some things lose their importance or maybe you stop living your life the way others expect you to. That's something you always knew, but I was too stubborn to let you teach me."

Matthew blinked and stared at his father. Now that he thought of it, his father hadn't been lecturing him. For the first time in he couldn't remember how long, they'd shared an actual conversation. He wouldn't have thought much about it, except that his father looked a bit thinner than the last time he'd seen him. "Are you feeling all right?"

He sighed. "Two weeks ago I started having chest pains on the golf course."

Matthew sat forward. "Why didn't you tell me?"

"I had enough doctors poking at me. Besides, it turned out not to be anything serious, yet. My doctor put me on a diet, put me on an exercise regime that includes more than a round of golf once a week. He made me give up my cigars."

"It's about time."

"Yes, well, I'm fine, son, but I've tasted my own mortality, so to speak."

"Have you told Mother?"

"No, and I don't want you to tell her either. No matter how you phrase it, she'll worry needlessly."

He grinned. "She thinks I'm having a second midlife crisis. She's been very nice to me lately."

Laughing, Matthew shook his head. As teenagers, he and Frankie had joked that their parents must have had sex at least three times, since there would have been three of them if Claire, the middle child, hadn't died in childhood. Yet, neither of them could imagine Peter and Margaret Hairston actually being hot for one another. Even as an adult, Matthew had never witnessed any great affection between them, but there must be something still there.

And, he appreciated the change in his father, no matter what the cause. Yet, Matthew intended to phone his father's doctor on Monday and get more details on his condition. He wouldn't tell his mother if his father didn't want him to, but that didn't mean he didn't intend to find out the truth himself.

"About this young lady, is she the one?"

He supposed, well or ill, his father was still his father. "I don't know, Dad. We've been on precisely one date."

"Why don't you invite her up for dinner while you're here? Let your old man have a look at her and help you decide."

Matthew shook his head. So far, Nina had no clue who he was aside from your friendly neighborhood pediatrician, and he wanted to keep it that way, for a little while longer at least. He wanted her to care for him, not the advantages an alliance with him could bring her. As long as she didn't know he was wealthy, he wouldn't have to look into her eyes and see dollar signs instead of his own reflection. "Maybe another time."

Peter Hairston shrugged. "If that's how you want it." He checked his watch. "I wonder when your sister is going to get here."

Frankie arrived fifteen minutes later. She came in jeans that were ripped at the knee, a T-shirt that didn't quite cover her stomach, and a baseball cap turned backward, just the sort of outfit sure to send their mother to the fainting couch, which was undoubtedly why she wore it. She bounded into their father's study and launched herself at Matthew.

"I missed you so much," she said against his ear.

"I missed you, too, munchkin," he said, setting her on her feet. He made a show of looking her up and down. "Going straight for the jugular, are you?"

She shrugged, but in a way that didn't fool him. "It's comfortable."

"Do you have one of those hugs for your old father?"

Both Matthew and his sister turned to face their father. His father's idea of a hug was to pat you on the back a few times while maintaining as much distance from the body as arm span allowed.

"Sure, Dad." Francesca walked over to their father, but rather than one of his usual numbers he enveloped her in a bear hug.

When Frankie glanced at Matthew questioningly, it was his turn to shrug. He supposed that if his father didn't want his wife to know about his condition, he wouldn't want his daughter to know either.

Stepping back from their father, Frankie asked, "Where's Mom?"

Obviously, Frankie was spoiling for the usual

fight, but it would have to wait. "She's resting," her father said.

"In that case, why don't you help me unpack?" She grabbed Matthew's arm and tried to hustle him out of the room.

He resisted only enough to be a nuisance. When they reached the foyer where her bags were stacked, he let out a whistle. "You and what army are staying here for a week?"

"Not an army, just me." She picked up a bag and slung it over her shoulder. "I'm not going back."

Matthew's eyebrows lifted. Last he'd heard, Frankie had been enjoying her position as soccer coach for a private girls' school in Atlanta. Then again, she'd received several more lucrative offers to coach elsewhere. He picked up one bag in each hand and followed her up the winding staircase. "You're moving on to somewhere else?"

She reached the top of the landing and turned to face him. "I'm not sure what I'm doing."

That surprised him, as Frankie was one of the most focused people he knew. He waited to question her further until they were inside her room with the door shut. He set her bags by the door. The room had remained unchanged from its state four years ago when she'd left home. It was decorated in various stages of blue, and trophies from every sport imaginable dominated the room. Every sport except basketball. At five feet two, Frankie was too short for anyone to take seriously as a player.

While Frankie flopped on the bed, he sat in one of the chairs by her vanity, an item of furniture he doubted she ever used. "So what's wrong with Atlanta? I thought you were enjoying your time down South."

"Too many southerners."

He chuckled. "What were you expecting? Eskimos?"

She made a face at him. "You know what I mean. The pace is so much slower. There's nothing to do there compared to New York. And I never got used to kids calling me ma'am. I felt like I should have a walker or a Seeing Eye dog or something."

He studied his sister. He knew her well enough to know when she lied and when she didn't. And she hadn't told him the truth, at least not the whole truth. He'd let it slide for now, seeing that it was her first day back. "Do Mom and Dad know you're staying?"

"No. I want to tell them when they're both together so I only have to do it once. By the way, what's with Dad? That's the first real hug he's given me since I was about six years old."

He shrugged. "According to Mom, he's having a second midlife crisis."

Her eyes narrowed in speculation. "What were you two talking about when I came in? Or should I ask, what was the day's lecture topic?"

"Actually, we had a nice conversation for a change."

Her eyes widened. "Do tell."

Matthew sighed. Now that he'd opened his big mouth, he had to tell her something. "He was trying to convince me to invite a woman up here for dinner."

Her eyebrows lifted. "A woman or *the* woman?"

"You're starting to sound like him, you know."

"And you're being evasive. Who is she?"

"Just a friend."

She crossed her arms in front of her. "And I'm the Tooth Fairy. If she was just a friend, you wouldn't have any problem letting her meet the Gruesome Twosome."

"It's too soon."

Her eyes narrowed again. "She doesn't know about all this, does she?" Frankie gestured in a way that encompassed the room and all that lay beyond.

"No."

"Then, as much as it shocks me to say this, I agree with Dad. You should invite her."

"Why is that?"

Frankie leaned forward, crossing her legs Indian style. "Has it occurred to you that you're being unfair to her? I'm figuring you must really care something for this woman if you're worried about how she'll take all of this. How do you expect a woman to really care for you if she hasn't seen you warts, trust funds and all? How do you think she'll feel later, knowing you kept part of your life secret from her?"

Honestly, he hadn't given it much thought. He'd considered only his own feelings, though he had to admit his sister had a point. "Maybe you're right."

"Of course I'm right. Has she ever given you any indication that she's a gold digger? And what if she is only after the family jewels? Isn't it better to know now than before you really lose your heart to her?"

He wondered if his sister wasn't a little late with

that bit of advice. But the most compelling argument his sister made was that he did Nina a disservice by not being honest with her. He'd invite Nina up and let her draw her own conclusions. Although he suspected she'd turn him down, he was more worried that she wouldn't.

Saturday afternoon, Nina opened her door to find Yasmin on the other side of it. "What are you doing here?"

"You didn't think I'd let you get away with hanging up on me, did you?"

Nina stepped aside to let her cousin enter. Yasmin pulled a wheeled carry-on bag behind her. "You came here straight from the airport?"

"Yup." Yasmin left her bag by the door, flopped onto the sofa, and propped her feet on the coffee table. "I figured we could go out for a late lunch if you haven't eaten already. Then I'll head downtown to my apartment."

"Um-hmm," Nina said. Yasmin intended to use the meal as an excuse to try to get her to talk about Matthew.

"Have you eaten yet?"

"Actually, no. She looked down her body to the faded jeans and worn T-shirt she had on. "Give me a moment to change and then we'll go."

Ten minutes later, dressed in cream-colored linen pants and a matching top, she rejoined Yasmin in the living room. "All set?"

Before Yasmin could answer, the phone rang. Nina was tempted to let the machine answer it, but thought better of it. She rushed to grab the cordless phone on the third ring. "Nina Ward."

"Hey, stranger, how's it going?"

"Matthew! Sending up the white flag already?" Out of the corner of her eye, she saw Yasmin eyeing her with interest. She turned so that her back was to her cousin.

"Not quite. Actually things are going better than I thought."

"I'm glad to hear it."

"Which brings me to the question of the hour. You wouldn't care to join me up here for dinner tomorrow night, would you?"

"Dinner?" she squeaked out. Completely stunned by his offer, her mind whirled, searching for something to say. Yasmin had moved into her field of vision again, frantically nodding her head and mouthing "yes." Nina waved her away. "I—I usually go to church with my grandmother on Sundays."

"I understand. Just thought I'd offer. I'll call you when I'm back in the city."

"Okay." She clicked off the phone, and sighed. Although meeting his parents was out of the question, she wished she didn't have to pass up on the prospect of seeing him. She turned to replace the phone in the cradle and almost bumped into Yasmin.

"Are you totally insane? Did I just hear you pass up the chance to spend the day with Matthew to go to church with your *grandmother?*"

Feeling defensive, she crossed her arms in front of her. "And what if I did?"

Yasmin rolled her eyes and sighed. "And I'm

supposed to be the one with no sense. A man does not invite you to meet his parents unless he's serious, or serious about something, at least."

"Do you think I don't know that?" That was the problem right there. She enjoyed being with him, anticipated having a bit of mind-blowing sex with him whenever they got around to it, but beyond that? He was the one who said they should go slow. Now he seemed to be changing the game plan on her.

"Then I would think you'd take this opportunity to find out if that's how you want it to go. Call him back and tell him you changed your mind. If it will make you feel better, I'll go to church with *Abuela* tomorrow."

"You? The whole church will probably cave in on you for daring to set foot in the place. Besides, even if I wanted to call him back, I don't have the number."

"I'm assuming you have caller ID."

"Why didn't I think of that?" Nina muttered. She huffed out a breath, letting her shoulders droop. She missed him and wanted to see him. Why deny herself if she didn't have to?

She dialed the number listed on the caller ID box. Matthew answered almost immediately. "If that offer for dinner is still open, I've changed my mind."

"Of course it's still open. I can send a car for you around three, if that's okay."

"You don't need to do that. I'm capable of getting on Metro North just like everyone else."

"I insist."

She sighed, knowing when to give up. "The Taxi and Limousine Commission must love you."

"I get a Christmas card every year. I'm really looking forward to seeing you."

In the span of one sentence his voice had gone from humor-filled to low and sensual. Knowing Yasmin listened to her end of the conversation, she said, "Me too," then hung up before they could venture into any more dangerous territory.

She turned to Yasmin, who stood in the same spot in the same position. "Happy now?"

"Very. Now what are you going to wear?"

Nina laughed. With Yasmin, everything boiled down to her three passions: men, fashion, and meddling in other people's affairs. "I'm sure you'll pick out something nice."

Six

The car arrived precisely on time and almost exactly an hour later pulled into the drive of a house hidden from the main road by a stand of maple trees. The drive up to the house wasn't a long one, but it gave her enough time to survey the well-tended lawn and the rows of manicured flowers that ran along the road. The house itself reminded her of one of those English country estates, old and drafty and occupied either in this world or the next by Vincent Price.

Part of her wanted to laugh. Now she knew what Yasmin meant by Matthew being more of a catch than she knew. Not that Matthew's financial status mattered to her one bit. More than anything, finding out that he came from a wealthy background surprised her, as he struck her as such an average guy, the boy next door. Sure, if your last name was Rockefeller.

Part of her wanted to beat Matthew to a pulp for

not divulging the financial status of his family. She supposed she should have had some idea he didn't come from hunger, considering his presence at the charity auction, his ease with spending money, but she hadn't really thought about it. And the only reason she could think of for him springing his family's wealth on her was to test her reaction to it.

She wondered what he'd say if she told him she'd prefer it if he were the boy next door, not the heir to whatever fortune his family possessed. As a favor to her brother, she lived in the apartment he'd bought before he married Daphne and didn't want to give up or leave empty. She saw Manhattan's wealthy every day and remained unimpressed.

Money changed people, made them feel entitled to what was not theirs, and gave them the hubris to look down on anyone not of their ilk. She hadn't seen this in Matthew yet, and hoped she never saw it.

By the time the driver pulled up in front of the house, both her humor and any violent impulses had subsided. As she stood at the front door, curiosity more than any other emotion rose within her. For better or worse, Matthew had grown up in this house. The people who occupied it probably knew him better than anyone else on the planet. What else would she find out about him here?

An elderly black man opened the door in answer to her knock. He wore a black suit that impressed her as more of a uniform than regular apparel. His face bore a kindly smile, which relaxed her. But whoever he was, she doubted he was Matthew's father. "Good afternoon, miss," he said in a gentle baritone voice.

"I'm Nina Ward. I'm here to see Matthew Peterson."

His smile broadened. "Yes, of course. Please come in."

She stepped inside and while she waited for him to close the door, she glanced around. The foyer where she stood opened into a large semicircular area. A sloping staircase to the left led to a gallery one floor above. Two floors up, an enormous chandelier made up of thousands of tiny crystals hung. Although she admired its beauty, she'd hate to be standing under that thing if the chain suspending it ever snapped.

"This way, miss," the butler said, drawing her attention from morbid thoughts. He led her through the house, past several open rooms and common areas. Given the age and obvious expense of the decor, she felt more as if she were touring some antiques museum rather than a home where people actually lived.

The butler stopped at a pair of French doors that opened onto the side of the house. "Mr. Matthew is outside with Miss Francesca."

He bowed and disappeared before she had a chance to ask, outside where or who the devil was Miss Francesca? She supposed she'd find out soon enough. She pushed through the door that opened onto a pillared overhang lined on both sides by tall hedges. After a short distance, the hedges on the right side opened, overlooking a half-size basket-ball court and hoop.

She recognized Matthew, dressed in a T-shirt and shorts. Whoever this Miss Francesca person was, she'd apparently left, as the only other occupant on the court was a young boy, maybe twelve or thirteen, who was doing an excellent job of whipping Matthew's butt. Smiling, she leaned her shoulder against one of the pillars watching, until the boy elbowed Matthew and gestured in her direction.

Matthew turned in the direction Frankie pointed. Seeing Nina standing there brought a smile to his lips. Not only was he glad to see her, she wore a prim dress that fell below her knees. He never would have suspected that such a proper garment had found its way into her closet. She looked lovely nonetheless.

Frankie elbowed him again, jarring him out of his long-distance perusal. "Shouldn't you get over there, or are you going to stare at her all day?"

He shot his sister a quelling look, then jogged over to where Nina stood. At close range he noticed the sardonic expression on her face. "Hey, stranger," he said.

"You never told me you were loaded."

He should have known Nina wouldn't waste time mincing words or pulling punches. "Would it have made a difference?" His breath held, his eyes intense, he waited for her answer.

She lifted one shoulder nonchalantly. "I'd have

ordered the steak two nights ago instead of the shrimp. After the play and the car, I thought I'd better give your wallet a rest."

He snorted, and both humor and relief washed through him as he realized she was teasing him. "My family is wealthy. I'm a poor working stiff."

She cocked her head to one side, offering him a droll look. "You're a physician. I doubt you're poor by any stretch of the imagination."

She had him there. Besides, they'd exhausted that topic of conversation, at least all he intended to say about if for the moment. He tugged at the neckline of his T-shirt. "I guess I should get changed, huh?"

"That might be an idea."

He laughed. "I'm sorry, I lost track of the time."

"Time flies when you are getting your butt whipped by a kid?"

He looked at her, confused for a moment, until he realized Nina thought Frankie was a boy. His sister would love that. "Something like that." He took her elbow and led her toward the house. Frankie had undoubtedly gone to change herself, and his mother was "resting." That left only his father to entertain Nina while he dressed. "Would you mind keeping company with my father for a few minutes while I make myself presentable?"

"Not at all."

As usual, Matthew's father was in his study, his chair turned around to face the large window overlooking the property. From that vantage point his father could have viewed the basketball courts, but not the sidelines where he and Nina had talked.

"Dad."

"Frankie ran you off the basketball court again?" The older man swiveled around. He knew the minute his father realized Nina was in the room, as a look of interest came into his eyes. "Oh, I didn't know you had your young lady with you."

"Nina, this is my father, Peter. Dad, this is Nina Ward."

His father came around the desk to shake Nina's hand. "It's a delight to meet you."

"Thank you," Nina said.

"Would you entertain Nina while I change?" Matthew said.

Peter rubbed his hands together. "It will give us a chance to get acquainted."

That's what Matthew feared. If it had been a week ago, he could have counted on his father to maintain a discreet silence, designed to make uncomfortable any other occupant of his domain, especially an occupant not of his class. In the past two days, his father had surprised him with a whole new side to his personality Matthew had never suspected existed. Heaven only knew what he might do.

He focused on Nina. "I'll be right back."

She nodded and smiled. "I'll be here."

He started toward the door, cringing inside when he heard his father say, "Tell me about your family, my dear."

Nina settled into the leather wingback chair Matthew's father motioned her toward. Rather than returning to his spot behind the desk, he sat in the chair beside hers. Nina recognize a crafty old cat when she saw one. She'd noticed his surreptitious perusal of her and assumed she'd passed the test in the looks department. But she knew he wasn't finished with her yet. Given the circumstances, it seemed logical that he would want to make sure she wasn't an opportunist, more interested in the family's fortune than its offspring. Frankly, she couldn't fault the man for wanting to protect his son, but she didn't intend to put up with too much of an interrogation.

Nina sat back, crossing her legs and steepling her fingers in her lap. "What do you want to know?"

"Where are your people from?"

"Queens," she said, knowing that was not the answer he sought.

"I meant your heritage."

No kidding. Given her complexion and her eye coloring, it was a question she heard often. People took her for anything from Puerto Rican to Cuban to Moroccan and everything else in between. One coworker had once assumed she was Sicilian, but admittedly that woman hadn't been the shiniest penny in the roll, either. "Why do you ask?"

"You have the look of someone, maybe that I know or have seen somewhere. You aren't related to the Braxtons, are you?"

"Not that I know of."

He shrugged and offered her an uneasy smile. "You must forgive me. I'm somewhat rusty at this."

"At what?"

"Giving the third degree to my son's paramours.

The last girl my son brought here stole a necklace from my wife and sold it to a pawnbroker for fifty dollars. I think Matthew was seventeen at the time."

She stared at him a moment, unsure what to make of that comment. What exactly was his point—that he feared she'd walk off with the family jewels or that Matthew surprised him by bringing home any woman at all?

"In other words," he said, as if reading her mind, "you must be very special to my son."

He smiled at her expectantly, as if he waited for her to confirm or deny that statement. She did neither. "Matthew and I are friends."

"I have met Matthew's friends, and he has never looked at any of them the way he looked at you. At least, I hope not."

Nina chuckled. He might not be the autocratic patriarch she assumed him to be, but he was relentless nonetheless. "You'll have to ask Matthew about that."

He scrutinized her for a moment, in which she kept her gaze steady and leveled at him. Then he nodded as if coming to a decision. "I think I like you. Would you care for a drink? I know I would."

"Yes, please."

He rose and walked to the bar cart in the corner of the room. He brought back a glass of wine for her and a tumbler of scotch for himself. Once each of them had a drink in their hand, he clinked his glass with hers. "To new *friends.*"

Smiling, she brought her glass to her lips. The wine was excellent, fruity but not too sweet. "My compliments to the bartender."

"Thank you, thank you." He inclined his head to the left and then the right, as if he were the recipient of applause.

He turned to face her again, and she studied him for a moment. Matthew must look like his mother, because the older man's face reflected nothing she saw in his son's.

"Did anybody miss me?" Matthew asked from the doorway.

Both she and Matthew's father turned to see him stride into the room. He'd changed into a short-sleeved shirt and a pair of black linen pants, a casual outfit that somehow looked elegant on him.

"We were having a drink. Care to join us?"

"Actually, if you don't mind, I'd like to give Nina a tour of the grounds."

"By all means. Enjoy yourselves." For a moment, father and son seemed to communicate something with a look, the meaning of which she wasn't privy to.

Once outside the study, he asked her, "What do you think of my father?"

"He's not quite what I expected."

"He hasn't been anything like I expected either, lately." She shot him a quizzical look. "Don't ask."

"I won't." They reached the double doors leading outside. "Where are we going?"

"Just like I said, I want to show you the grounds."

She cast him a skeptical look, but didn't question him further. As they walked down the path he laced his fingers with hers. "I never asked you about your trip up. How was it?"

"Uneventful, except for a traffic jam in the Bronx."

A little past the basketball court, the path opened on the left, facing away from the house. Lush, green lawn extended as far as she could see, interrupted only by a series of tall hedges that seemed to zigzag across the property.

They walked on in silence, but a sense of anticipation filled her. He walked with too much purpose for a casual stroll around the grounds. She suspected that wherever he planned to take her lay on the other side of those hedges. She liked the feel of his warm, strong hand joined with hers, and the quiet sensuality that emanated from him. She had always been with men who clubbed you over the head with their machismo. Simply being with Matthew excited her, he didn't need any extra trappings.

Nestled at the center of the hedges was a little pond, obviously man-made, with a small fountain rimmed by multicolored flowers. Three white stone benches arched around the pond. A red-and-white-checked blanket had been spread between the benches and the pond. A small wicker basket held down one of the corners.

Matthew squeezed her hand. "How do you feel about a little picnic before dinner?"

"Won't that spoil our appetites?"

"Not if we do it right. Besides, dinner is not for at least another hour and I'm starved."

The way he looked at her, she wondered exactly what he was hungering for. She hoped he hadn't brought her out here for some tryst, not because she didn't want to be with him, because she did. But here in this idyllic setting she wondered how much resistance she'd muster up, if any. Showing up at the dinner table with grass in her hair was not the best way to make a good impression on his family.

They settled on the blanket, Matthew next to the basket and Nina at the other end. From the basket he pulled a bottle of white wine, two glasses, chilled fruit, and an assortment of cubed cheeses. He filled a glass and offered it to her. Nina accepted the glass, but demurred at the food he'd laid out on a small china plate. Despite his complaint about being hungry, he didn't seem too interested in the food either. After taking a cursory sip from his glass, he stretched out on the blanket, leaning back on his elbows.

He glanced over at her. "You haven't asked me the one question I know you must be wondering."

"What question is that?"

"What on earth did a black family do to earn so much money?"

She lifted one shoulder and let it drop. "That question has crossed my mind."

"The answer is not much. Have you heard of Montgomery DeWitt?"

"No, should I?"

"Probably not. He was an obscure businessman and a recluse. He made a fortune during World War II hoarding and selling commodities made scarce by the war. He made millions that way, although he was a millionaire many times over before that."

"What has he got to do with your family?"

"My maternal grandmother was his nurse in his later years. When he died right after the war, lacking a single living relation, he left his estate to his servants, the lion's share of which went to my grandmother, including this place. Apparently, she'd been very good to him."

He looked off into the distance, a somber expression on his face.

"And that bothers you?"

"That my grandmother inherited the money?" He shook his head. "No. I remember her as a sweet, caring woman worth several old men's fortunes. My parents are another matter, particularly my mother." He shook his head, grinning at her. "She was born poor, but you'd swear she'd read the book *Obnoxious Habits of the Filthy Rich*, and adopted every one of them."

She tilted her head to one side, studying him. She'd met his father, and he'd been more gracious than she'd expected. "What do you mean?"

"Take Anderson, for example. His sole job here is to open the door and answer the main phone."

She grinned. "I have to admit, I've heard of butlers, I've seen them on TV, but I've never actually seen anyone butle before."

"Don't get me wrong. I'm not trying to sound like some rich kid crying 'poor me.' I know I had every advantage, every door of opportunity opened for me that money could buy. But I realized at a very early age that my parents were nouveau riche snobs. Granted my father's family was comfortable, but neither of my parents did anything save be born to earn any of this." He gestured in a way that encompassed the property.

Nina looked down at her lap. Whatever his parents were, at least he had two of them. She had never known her father, and time had dimmed what few memories she had of her mother. But rather than sink into maudlin thoughts, she tried humor instead. "Did you really bring a girl here who stole your mother's jewelry?"

He nodded. "A necklace, a fifty-thousand-dollar necklace at that. The girl had no idea what she'd taken, but the pawnbroker she sold it to did. He let my father have it back after extracting a significant finder's fee."

"Ouch!"

He sighed. "It's funny, but yesterday my father praised me for living my life on my own terms, but there was a time when my whole existence centered on rebelling against my parents and everything they stood for. I kept my grades up, I wasn't stupid. But I tried every other way to let them know I didn't approve of their elitism and their sense of privilege."

"Somehow, I wouldn't imagine you as being much of a hell-raiser. What changed things for you?"

"Realizing that I had choices, that I didn't have to live the life my parents had set out for me. I could spend or not my money as I wished." He lay back, taking her hand and pulling her down beside him. He rolled onto his side facing her, propping his head on his hand to look down at her. "I have to make another confession."

"What's that?"

"I really didn't bring you out here to talk about my family."

The picture of innocence, she asked, "No?"

He shook his head. "I haven't gotten so much as a kiss hello from you, yet."

Her eyes narrowed and a siren's smile tilted her lips. "Whose fault is that?"

"Mine, I guess. I thought I ought to keep my distance, since I wasn't exactly at my fragrant best when you got here."

She laughed, though she wouldn't have minded if he'd kissed her then. He'd smelled of himself and hard-earned male sweat, which, no matter what any woman said, could be a powerful turn-on. "I hope you're planning to make up for the oversight now."

"You tell me."

Anticipation flooded her belly as she watched his head lower toward hers. But the moment his lips touched hers, her eyes squeezed shut from the unexpected intensity of his kiss. His tongue plunged into her mouth, capturing hers in an erotic dance. He sank against her until his body covered hers and one of his thighs rested between her two. Her arms wound around him, her fingers splaying over his muscled back. She moaned her pleasure into his mouth, and his answering groan sent a wave of desire, white-hot and potent, flooding through her body.

He broke the kiss and she called his name, not wanting him to leave her. And then his lips touched down at the sensitive skin between her breasts exposed by her dress, and his hand rose to cover one breast. She jerked and arched against him. He rolled her nipple between his thumb and index finger, intensifying the ache at the very core of her. She wrapped her leg around him, wanting him *there*, wanting him inside her. In response, his hand traveled upward, underneath the cover of her dress, along her bare leg, to grasp one cheek in his palm.

The contact jolted her and she felt a shudder pass through him, too. He pulled back from her then, his hand coming to rest on her waist. He offered her a smile that was at once smug and rueful.

"Part of me knew I shouldn't come out here with you. I only wanted a few moments alone together, but you make me lose my head."

He did the same to her. "What's wrong with that?" she asked.

He exhaled a heavy breath. "Aside from this being the wrong place at the wrong time, it's too soon, Nina. We both know that." He stroked a finger across her cheek. "I don't want this to be some fly-by-night thing between us, over before it's begun."

Neither did she. The more she knew of him, the more she wanted to know. And the more she wanted him. But she understood his desire to wait, had in fact thought the same thing herself only minutes before. And she knew the answer to her own question: how much resistance did she offer? Absolutely none. Doubting she'd be any less pliant if he changed his mind, she said, "Maybe we'd better get back to the house."

He nodded, and together they got ready to go inside.

Seven

By the time they got back to the house, the rest of the family had assembled in the great room. Frankie sprawled on one of the sofas with her feet propped up on the coffee table, while his parents stood near the fireplace talking quietly. "We're back," Matthew said as they entered the room, drawing three pairs of eyes in his and Nina's direction.

His mother was the first to respond, placing her glass on the fireplace mantel and stepping forward. She wore a smile that contained surprise and recognition. Nina's face bore a similar expression with humor mixed in as well.

"Nina Ward, this is my mother, Margaret Hairston. Mother, this is Nina Ward."

"Yes, I know," Margaret said, extending her hand. "We met at the charity auction."

"It's good to see you again."

He smiled as Nina did her best to accommodate

his mother's usual limp-fish handshake. "I thought I had seen you two talking at one point."

"I was trying to arrange an introduction for you two, but I see my efforts were wasted."

Matthew tamped down on a smile. He could imagine that Nina's reaction to his mother's attempt at matchmaking had been to run as quickly as possible in the opposite direction. In the periphery of his vision he saw his sister moving toward them. She wore the same jeans she'd had on earlier, the same cap faced the same way, but she'd changed her shirt to one that covered her navel. He gathered she'd made that gesture toward looking presentable for Nina's sake, as she normally didn't back down until their mother had suffered at least one migraine.

Frankie sidled up to the group. His mother stepped back and placed a hand on Frankie's back. "This is Matthew's sister, Francesca, who at the advanced age of twenty-seven has yet to realize she's a girl."

Frankie gave their mother a sour look before extending her hand toward Nina. "Call me Frankie."

Nina shook Frankie's hand, but her gaze, full of mischief, slid to him. "The boy on the basketball court?"

Matthew shrugged. "Frankie cheats."

"I do not," Frankie protested, full of fake indignation.

"She knows I won't knock her on her butt the way I would a guy who pulled the same nonsense."

Frankie stuck her tongue out at him, her usual response to him saying anything she didn't like.

His mother harrumphed, focusing on Frankie. "What kind of name is Frankie for a young lady?"

"It's no kind of a name for a young lady, which is why it's perfect for me."

His mother threw up her hands in disgust and walked back to the fireplace to reclaim her drink.

Matthew glared at his sister, a stare she pointedly ignored. She turned her gaze on Nina. "So how did my brother manage to drag you to a Hairston family dinner? You don't look drugged."

"Behave, munchkin," he warned.

She flashed him a dazzling plastic smile. "I will, but only because I want to ask you for a favor later."

That didn't surprise him. Considering that she didn't intend to go back to Atlanta, he thought he knew what that favor might be. "I'll take what I can get."

Anderson, the butler, appeared at the door to inform them that dinner awaited them in the family dining room. Matthew glanced at his mother. She was pulling out all the stops tonight. She'd even dressed in her battle jewelry, pieces expensive enough to require a home in the family vault. What Matthew hadn't figured out is whether she'd worn them to impress Nina with the merits of a marriage into the Hairston clan or to emphasize the difference between Nina's financial status and his own.

As often as his mother pressed him to marry so as not to lose part of his inheritance, he'd always wondered if only a debutante daughter-in-law would really satisfy her. Since he harbored no plans to marry anyone just to suit his family, it didn't matter. But he often wondered at the depth of his mother's shallowness.

As the family made its way toward the dining room, Matthew steered Nina to the back of the pack. He draped his arm around her shoulders and leaned down to whisper in her ear, "Want to make a break for it while no one's looking?"

She laughed softly. "They're not that bad. Everyone thinks his family is worse than it really is. Only let's not get Yasmin and Frankie together. The two of them might take over the world, and I shudder to think what they'd do with it."

He threw back his head and laughed, drawing over-the-shoulder stares from the three Hairstons. He didn't care. The more he got to know Nina, the more she charmed him. His family might as well get used to it now.

He squeezed her shoulder. "You've got a deal." He glanced at his sister, who gave him a surreptitious thumbs-up sign. He could always count on her to be in his corner. Then again, she wanted something from him, undoubtedly a few nights' reprieve from their parents in his spare bedroom. He shuddered to consider that, too.

At the end of dinner, Nina dabbed her mouth with her napkin and laid it beside her plate. The meal had been divine: cold potato soup, mesclun salad, and chicken with a light sauce flavored with lemon and herbs. She glanced up at the portrait hanging on the wall opposite her. A woman with kind, deep-set eyes stared down at her, Matthew's grandmother, she supposed.

Aside from the woman on the wall, Matthew was the only family member that hadn't asked her pointed questions about her job, her life, her family. At first, she'd thought they were simply inquisitive about her. After a while, she'd felt more as if she were being interrogated, but for what purpose she couldn't imagine. Peter Hairston might be rusty at giving the third degree, but his wife more than made up for it. To Matthew's credit, he had deflected most of the more intrusive questions. However, his mother gave new meaning to the word *relentless*.

Margaret dabbed a spot of sauce from her lips. To Nina's chagrin, she sighed, which indicated that another question was at hand. "What is your position on children?"

She couldn't help smiling at the roundabout question. What was her position? "I'm for them."

"I meant, do you want children of your own?"

"That's none of your business, Mother," Matthew said.

Margaret huffed, but Nina's attention was taken up by Frankie leaning across the table toward her. "What my brother hasn't told you is that he's in line to inherit five million dollars if he gets married before he turns forty in a couple of months. Mama Hen here is trying to speed the process along."

She heard Matthew's mother gasp, but his attention centered on Frankie. He glared across the table at his sister, who seemed to shrink visibly. He threw his napkin on the table. "If you'll excuse us."

He slid from his seat and held out his hand to her. Without hesitation, she took it and let him lead her from the room. He took her to a door at the back of the house that opened onto a lanai. Farther ahead was a large oblong pool. Lights embedded just below the surface illuminated the chlorinated water.

Nina inhaled. The night was warm, sultry, with a gentle breeze that stirred her hair and wafted the scent of flowers from the garden. She perched on one of the white-on-white stuffed chairs that ringed the pool, watching Matthew. He looked up at the stars, rocking back on his heels with his hands in his pockets. He seemed more pensive than upset, so she let him be. She leaned back in the chair and propped her feet up on the cushion.

He huffed out a breath and turned to her. "Ready to revise your opinion of my family now?"

She lifted one shoulder. "If you knew some of the things Yasmin has pulled over the years, this is light stuff."

He sighed. "So now you know my dark, dirty secret. My mother wants to marry me off to keep the money in the family."

She elbowed him playfully. "I thought you might have been hiding a deformed relative in the attic who'd come down and tag me and make me 'it.' "

He chuckled, a combination of mirth and resignation. "Don't laugh. You don't know how embarrassing it is to have your mother parading every eligible and not so eligible female in the tristate area under your nose in the hopes that one of them will catch your attention."

"Well, if I'd known you were the son she wanted me to meet, I'd have stuck around for the introduction."

"That's just the problem. You dangle the Hairston name or some of my mother's jewels in front of some women and they wouldn't care what the son looked like, as long as they might get their hands on said money or jewels one day."

She studied him for a moment. She'd wondered before why he'd never married and she supposed she'd learned the answer in part. She'd known a few men who assumed she lived on her brother's largesse and who courted her wanting a piece of the action. She'd set them straight, but the experiences left a foul taste in her mouth. "Is that why you don't use your family name?"

"Peterson is my family name. My biological father's name. He died before I was born. My mother remarried when I was two." He shrugged. "Peter Hairston is the only father I've ever known, and he's never treated me as anything except his."

Nina looked down at the blue water before her. That never would have happened if Margaret Hairston had been born into the Ward family. No, the women in her family couldn't keep a man, and after he'd gone they spent the rest of their lives bemoaning his departure. She thought of her own mother, an unsmiling woman who found little pleasure in her daughter or in life. Or her aunts, who were like a gaggle of dissatisfied chickens, always pecking about something. Her grandmother had raised her with love, but came from a generation whose beliefs she didn't share.

Of all her female relatives, she was closest to Yasmin. But Yasmin wanted to shake up the world; Nina wanted to find a place where she belonged.

She slanted a glance at Matthew, who watched her with a hawkish glare. Again, she opted for humor instead of a darker emotion. "You could always marry me. If you think your family is anxious to marry you off, you ought to see mine. You'd swear a woman still became a spinster if she wasn't married by the age of thirty, the way my grandmother carries on."

"That bad?"

Nina nodded with mock gravity. "She claims she wants to see me settled before she dies."

He chuckled again. "How serious about this are you?"

She studied him for a moment, unable to gauge his own sincerity. "About two or three," she said, deciding on a flippant response. "You probably leave the toilet seat up and throw your dirty socks on the floor."

"True. But I live alone so I have no one to scold me. Let me know when you get to nine or ten. Then we'll talk."

He was teasing her, but she noted he said when, not if, as if he expected her to get to that point. But the only way she saw herself getting there was if she fell in love with him, and she couldn't see that happening. She liked him; she admired his convictions and his sense of obligation to the rest of the world. She craved the excitement she felt when she was with him and the feeling of connection they shared. He was probably the most stable man she knew. But love? She didn't know what that was, not the man/woman kind, anyway. To fall in love you had to make yourself vulnerable, to open that innermost core and share it. Nina didn't do that with anyone, man or woman. She wouldn't know how.

She looked away from him, unable to look him in the eye when she said her next words. "Is it so wrong to marry for a reason other than love?"

"I wouldn't say wrong, but I wouldn't consider it preferable. If you're going to spend the next forty or fifty years staring at someone else across the breakfast table, you should be able to say more to each other than pass the corn flakes."

He either hadn't caught on to the shift in her mood or he ignored it. Either way she was grateful. She didn't need him to acknowledge that for one crazy minute, she'd honestly considered marriage to a man she barely knew. And not for the sake of any inheritance that neither of them needed, but simply because she was tired of being alone.

"All jokes aside, my seeing you has nothing to do with fulfilling the conditions of my great-aunt's will. I don't even want the money."

"Why not?"

"I don't like dancing to someone else's tune." He sighed. "What do you say we go inside for some dessert? Frankie will behave this time, I promise."

"That depends. What's for dessert?"

He took her hand and helped her to her feet. When she stood, he captured her lips for a brief kiss. "Whatever it is, it can't be any better than that."

* * *

The remaining Hairstons had moved into the great room for coffee and chocolate mousse cake. He supposed he was responsible for the subdued atmosphere of the gathering, considering he, the least dramatic of the Hairston clan, had just left the dining room in a huff. While Nina spoke with his parents, he took his sister aside.

"You had a favor you wanted to ask me?"

His sister sighed, relieved. "I thought you were going to light into me for what I said before."

"Later. For now, tell me what you want."

She tilted her head to the side and crossed her arms. "You know what I want. To crash at your place for a few days. Are you planning on making me beg?"

"No, you know you can stay with me if you want to. But know this: I don't know how or when or why this feud between you and Mother started and I don't care. But I don't intend to be dragged into it by either you or her."

"Point taken." She grinned. "I thought you weren't going to lecture me about what I said."

He snorted. "Believe me, I haven't even begun."

She rolled her eyes, comically. "I can't wait. But seriously, at least you have the answer to how Nina would take family night in Scarsdale."

"True." He glanced at Nina, whose eyes seemed about to glaze over as his father rambled on about something. She seemed completely indifferent to it. The only reaction she'd shown to Frankie's revelation was indignation on his behalf.

He turned his attention to his sister. "Go pack whatever you plan to take to my place. I want to be out of here in an hour."

* * *

When they reached Nina's apartment, Matthew took her key and opened the door, but as usual didn't step over the threshold. Instead, he pulled her close, until her cheek rested against his chest. His hands roved over her back, warming her in ways that had nothing to do with the physical.

Sinking into his embrace, she inhaled, breathing in his scent, and let her breath out on a sigh. She wondered if he knew how profoundly these simple caresses moved her.

He touched his lips to her temple. "Would I be pressing my luck if I asked you if you had a good time?"

"I enjoyed meeting your family." She pulled back enough to see his face. She expected to see the same tenderness he'd shown her there, but instead she saw desire, the same want that left her with an ache in the pit of her belly. But it wasn't their time yet. "Your sister is waiting for you."

"She'll keep." He drew her to him with his hands at her waist. "Kiss me good night; then I'll let you go."

She smiled, remembering those words being ones she'd told him the last time they were in this position. Then he'd kissed her silly. She decided to return the favor. She took his face in her hands and pressed her mouth to his. Her tongue slid past his lips to tantalize and tease. But his arms wound around her back, squeezing her to him. The heat and heaviness of his erection pressed against her pelvis. She moaned and her back arched as his hands slid down to grasp her buttocks in his palms.

He pulled away from her by slow degrees, until a centimeter or two separated them. Her lashes flicked open. Her lids felt heavy and her body languid. Damn! He'd zonked her again. This time there was no smugness in his gaze, only the same longing that tormented her.

She took a step away from him. "You'd better go."

"I know. Have dinner with me tomorrow night."

"Don't you have to entertain your sister?"

"Are you kidding? She only wants to stay with me so she can run up my phone bill and hang out with her friends in the city."

"All right. Where should I meet you?"

"Unfortunately, I'm on call tomorrow night, so we need to stay near the hospital. There's a jazz supper club on Broadway and 116th. How does that sound?"

"Fine."

"Do you mind picking me up at work? That's probably the only way I'll get out of there on time."

"Not at all." In fact, she looked forward to seeing him in action when said action concerned none of her own relatives. "I'll call you tomorrow afternoon and we can go over the details."

"Sounds like a plan." He curled one hand around her nape and drew her to him for a brief but nonetheless stirring kiss. "See you tomorrow."

She stepped away from him and watched him leave. For a fleeting moment, she wondered if he would have stayed if his sister weren't waiting in the car. She smiled to herself. If it weren't for his sister, she wouldn't have let him go.

* * *

Matthew slid into the driver's seat of the car and glanced at his sister. She'd taken Nina's seat beside him. She had her eyes closed, feigning sleep. If she thought she could avoid talking about her behavior at dinner, she was mistaken. He slammed the door shut and started the engine. "Don't think you're fooling anybody by pretending to be asleep."

She opened her eyes and shot him a penitent look. "I'm not. I already know what you're going to say, and I'm sorry."

He pulled away from the curb, easing into surprisingly heavy traffic for that time of night. "When do you plan to cut our mother some slack?"

She shrugged and huffed. "Maybe if she hadn't spent the first eighteen years of my life trying to make me into a *young lady.*"

"And you've spent the last ten years making her pay for that."

"For God's sake, Matthew, she made me go to charm school. Until then, I'd thought they'd abolished it in the Stone Age."

"And you were so charming tonight. I guess you must have skipped the lesson on common courtesy."

"Honestly, I don't know what comes over me when I'm there. I must regress or something. I'm sorry if I embarrassed you in front of Nina."

He snorted. "You didn't. She's got a cousin that's more of a pain in the neck than you are."

She crossed her arms in front of her. "Gee, thanks. If it makes any difference to you, I like Nina a lot."

"It does mean something to me, and I'm glad."

When Frankie remained silent he darted a glance at her. She stared back at him with a narrow-eyed speculative glare. He focused on the road in front of him. "What?"

"So, she's the one, huh?"

Matthew smiled, more for his own benefit than his sister's. He was old enough and had been around enough to know what he wanted when he saw it, and he'd found it in Nina. "Yes."

Frankie whooped. "Alert the media, Matthew Confirmed-Bachelor Peterson has fallen in love."

"I didn't say that." But he knew it wouldn't take much to topple him over. If he were a less cautious man, he'd probably be a goner already. "Keep this to yourself, would you? As it is, our mother probably called the caterer the moment we were out of the house."

She used her right index finger to make an X on her chest and spoke their most solemn childhood oath, "Cross my heart, hope to die, stick a needle in my eye."

"I don't think you have to go that far."

"Seriously, Matt, have you told her what you've done to yourself?"

She asked that as if he'd performed some ancient scarification ritual on himself instead of having had a vasectomy performed by a competent doctor. "No, I haven't told her." His grip on the steering wheel tightened. "It hasn't come up."

"It or the subject?"

He stole a glance at her. She grinned back, enjoying her own impudence. "We're straying into none-of-your-business territory." Actually none of it was her business, but that wouldn't stop her from being nosy if she chose to.

She shrugged. "I know, but you have to admit you set yourself up for that one."

He didn't have to admit anything, including the fact that for one crazy moment when Nina'd suggested he marry her, he'd been willing to forget his convictions and agree. That's what she did to him, made him lose every shred of common sense with which the Lord had blessed him. Not that the prospect of being married to Nina would give him nightmares. They were compatible; they enjoyed each other's company. Then there was the chemistry they shared, which crackled between them like an electrical charge.

But most of all, he knew she was ready to nest, if not with him with somebody else. He didn't think he could bear that.

"What if she wants children?" Frankie asked, serious at last.

That was the rub, the thing that had kept him from pursuing her as he would have liked. It wasn't a question: she wanted children. And despite the strength of his feelings, he owed it to her to tell her and let her decide if she wanted things between them to proceed any further.

Eight

The following day dragged for Nina. She'd come to a decision the previous night. On call or not, wanting to take things slow or not, Matthew Peterson was going to be hers tonight. They had agreed that they didn't want what was between them to be some fly-by-night thing, but hadn't they passed that point already?

She didn't know what name to give the feelings he inspired in her. Physically they went beyond lust and emotionally they went beyond caring, to what she couldn't say. All she knew for certain was that she wanted him. For now, that had to be enough.

At four o'clock, she tidied her office and headed home. She straightened her apartment, took a brief shower, and dressed in black silk undies and a wraparound dress that looked pretty and was easily removed. She left her legs bare and tied on a pair of strappy, high-heeled sandals. She checked her watch. She had just enough time to make it to the hospital at five-thirty to pick up Matthew.

She'd expected him to be waiting for her at the small receptionist's desk at the front of the pediatric emergency area. A grim-faced nurse pointed her toward the examination rooms on the left-hand side of the room. She wondered if this was usual hospital protocol for nurses to send doctors' guests in search of them. But as she slid open the curtain that closed off exam room 1, she thought she knew why the nurse had.

Matthew sat on the examination table at the far end of the room, his head down, his hands clasped between his knees. Yet, he didn't present the picture of a man in repose. He seemed dejected beyond words or her understanding. She wanted to go to him, but something about his posture also indicated that he wanted to be left alone.

She leaned her back against the wall, just inside the curtain. "Matthew?"

His head snapped up and his eyes trained on her. The bleakness in his gaze made her gasp. He blinked and shook his head, schooling his features into a more benign expression "Nina." He slid off the table to stand facing her. "I'm sorry. I forgot."

If he weren't such a considerate man, she might have been upset about his admission, but given the unguarded, disconsolate look on his face when she called his name, she knew her arrival hadn't simply slipped his mind. "What happened?"

He leaned back against the examination table,

crossing his arms. "Maybe we should cancel dinner tonight. I'm not going to be good company."

"Tell me what happened," she repeated.

He was silent so long that she feared he wouldn't tell her. When he finally spoke it was in a voice so low she had to strain to hear him.

"Two kids came in tonight, brother and sister. Their mom had double-parked outside a candy store to get treats for them. Some idiot in an SUV plowed into them."

Nina's heart raced and her stomach cramped, knowing that the ending to this story couldn't be a happy one. In truth, she didn't want to know, but she sensed in him a need to tell her, even if he didn't acknowledge its existence. "What happened?"

His grim, red-eyed gaze met hers. "We lost them. The girl should have been declared DOA at the scene, but the EMTs didn't want to give up. We thought we could save the boy . . ."

His voice trailed off. Her heart ached for him, for his sorrow at being unable to save two children he didn't know. And more than that, she sensed his anger at his own impotence. She didn't know if he'd welcome any overture from her, but she decided to take her chances. She went to him, wrapping her arms around his neck and burying her nose at the crook of his shoulder. "I'm sorry."

"Don't, Nina." His hands rose to her shoulders, but he didn't push her away. "You should go. I'm not fit company tonight."

"I don't care about that. I don't care about dinner." She placed a soft kiss against his ear. "Don't shut me out."

She felt his resistance melt one degree at a time. His arms closed around her, tightening until he held her in a fierce grip. She clung to him, whispering soothing words, Spanish words of comfort she'd learned at her grandmother's knee.

After a while his hold eased. She pulled back enough to see his face. A resigned expression took the place of the ravaged one she'd seen a moment ago. "Better?" she asked.

He nodded. He tucked a stray strand of hair behind her ear. "You must think I'm the biggest wuss in North America."

She shook her head. If anything, he'd shown her a sensitive man unused to sharing that side of himself with anyone. "Actually," she teased, "you've just gone up a notch or two on the marriage-o-meter scale."

He narrowed his eyes. "Really?"

"Sure. What woman doesn't love a guy that loves kids?"

He dropped his hands to his sides, releasing her. "Sometimes I really hate this job." He sighed. "It's not as if we never lose kids here or have outcomes less than what we hoped. That's why medicine is an art, not a science. Most of the time I can deal with that. But these kids were sitting in a parked car with the blinkers on when some jackass too drunk to notice rammed into them. A witness at the scene said he was doing seventy-five on a city street. I had to look that mother in the eye and tell her that both her children were gone. It's not a task I would wish on anybody."

"What happened to the driver?"

"He's on the other side of the floor, complaining because he banged up his knee. I heard from one of the nurses that this isn't the first time he's been in here after smashing into something, but it's the first time he took someone with him."

She noticed the rigidity of his posture and doubted he realized he'd curled his hands into fists at his sides. And she understood that reserved much of his anger for the man who'd caused the accident and had probably come in here to avoid bashing that man's head in.

She took one of his hands in both of hers and kissed his knuckles. Oh, well, her seduction plans for the evening were off. Sexual healing wasn't what the doctor ordered. Matthew Peterson needed some good old-fashioned TLC, and she planned to give it to him.

"What do you say I take you out of here to my place? It's not that far from here. We can order in some Chinese." She let a playful smile turn up her lips. "Unless you're still afraid to be alone with me."

His expression sobered as he traced her lower lip with the tip of his thumb. "I am scared of you, Nina Ward, but it's not my body I'm worried about."

His mouth was on hers before she could ask him what he meant by that, and after a moment she didn't care.

When they reached Nina's apartment a half hour later, Matthew reached for her key as he always did. This time, rather than hand it over, she held it aloft.

"You're not going to turn into some sort of ravening beast if I let you in, are you?"

He focused on the teasing smile turning up her sassy mouth. If that kiss she'd laid on him at the hospital hadn't done it, he figured he could manage to behave. "We'll see."

She shot him a droll look. "That's the best guarantee you can give me?"

He took a step toward her, imprisoning her against the wall. He studied her with an intense gaze. "I'm not guaranteeing anything." Let her mull that one over. She didn't fool him either. With that dress and those heels, he knew how she wanted to end the evening, or at least what she'd wanted until she walked into the exam room and found him brooding. Rather than backing away, as almost every woman he'd ever known would have, she'd asked him to share his burden with her. Having her hold him so tenderly was a rare balm to his spirit at a time when he needed it most.

He was falling for her, hard and fast, and he hadn't bothered to pack a parachute. He cradled the side of her face in his palm and brushed his thumb across her cheek. Despite her plans or his feelings, he knew he couldn't allow their relationship to progress physically until he'd come clean with her about his inability to father the children she obviously wanted.

How much would that admission change things between them? Would she send him packing, knowing he couldn't give her what she wanted? As much as he dreaded finding out, he knew he had to tell her.

This time when he reached for the key, she relinquished it. He unlocked the door and pushed it wide to allow her to enter. She paused long enough to flip on the overhead light. The apartment opened onto a spacious living room decorated with pale peach walls, an overstuffed sofa and love seat, and glass and black faux granite tables. Bookshelves lined the walls, save for the areas reserved for windows. Nina Ward, bibliophile, at home. He shut the door and dropped her keys onto the end table closest to the door.

She turned to face him. "Welcome to my not so humble abode. Actually, it's my brother's abode. I could never afford this place. Come on, I'll give you the grand tour."

As she led him through the apartment, he could see why she couldn't afford it, considering the apartment's choice location on Central Park West and the size of the rooms, huge by New York standards.

She stopped outside the door to what was obviously her bedroom, a feminine room decorated in shades of lavender and cream. "Here's the one drawback to the place. Only one bedroom. No room for a home office."

She led him back to the kitchen, which was straight out of a designer's showroom with countertops, cabinets, and appliances rendered in the same faux granite pattern.

"Would you like something to drink? I've got some wine or some stronger stuff if you like."

"Wine is fine."

"Good. Then you can do the honors. I'm a hazard with a corkscrew."

She handed him a corkscrew and bottle of wine, not the caliber of his father's selection, but a decent vintage. While he set about getting the bottle open, she rooted around in one of the drawers, eventually pulling out a stack of menus.

"You have almost as many take-out menus as I do."

She lifted one shoulder. "Cooking for one seems like such a waste of time. Then if I do cook, I'm eating the same leftovers for days."

"Same here, and it's hard enough to stomach my own cooking once."

"You can't be that bad."

"Yes, I can. Growing up, we always had a cook. I never had to fix a meal until I was in college. Everything I know about cooking I learned from the back of a macaroni and cheese box."

She looked at him, laughing, her eyes twinkling. "Honestly, I'm not much better. Let's make a deal. You cook Mondays, Wednesdays, and Fridays. I'll cook Tuesdays, Thursdays, and Sundays, just to keep us from having to eat our own cooking, of course."

"Of course. What happens Saturdays?"

"We go out. There's no sense being gluttons for culinary punishment."

She was teasing him, but damn if that didn't sound like a cozy arrangement to him. He could see himself coming home to Nina every night, to eat and enjoy other pleasures that had nothing to do with food. That thought sent a wave of heat crashing through his body. His smile was taut, not playful, as he said, "It's a deal."

"Voila," she said, holding aloft a single menu. "This place has the best shrimp with garlic sauce."

"Sounds good. Order some for me, too."

He busied himself getting the bottle open and pouring them each a glass while she placed the order. He handed Nina hers as she switched off the cordless phone.

She sipped, her eyebrows arching. "Not bad."

After a first taste, he agreed.

"What do you want to do now?"

She didn't really want him to answer that question.

"There's a Knicks game on tonight."

She shot him a warning look. "Don't even think about it."

He draped an arm across her shoulders, laughing. "Even if there were a game on tonight, it wouldn't start for another couple of hours."

"Good thing. How about some music, instead?"

"I'm game."

He settled on her sofa while she loaded some discs into the CD player. A mellow saxophone solo filled the air as she came to sit beside him with her feet tucked under her. In that position, her dress rode high on her thighs. Too much temptation for any man to withstand. He focused instead on the bookcases just behind her and steered the conversation to a neutral subject. "Have you read all these books?"

She glanced at the bookcases behind the sofa and nodded. "Most of them, although some of them are duplicate copies of my clients' books." She fastened a narrow-eyed stare on him. "I hope you're not going to ask to borrow something. The last book I lent out, I didn't get back for three years and it was minus the cover."

He chuckled. "No, I wasn't thinking of borrowing anything. Outside of professional journals and the morning paper, I'm not much of a reader."

Tsking, she shook her head. "You're an educated man. How could you not want to read?"

"I didn't say I didn't want to. I don't have time."

"And when you do, you probably read Stephen King or some horribly gory murder mysteries."

"How did you know?"

"You medical types with your blood and guts. Your friend Garrett is a big fan of one of my authors who writes about serial killers."

"Maybe I'll go borrow some books from him."

"If he'll let you. He guards his stash almost as zealously as I guard mine."

He tucked a strand of hair behind her ear. "Tell me, what do you find so fascinating about books, enough to make a career out of them?"

"Two careers actually. I was an editor first, remember?"

He nodded, more of a prod for her to continue than an acquiescence.

She shrugged. "Books have always been my friends, I guess. I always loved to read, when I wasn't beating up the neighborhood boys. I loved reading about different places and about different people's lives. Finding out new things." She shrugged again. "For a long time, I wanted to be a writer, but lacking any talent in that regard, I settled for helping others to bring their stories to fruition."

She conveyed a wealth of unspoken information in the few words she'd spoken. He knew from her brother, Nathan, that their mother had died when they were both very young. He'd bet Nina had found comfort in dealing with that loss in solitude and the escape of reading. He wondered how much her mother's death affected her and shaped the woman she was today.

"Do you enjoy your work?"

"Most of the time. I hate rejecting people, but overall, I enjoy working with authors and helping them get the best deal they possibly can. And the free books aren't bad either." She shifted into a sitting position, still facing him. "Can I ask you something?"

"Sure."

"Why don't you want your great-aunt's money? I mean, I can understand you not wanting to conform to the conditions of her will, but I'd think some part of you would want the inheritance left to you."

He wondered what brought that question on. "Not enough to change my whole life for it. Why do you ask?"

She lifted one shoulder. "Think of all the things you could do with that money. That charity your mother gave the auction for, for instance. I understand they fund some promising research. Wouldn't it give you pleasure to make sure that money did some good for someone?"

He exhaled, as relief flooded through him. For

a minute he thought he'd misjudged her interest in his family's wealth, a disquieting notion. "You know I would."

"What happens to the money if you don't take it?"

"I have no idea. For all I know, it goes to my great-aunt's best friend, a crazy woman from Arizona who has a tiger preserve in her backyard."

"I have nothing against cats, domestic or otherwise, but wouldn't some people be better served with that money? I'm all for taking care of our own species first."

Despite the humor of her words, the earnestness of her gaze got to him. "What are you really trying to say?"

"I just wonder why someone would put such a stipulation in their will, nowadays. It seems to me she must have had some reason for doing so."

"How about pure cussedness? She wrote me a letter that I received after her death. She says the greatest mistake of her life was never marrying when she got the opportunity, which turned her into, in her words, a mean-spirited harpie. She wanted better for Francesca and me. Incidentally, Frankie is under the same gun, so to speak, if she doesn't marry before thirty. Although, knowing Frankie, she'll probably just hog-tie some guy to the altar and pester him until he says I do."

"But you've made up your mind not to comply?"

"Yes."

"You're sure this isn't one final act of rebellion against your parents and all they stand for, one you won't regret after the deadline passes?"

He'd never thought about it that way, but he admitted to himself she might have a point. Even if it were, he didn't see how that changed things any. "Why are you so interested? Are you offering yourself up as sacrificial bride?"

"No. Maybe. I don't know. The idea has merit. She didn't make any other stipulations to the will, like the duration of the marriage or whether you had children?"

"Aside from the marriage lasting at least six months, no."

"That's not too much to ask."

He swallowed. "Maybe not, but if I were to actually go through with this, I would expect it to be a real marriage. Do you know what I mean?"

She grinned. "I think so. That wouldn't be a problem."

He sighed. She thought he meant he wanted sex, when what he referred to was a commitment to build a life together. "Are you in love with me, Nina?"

"No, but I care for you, I respect you, you do wicked things to my nervous system, and we haven't even made love yet. We would both have our eyes open. If things didn't work out, we could walk away without rancor."

What she offered sounded cold and barren, and ultimately more practical a foundation for marriage than most of the rose-colored vows spoken by the true romantics who took the leap. Worse yet, she implied that she expected no more from a union with him or any other man. But what got to him most was that she obviously lacked any insight into the depth of his feelings for her.

He laughed without mirth. For some reason the old Meatloaf song popped into his head, the one about the man who claimed to need and want the woman in his life but was incapable of loving her. Two out of three might not be bad, but Nina neither needed him nor loved him. One out of three stunk.

On second thought, she did need him for something. "And you would be satisfied with this arrangement? All you want is to help me preserve my inheritance?"

"I didn't say that. I'd get my family off my back, for one thing."

She didn't say what the other thing was, but he knew what she wanted from the relationship she proposed: children. The one thing, as his circumstances were now, that he couldn't give her.

He moved closer to her and took her hand. "Sweetheart, there's something about me you should know before you get any further along with this plan of yours."

She cast him a scoffing look, as if she believed he was simply trying to scare her off. "What's that?"

He exhaled, searching for the words to convey what he'd done and his motivation for doing it. Before he got a word out, his beeper went off. *Damn!* Saved by the bell, though he didn't want salvation. He wanted Nina to know precisely what she would be getting herself into, and to what degree that altered her plans.

He unclipped the beeper from his belt and read the hospital's number on the display. "I need to call in."

He felt her eyes on him as he rose from the sofa, retrieved his cell phone, and dialed the number. Secretly, he hoped it was something innocuous, like a question that could be easily answered over the phone. Anything that wouldn't take him away from Nina at this moment. But there had been a major accident on the West Side Highway just off the 116th Street exit.

He turned to Nina, who sat with her legs drawn up underneath her. "I'm sorry, but I have to go."

She lifted one shoulder. "I figured. Are you going to be all right?"

Now he'd gone and done it—labeled himself an emotional weakling in her eyes. "I promise not to have a repeat performance."

Her eyes narrowed. "I wasn't talking about before. I meant that we haven't had dinner yet. I wouldn't want you to pass out from low blood sugar at the operating table."

"I'm not a surgeon."

"No, but you're very literal, aren't you?"

She rose from the sofa to walk him to the door. At the threshold, she stopped and wrapped her arms around his neck. "You take care of yourself, Doctor."

He scrubbed his hands up and down her sides, pulling her closer at the same time. "You do the same." He pressed his lips to hers briefly, as any deeper contact might have made him forget his obligation and lose himself in her arms. He pulled away and winked at her. "Don't forget, you're cooking dinner tomorrow night."

"Yeah, at this rate, leftovers."

He touched his fingertip to the tip of her nose. "Sleep tight." Then he headed down the hallway to wait for the elevator.

Matthew walked into his apartment a little after midnight, surprised to find his sister on the sofa with a box of tissues beside her. She had some black-and-white tearjerker on the tube, not usually her kind of movie. Usually, movies in which at least one person didn't get his butt kicked didn't interest her.

Besides that, he would have sworn he'd have beaten her in for the night, but she must have been in for a while, as she had on her pajamas, his robe, and a pair of fuzzy slippers with monster toes poking out the front.

"Early night?" he asked, coming to sit beside her.

"I didn't go out."

His eyebrows lifted. Now that surprised him most of all. "Are you feeling all right?" He extended his hand, intending to feel her forehead for signs of fever.

She smacked his hand away. "Quit being a doctor. I'm fine."

"If you say so." He sat back and propped his feet on the coffee table, mimicking her posture. "Is there any particular reason you're watching this?"

"What do you mean?"

"I thought maybe you'd lost a bet or something and were forced to watch this thing. Or does Rambo show up in a few minutes and mow everybody down?"

"Very funny. How did things go with Nina?"

He sighed. "Fine, until the moment that my beeper went off and I had to go back to work."

"That stinks. So you didn't tell her?"

"No."

"Do it, Matt. Do it soon."

He turned his head in her direction to study her profile. She sounded so somber and her expression had turned so grim that he wondered if there wasn't a deeper reason for her admonishment. "Why are you so worried about it?"

She glanced his way and huffed in a way that told him she expected him to already know the answer. "Because I'm your sister and I care about you. And it seems to me that if you have a chance to be happy you shouldn't screw around and blow it."

"Is that a general warning or does that advice come from personal experience?" He tugged on a strand of her long brown hair that had come free of her ponytail.

She brushed his hand away. "Never mind where it comes from. It's true."

Her evasiveness deepened his suspicion that some idiot had broken her heart, or damaged it at the very least. "You know, if there's anything you want to talk about, you can always come to me."

"Yeah, I know. But shouldn't you be in bed or something? Don't you have to go to work in the morning?"

"Unfortunately, yes. You sure you don't want some company?"

"Why? So you can fall asleep in five minutes and snore through the rest of my program?"

"I see your point." He leaned over and kissed his sister's cheek. "See you tomorrow." He rose from the sofa and started to make his way toward his bedroom.

"Matt."

He turned to face her. "Yes?"

"Thanks for letting me stay here. I know I really pushed it back at the house. I called Mom and told her I was sorry, too."

He blinked and pretended to sway. "I really must be out of it. I could have sworn I heard you say you apologized to our mother."

Frankie flung a sofa pillow that would have hit him right in the head if he hadn't caught it first. "I don't know why I tell you anything," she said.

He tossed the pillow back to her. He wondered why she wouldn't tell him enough.

Nine

Nina glanced at her beside clock. Two in the morning, and still she couldn't sleep. She hadn't been plagued by insomnia since childhood. Her cure then had been to get one of her treasured books and read until she felt drowsy. She'd been staring at the pages of James Patterson's latest thriller for hours and she remained as awake as ever. Worse yet, she hadn't a clue as to what she'd supposedly read.

She threw off her covers and padded to the living room barefoot. She sat on the sofa and flicked on the television. At this hour, it wouldn't be hard to find something simple and brainless to take her mind off what really occupied her. Dr. Matthew Peterson and the feelings he inspired in her.

He'd asked her if she loved him, and she'd answered honestly but not truthfully. He aroused feelings in her that terrified her, all those warm fuzzy feelings she'd read about but never experienced, coupled with an incredible case of lust. The lust she could handle, but what of the more tender emotions he engendered in her? They were the reason she'd brought up his inheritance, the desire to make sure he didn't regret his decision to walk away from it.

Those feelings, if not love yet, could soon be. That thought terrified her more than a little. It left her vulnerable in a way she had sworn she would never be to a man. Maybe she should walk away now, before she got in too deep, before she couldn't let him go.

But what sort of life would she have if she did that? In her heart she knew she could go on simply as she was, alone. Maybe she could find another Ron, a man who would fulfill her sexually but leave her untouched in every other way. She might protect her heart and save herself from the same misery her mother faced. Or maybe she'd end up like his aunt, a bitter old woman, who in death challenged her relatives to do what she had been afraid to do in life.

He hadn't said he loved her either, though she knew he cared for her in a way no man ever had before, as a person, not simply as the woman he happened to be sleeping with at the time. Even Ron, as much as he had professed to love her, saw her more as the means by which to satisfy his own domestic fantasy—marriage to an independent woman who wouldn't ask too much of him, who would take care of his children without much input from him, leaving him free to pursue his true love: writing.

She laughed without humor, realizing what she'd thought she'd wanted all these years—marriage to a man who would give her children but wouldn't claim too much of her heart—was exactly what Ron would have provided. And she'd rejected it. She'd rejected him until the point he found what he wanted in someone else.

And what of her own desire to have children? She'd always considered children on the level with her books—safe to love. As long as you fed them, clothed them, put a roof over their heads and treated them halfway decently, you'd have a few good years with them before they decided you were too old and out of it to understand anything about them. And when they left home and got their own places, that was the natural order of things. She'd wanted someone to lavish her affection on, without fear of desertion. Someone to belong to. Men might come and go, but children were for keeps.

So, where did that leave her? She thought of Matthew and the easy way they'd agreed to spend their evenings together. She could imagine that as her life, spending together whatever time their jobs allowed them, going to sleep each night and waking in the morning with Matthew beside her. And that had nothing to do with her fear of being alone and everything to do with wanting to be with him.

She couldn't go back; she could only move forward. Matthew was a good man, the most stable man she knew. If she stood any chance of building a secure relationship, it would be with him. Despite his words, she sensed his ambivalence about the inheritance. If she had to use that as a lever to pull him forward with her, she would use it.

Nina huffed out a resolute breath. She knew what she was going to do.

The next day dragged for Matthew, as the ER wasn't busy and he was impatient to see Nina later that night. With his sister's words ringing in his ears coupled with his own desire to come clean with her, he was anxious to tell her what he hadn't been able to the night before. If she saw no future for them, he wanted to know now.

He'd just finished diagnosing his second ear infection of the day when the intercom on the wall phone buzzed to life. "Matt, you have a visitor at the front desk."

Anticipation shot through him until he checked his watch. At two o'clock it was too early for Nina to be here. Who else could it be? Maybe his sister had gotten bored and decided to pester him for the afternoon. He pressed the appropriate button. "I'll be out in a moment."

He finished up with his patient and went out to reception. A girl of about sixteen stood at the reception desk. She obviously recognized him, but he hadn't a clue who she was.

"Dr. Matt, don't you remember me?"

Dressed in jeans and what in his day would have been called a peasant blouse, she looked like any other young woman. He scanned her face for signs of familiarity. "Michelle?" The last time he'd seen Michelle Turner she'd been fourteen years old, recuperating in a hospital bed from surgery to correct a defect in her heart. She'd been small and painfully skinny, the antithesis of the healthy-looking young woman that stood before him. "What are you doing here?"

"I was thinking about you and I found out you worked here." She shrugged in the offhand way teenagers do. "I'm taking classes at Columbia." She grinned. "I'm premed."

And obviously summer school at that. "You poor thing. Are they working you hard?"

She lifted one shoulder. "Nothing I can't handle."

Self-assurance. It suited her. "If you need any pointers, you know where to find me."

She motioned toward the exit. "I've got to go. I've got someone waiting downstairs for me. I just wanted to say thanks again." She embraced him hastily, as if she wasn't sure she should. "Bye, Dr. Matt."

"Tell your mother I say hello."

"I will."

Matthew watched her as she hurried off toward the elevators. It seemed like a lifetime ago that a colleague had lamented to him that he had a patient who needed surgery and the family lacked insurance. Between the two of them, they had convinced the doctors involved to waive their operating room fees. Matthew had paid for the rest out of his own pocket. The family would have been staggered to know what the total bill had come to.

If he had money to blow, that's what he'd blow it on. That's what caused the ambivalence Nina sensed in him. But he'd meant it when he said it wasn't worth changing his life over. If he really wanted the money that badly, he'd petition the court to release it to him. Considering that his aunt had been a crazy old bat, he'd probably win. But he couldn't see spending the effort on that either.

His beeper went off and he checked the number on the display—Garrett Taylor's office number. He borrowed one of the phones at the desk and dialed the number.

"What's up?" he asked when Garrett picked up. "You busy?"

"Not too. Why?"

"I heard on the family grapevine that Nina's grandmother was brought in. Sounds like a stroke. I don't know how bad."

"Damn," he muttered. "Does Nina know?"

"They were together."

Which meant she probably came in right behind the ambulance. "Thanks." He hung up the phone, told the receptionist where he was headed, and went to the other side of the building to the adult emergency room.

He found Nina right away, standing alone, leaning against a wall, her eyes closed, her arms folded. The quiet tapping of her right foot served as the only sign of her distress.

As he approached, she opened her eyes and straightened. Their gazes met and the despair in hers nearly undid him. Part of him wished she would run to him, seeking his comfort, but that wasn't Nina's style. He made do with the welcome she provided: opening her arms to him. And when he entered them she buried her nose against his neck.

She gulped in a breath of air. "I didn't expect you to come."

He smoothed his hand over her hair. "I was right next door. Why didn't you call me?"

She shrugged, but he knew the answer. She was used to coping alone. He coaxed her head up with a finger under her chin. "How are you doing?"

"I'm not worried about me."

"I know, sweetheart. What happened?"

"She came into the city to have lunch with me. She didn't look right. I don't know how to describe it. Her left side seemed to sag and she couldn't read the menu. Normally, my grandmother has better eyesight than I do."

From what she'd told him, he'd guess that Garrett was right. If so, they could only hope the stroke was a mild one and that it wasn't caused by bleeding in the brain. "Have they told you anything yet?"

"No."

"Do you want me to see what I can find out?"

She nodded.

He tucked her hair behind her ear, offering her an encouraging smile. "I'll be right back."

She nodded and stepped away from him. "Hurry."

He found the room where Nina's grandmother had been worked on just as they were wheeling her out. She looked pale and small, hooked up to an IV, but she had enough presence of mind to recognize him and warn him to look after her granddaughter. He breathed out a sigh of relief. For all he knew, she might not be out of danger yet, but for the present he didn't have to look Nina in the face and tell her that her grandmother was gone.

After speaking with the doctor who'd seen Nina's grandmother, Matthew went back to the waiting room. Nina's brother and his wife had arrived in the meantime. Nathan had his arm around his wife's waist and his sister's shoulders. All three turned to him with expectant faces.

Nina slid out of her brother's embrace and stepped toward him. "How is she?"

He took her hand and gave her fingers a gentle squeeze. "Alert enough to fuss at me for wasting my time looking after her when I should be taking care of you."

Nina snorted, while Nathan eyed him with an expression that was more questioning than confrontational. Obviously neither Nina nor her doorman had bothered to share with him the fact that he and Nina were seeing each other.

"I spoke with her doctor, too. He thinks it's a mild stroke. The neurological was normal, though she has a slight weakness in her left arm. They're taking her upstairs for a CAT scan to make sure the stroke is aeschemic, not hemorrhagic."

"What's the difference?" Daphne asked.

"An aeschemic stroke is caused by a blood clot rather than by bleeding in the brain. In that case, they would give her TPA, a thrombolitic that basically reverses the effect of the stroke. It's as if it never happened. Otherwise it might take weeks or months of rehabilitation to get the patient back to where they were prestroke, if at all."

His gaze slid from Daphne to Nina. She presented a stoic front, but he wondered how well she was holding together on the inside where it counted. "It should be at least a half hour before she comes back down. Want to get some coffee?"

She nodded and turned to face the others. "Do you guys want anything?"

Both Nathan and Daphne declined. With a hand on Nina's back, he led her toward the bank of elevators on the other side of the floor. As they waited, he slid his arm around her waist. "How are you doing, really?"

She leaned her cheek against his shoulder. "I'm scared, Matthew. It sounds like a crazy thing to say since my grandmother is over eighty years old, but I never really considered her mortality before. She's always been healthy as an ox."

He tightened his grip on her waist. "You two are very close?"

She nodded. "Nathan always had his music or Daphne to occupy him. He's been in love with her since they were kids. Yasmin isn't interested in anything that doesn't have either bulging pectorals or matching accessories. The rest of my relatives think I'm a cold fish and ignore me. My grandmother is the only one who's always been there for me."

She lifted her head and tried to pull away from him, perhaps realizing she'd said more than she intended. He refused to let her withdraw from him. He scrubbed his arm up and down her side. "Sweetheart, you can't be losing hope already when we don't even know for sure what's wrong yet."

"I know. But it's the first time I've thought about losing her."

He didn't know what to say to that. Receiving a medical degree didn't automatically confer on the bearer a mystical ability to summon up the appropriate words of comfort for any occasion. The elevator came and they got on.

The cafeteria was a large L-shaped room where staffers joked you could find everything from soup to nuts—the human kind that talked to people who weren't really there.

"How's the food here?" Nina asked him, looking around.

"As institutional fare goes, it's not too bad. Only gives me indigestion once or twice a week."

She glanced up at him, smiling. "What's the safest bet?"

"They make a mean can of beef barley. It's the special today."

"Sounds tempting."

He took her arm and led her to the appropriate line. Once they'd each gotten a cup of coffee, he paid for their meal and led her to one of the small square tables in the eating area. Nina dipped her spoon in the steaming soup and brought the sample to her lips. "How is it?" he asked.

She lifted one shoulder and tilted her head to one side. "Not bad if you like bland. Could use some salt."

There was a shaker on the table, but she made no move to use it. Nor did she take her eyes off her soup bowl. She ate rapidly and mechanically, as though trying to force down sustenance because she needed it, not caring about the taste. Obviously neither his presence nor the food offered much of a diversion from what really bothered her. Not yet.

He took a sip of coffee and set his cup on the table. "Why didn't you tell your brother about us?"

She did look at him then. "It never came up. Truthfully, I haven't seen him since Emily's birthday party. Does that bother you?"

"No. He seemed surprised, that's all."

"Nathan is used to seeing me with a different kind of man."

Maybe he was looking for trouble, but he couldn't resist asking, "What kind of man is that?"

"You know, someone flashy and macho. The type to break a girl's heart if she lets him. Someone he can relate to, or could until he found Daphne again."

"Does that hold true for the man you just broke up with?"

"I suppose. Ron is a fairly well known mystery author who doesn't mind flashing either his money or his testosterone."

"So why did you break things off with him?"

"I didn't. He married someone else."

His eyebrows lifted. He wouldn't have expected any human male to be capable of walking away from Nina if she wanted him to stay. He knew he couldn't. "His loss."

"True, in more ways than you know. But can we drop the subject? It's a little weird discussing the men in my life with you."

He feigned innocence. "Why?"

He didn't fool her. She tilted her head to the side, offering him a droll look. "For one thing, it occurs to me that you know a hell of a lot about my former love life while I know nothing about yours."

"You never asked."

"Okay, so I'm asking."

"I've been around the block a few times, but I'm no heartbreaker."

She considered him for a long moment, with an expression much too intense for their lighthearted banter. "You better not be." She pushed her bowl away from her. "We should get back."

By the time they got back downstairs, Yasmin had arrived. Of all of them she looked the most shaken. Matthew stepped out of the way as the younger woman rushed forward to throw her arms around Nina. Nina's arms closed around her cousin, rubbing her back in a soothing motion, as she whispered comforting words, some of the same ones she'd whispered to him when he'd needed them.

This woman he loved had so much love inside her. That thought came to him, and he accepted it with no surprise but with a little bit of wonderment. He was in love with Nina Ward. As he watched her walk her cousin toward the chairs and settle her into one, he wondered what it would take to get her to direct her love fully toward him. She'd told him that she cared for him, that she wanted him, but it wasn't enough. He wanted all of her.

"I can't believe this is happening," he heard

Yasmin say as he walked forward to join the others. "She's always been in perfect health. She doesn't even have arthritis. Thank God you were with her and got her to the hospital in time."

"Shh," Nina said. "You sound like *Abuela* is on death's doorstep, when in all likelihood she's only had a mild stroke. Let's wait until we find out what's wrong before we have the panic attack."

Nina's gaze met his and she smiled, a silent thank you for giving her similar advice only a few minutes ago. He winked at her, but a moment later, Stu Gardner, the attending physician for the emergency room, came out of the double doors leading to the ward.

Matthew stood as Stu came directly to him. "You're here with the Ward family?"

He gestured in a way that encompassed all of them. "These are her grandchildren." He introduced each of them, who in turn shook hands with Stu.

"Your grandmother is doing fine. Our initial diagnosis was correct. She's had a mild stroke. She's got a blot clot in her brain that needs to be addressed, but we're confident she can make a full recovery."

"Can we see her?" Nina asked.

Stu nodded. "I'll let two of you in. We need to admit her and she needs to make a decision about her treatment options."

Matthew took Nina's hand as she and Nathan stepped forward as the chosen delegates. Stu led them to an exam room on the perimeter of the ward and pulled aside the curtain. "Luz, your grandchildren are here."

Nina entered and pulled the chair beside the bed closer to her grandmother, while Nathan stood beside her. Matthew was glad to see that her condition didn't seem to have worsened any, as that would indicate that more areas of the brain were being affected.

"How are you feeling?" Nina asked.

"Def-finitely been better."

Nina snorted, then turned to Stu. "You said my grandmother had to make a decision about her treatment options?"

"Yes. In cases like hers, we usually prescribe TPA as the course of treatment. Without getting into medical jargon, it basically reverses the effects of the stroke, as if it never happened."

"What are the side effects?" Nathan asked.

"Basically, there aren't any. TPA does promote systemic bleeding in order to break up the clot, but your grandmother doesn't have any preexisting conditions that would contraindicate its use."

"What is the alternative?"

"We can administer heparin to help break up the clot and let the stroke run its course, but I wouldn't advise it. It might take your grandmother much longer to recover. With TPA, she should be back to being herself within twenty-four hours."

While Nathan and Daphne exchanged a look, Stu glanced at him, obviously wondering what his relationship was to this family. Matthew decided to let him wonder.

Stu shrugged. "Take a few minutes to decide, but if you decide to go with TPA, we need to administer it within four hours of the onset of the stroke."

Stu turned to leave, but Luz urged him back with a wave of her unaffected arm. "Shtay," Luz said, but her gaze was on Matthew. "Shtu is s-s-single."

Wily old woman, Matthew thought. She was challenging him to make a claim on Nina, and he didn't mind doing so.

"I'll make sure he gets a better look at Yasmin," he said. Nina's grandmother chuckled, while Stu turned as red as a black man's complexion allowed.

"I'll be back," Stu said, then bolted before he could be embarrassed any further.

"What do you want to do, *Abuela?*" Nina asked when Stu was out the door. "Do you want the TPA?"

Luz glanced at him and he nodded. She held up her good hand. "Cons-sen-nt form."

Later, after Nina's grandmother had been settled into a private room and the drug administered, Matthew took Nina home. Nathan and Daphne had agreed to drop Yasmin off and bring Luz some articles to make her more comfortable. When they got to her apartment, he nuked some of the uneaten Chinese food for himself and Nina. Ever since they'd left the hospital she'd been uncharacteristically silent and more withdrawn than he'd ever seen her.

They sat on her sofa, resting their food on the

coffee table. Nina had barely touched hers, and he hadn't done much better. "What is it, sweetheart? Are you still worried about your grandmother?"

"It's not that. I . . ." She trailed off, shaking her head.

"Come here, sweetheart." He pulled her closer so that her head rested against his shoulder. "What can I do?"

She was silent for a long moment; then she lifted her face to his. "You can marry me, Matthew."

He wouldn't have been more surprised if his eyes had bugged clean out of his head. Of all the possible answers she could have given to that question, he expected that one the least. Yet, he thought he knew what had prompted her request, and he didn't like the implications. "Why?"

"It makes sense. I don't want to see you lose your inheritance because you're too stubborn to admit you want it. I—"

"Stop." He cut her off, not wanting to hear another dry accounting of her reasons. "How much of your sudden desire to walk down the aisle has to do with your grandmother becoming ill, her desire to see you married before she dies?"

"It's not all that sudden, not any more sudden than anything else that's happened between us."

True. In a few weeks they'd gone from virtual strangers to discussing marriage, albeit not in the way most people would. He could kill his sister for ever mentioned the damn money. He couldn't put off telling Nina any longer, which was probably for the best. It might end this ludicrous conversation. Matthew swallowed. But it might end all that had developed between them, too, the thing he dreaded most.

He shifted so that he faced her and took her hand. "Listen, Nina. About five years ago, I decided I didn't want children. I made sure I didn't have any. I had a vasectomy."

She laughed in the way people do when they've heard something shocking. "You what?"

"I don't know if it's reversible. I don't know if I would reverse it if I could. My reasons for doing it haven't changed."

She viewed him through narrowed eyes. "What reasons were those?"

"I told you once, the world is often not a very nice place for children. Working in a hospital I've seen plenty of the gruesome things we adults can do to children. I've seen the sorrow brought on by illness or death. I didn't want to live through any of that firsthand."

He hadn't told her everything, but he'd told her enough to make her understand. Or he'd thought so, until she pulled away from him to pace the area on the opposite side of the coffee table.

Finally, she turned to face him with her arms wrapped around her middle. "You know something, Matthew, a month ago, I would have said having children was the most important thing to me, that I wouldn't consider my life complete without them. But in the last few weeks, I've found every assumption I made about myself, everything I thought I wanted, challenged in one way or another. I can't say I don't still want children. I can't say if what you've told me changes anything. I don't know."

"Then don't you think you should make up your mind before we make any decisions?"

"That's just it, Matthew. We don't have time. When is your birthday?"

"September fifteenth."

"That's only a month and a half away. I don't know about your family, but mine would never let me get away with not having a proper wedding, in church, with bridesmaids, the whole nine yards— all of it French lace."

"Nina—" he began.

"It's six months, Matthew. Aren't six short months worth five million dollars?"

She offered him months when what he wanted was a lifetime. "Can you meet me tomorrow afternoon?"

"Sure. Why?"

"You're going to need an engagement ring."

She stared at him a long time, as surprise, acceptance, and finally resignation played across her face. He realized that at least in some part she hadn't expected him to say yes. She licked her lips. "When do you want to get married?"

"How does three weeks sound?"

"I think I could swing that." She wrapped her arms around her waist. "One more thing. I would need you to sign a prenuptial agreement. You know, all my assets stay my assets except for those I give you. That sort of thing."

He knew she requested that for his protection,

not her own. "I'll have my lawyer draft one. I need something, too."

"What's that?"

"I'm assuming you would want to live here. In that case, I would need your brother to sell me this apartment."

"Why?"

"I'm too old to be living under another man's roof."

She smiled, the first smile he'd seen on her face all day. "So the macho finally comes out."

"Damn straight. If he won't sell, we live at my place. That is, if I can get my sister to go home."

"All right."

For the first time since he'd known her she seemed fragile and unsteady. He got up and went to her, stopping when their bodies were only inches apart. He threaded his fingers through her hair, cradling her head and forcing her to look up at him. "Are you sure this is what you want?"

"Yes."

He closed his eyes and shook his head. How had he agreed to this farce, when what he really wanted was a real marriage with a chance for a real future?

"Matthew?"

That one softly spoken word, full of concern, got to him. It reminded him that she did care for him, even if it wasn't in the way he wanted. Not yet, anyway. She offered him six months, but maybe that was all the time he'd need to convince her they belonged together.

He lowered his mouth to hers for a gentle kiss full of all the tenderness, all the love he felt for her. When he pulled away, she swayed against him, a closed-eyed, dreamy expression on her face.

"One more thing," he said. "I'm paying for the wedding."

She opened her eyes and grinned up at him. "You'll have to fight that one out with Nathan."

Ten

Nina woke late the following morning since she hadn't bothered to set her alarm clock. She stretched and reached for the phone to leave a message on the office answering machine to say she wouldn't be in except to pick up some work to complete at home.

With a sigh, she settled back against the pillows. After Matthew left the night before, she'd called Yasmin to tell her the news. She'd wanted to speak to another person and verify she was still on planet Earth and she hadn't dreamt most of what happened that day. In a way, it had all seemed surreal—her grandmother's illness, Matthew's somewhat easy acquiescence to her proposal.

She'd thought for sure she'd have to beat him over the head to get him to agree to it, but she hadn't needed to call out the big guns. Or reveal that her desire for marriage had nothing to do with his inheritance. She'd save that for later when she was sure she hadn't talked them both into making a big mistake.

But he'd absolutely shocked her with his own revelation, not so much the vasectomy part, but the admission that he didn't want children of his own. With his obvious love of children, she had assumed the opposite was true. She didn't know what to make of that, but she didn't buy that explanation of his as to why he'd come to that decision. She suspected a more personal reason lay at its core, though she couldn't imagine what that might be. In any event, she had six months to convince him of the error in his thinking.

Even if the vasectomy wasn't reversible, they could always adopt. Every year, millions of black children languished in foster care because there weren't enough black families to adopt them. And given that Matthew was a doctor and she a businesswoman, they would certainly qualify as an acceptable household.

She rolled that plan around in her mind for a while, relishing the future she envisioned for them. But she couldn't lie in bed all day. She had to meet Matthew. She had to stop by her office. She wanted to be at the hospital by one o'clock when visiting hours began. After that, she needed to get over to Yasmin's studio for measurements for her gown, which Yasmin insisted on designing, and begin planning all the other details of the wedding, from the church to a reception hall to flowers, and all in three weeks. She must be insane.

She threw off her covers and headed for the shower. She'd just finished styling her hair when the phone rang. She smiled hearing Matthew's voice on the other end of the line. "What can I do for you so early in the morning?"

"There's been a change in plans. Can you meet me on Forty-seventh and Seventh at eight-thirty?"

"Sure, but you're just going to be standing on the corner?"

"Something like that."

"Okay."

"See you then." The line went dead before she had time to respond.

She hung up the phone, shaking her head, wondering what this man was up to. She threw off her robe and dressed in one of her favorite summer outfits, a short red skirt and matching red and orange sweater set. She checked the clock again. Downtown traffic in rush hour was always a bear. She'd be lucky to find a cab at this hour.

She made it to the appropriate corner only five minutes late. Matthew was already waiting for her. He paid the driver before helping her out of the cab.

Stepping onto the curb, Nina glanced at her surroundings. They stood in the heart of the diamond district, which just seemed to be opening its doors for business. He'd said he wanted to buy her a ring, and she guessed he wasn't kidding. So his first words other than hello surprised her.

"Have you had breakfast yet?"

"No."

"Good. I'm starved." He led her to a little diner a step up from being a greasy spoon. They were seated by a window booth that overlooked Seventh

Avenue. Matthew picked up one of the menus the waitress left with them. "What do you feel like eating?"

"Nothing, until you tell me what we're doing here."

"Eating." He put down the menu and pulled something metallic from his pocket. "Give me your left hand."

She complied more out of curiosity than anything else. "Are you going to tell my fortune?"

"Not exactly." He fiddled with the metallic thing, which she realized was a jeweler's ring sizer. He slid one of the loops over her ring finger. He slid it off again. "Excuse me for a second." He pulled out his cell phone and dialed a number. Whoever was on the other end must have picked up immediately, as it seemed only a second before Matthew said, "Five and a half. Perfect." He disconnected the call and replaced the phone in his breast pocket. He grinned at her. "Where were we?"

"You're really enjoying yourself, aren't you?"

"Yup."

She decided to let him have his fun. Obviously he planned to surprise her with a ring, though it wasn't much of a surprise. Truthfully, she didn't care about a ring one way or the other, but she enjoyed seeing him like this, the mischievous little boy inside the man. "What's good here?"

"Almost nothing, but they won't poison you."

She decided on a bagel with cream cheese, while Matthew ordered steak and eggs. When their meal arrived, she said, "You're a doctor. Don't you know all that cholesterol is bad for you?"

"Actually, refined carbohydrates are worse. Recent studies have shown that diets high in protein are actually better for you. Protein burns off as fat, while carbs turn to sugar. Which explains in part the rampant diabetes in the black community. Too much starch in the diet."

Nina's shoulder's drooped. "So this bagel is going straight to my hips?"

"Pretty much. Mind you, I'm not complaining."

She shook her head, laughing. "Is that a compliment from you? If so, it needs work."

"Telling you you're a beautiful woman is like telling the sun it's bright. That's a given. Besides, I already told you."

She remembered. The night Justin was sick. "But then you said it to put me in my place."

"I wasn't trying to put you in your place, that was self-protection. I knew you knew I was attracted to you. And there you were thinking of me as Dr. Frumpy."

Her mouth fell open and she snapped it shut. "You knew about that?"

He chuckled. "Not then, but Yasmin let it slip. I swear, if there's anything that girl knows that she hasn't blabbed to someone, I can't imagine what it is."

"As a kid we used to call her Motor Mouth." She sipped from her cup. "Remind me to kill her later."

He laughed. "She's not that bad. Nothing a little maturity won't cure."

"We can only hope." Nina pushed her plate away. "Are we finished eating yet?"

"Almost." Matthew turned to watch a man rushing by the window on his way into the coffee shop. The man, a tall drink of water with graying hair and mustache, came to stand by their table. "Nina, this is a friend of mine, Jackie Spenser. Jackie, this is my fiancée, Nina Ward."

Jackie stuck out his hand. "Nina, it's a pleasure. Though I never thought I'd see the day when this one called me up first thing in the morning needing my services."

Nina shook his hand. "It's good to meet you. I suppose you're the reason this one has been very secretive this morning." She cast a look at Matthew.

"Go ahead, discuss me like I'm not here."

"We already were." He punched Matthew on the shoulder. "Step into my office over here, so I can get out of here. I have real customers waiting for me."

Matthew excused himself and the two men went over to the counter. Matthew had his back to her, so she couldn't see what he was up to. After a moment, the men embraced and Jackie headed out the door the way he'd come.

But instead of taking his seat, Matthew tossed some bills on the table to cover their meal. "Are you ready to go?"

"That's it? We're leaving?"

"Unless you want more coffee."

Nina made a face. The one cup she'd drunk was now giving her indigestion. "I have to be at Yasmin's in less than an hour."

"You'll make it in plenty of time."

She took the hand he extended toward her and let him help her slide from the booth. "Where are we going?"

"You'll see."

Once outside the restaurant, they took a cab to the corner of Thirty-fourth Street and Fifth Avenue. Matthew checked his watch. "We're right on time."

"On time for what?"

With his hand around her waist he led her toward the entrance at the middle of the block. "A trip to the top of the Empire State Building."

"You've got to be kidding?"

"Nope. Have you ever been here before?"

"No. I'm like most New Yorkers. It's here, so I always figured I'd get around to it eventually."

"I guess today is eventually, then."

She laughed, willing to indulge him, if only to find out what this was all about. They had to go to the lower level to buy tickets for the elevator that would take them to the observatory on the top floor. The swift ride up made her stomach lurch and her ears pop. "Now I know why I haven't been here before," she joked as they stepped out of the elevator.

He led her through the indoor section, where overpriced food as well as every conceivable souvenir for the Empire State Building was sold, to the outside observation deck. They took a place along the railing that faced Lower Manhattan. Even though it was a warm summer day at ground level, at this altitude a chilly breeze whipped around them.

Matthew stood behind her, wrapping his arm around her waist. His warm breath fanned her face as he leaned down to kiss her cheek. "Isn't the trip worth it for this glorious view?"

She smiled. "I guess." Her gaze swept over the city, as she picked out the buildings she knew by name or location. Way to the south there was nothing where the buildings of the Trade Center once stood.

Matthew squeezed her waist. "The last time I was here I was in the sixth grade, a class trip. The Twin Towers had opened a couple of years before. I remembered standing at this spot and wondering what the big deal was about two tall buildings. Now they're gone, and I actually miss them. It's as if a part of the city was lost when they collapsed."

She nodded. Like most New Yorkers, she had mourned the loss of life on that tragic day, but the loss of such an integral part of the landscape was felt almost as keenly.

"If that day reminded me of anything, it was that nothing in this life is guaranteed, Nina. Nothing."

She shifted to gaze back at him. "Boy, you're a bundle of cheer this morning."

He smiled and tucked a strand of her hair behind her ear. "I just meant that all we can live by are our intentions, because seeing our plans come to fruition isn't always up to us."

"That's supposed to be better?"

He sighed. "This isn't coming out quite how I meant it."

"Thank goodness."

He turned her in his arms so that she faced him. "Will you marry me, Nina? I'd get down on one knee, but there's a big wad of gum on the floor."

"You know that I will."

"No, what I'm asking now has nothing to do with our arrangement or the money. Will you marry me?"

She bit her lip, not knowing how to answer him. She shook her head, confused. What exactly was he asking her? And why? She'd thought they'd settled all this last night. Did he think she needed the appearance of a real marriage to justify her actions? Or was he trying to tell her in his own convoluted way that he wanted more from her than just the sham? "Matthew . . ."

He closed his eyes for a moment and when he opened them a rueful expression came over his face. "I guess I have your answer." He pulled a jeweler's box from his pocket. "This is what I had Jackie make up for you. I hope you like it."

He opened the box. Inside lay an emerald-cut diamond ring in a platinum setting. The stone was easily three carats. She glanced from the stone to him. "My God, Matthew. It's beautiful."

He took the ring from the box and slid it on her finger. "It looks beautiful on you."

He touched his lips to hers, a brief caress that left her wanting more. When he pulled away, she gazed up at him,

He laid a finger across her lips to silence her. "We'd better go before you're late to meet your cousin."

On the ride down on the elevator she stared at the light panel, convinced she'd lost an opportunity with him because of her indecision.

* * *

By the time Matthew brought Nina home to her apartment, he wished he'd never agreed to this hasty wedding in the first place. He'd accompanied her to Yasmin's studio, where the younger woman had embraced him as her new cousin-in-law and oohed over Nina's ring. The women in her office had congratulated Nina and offered ribald marital advice. Nina's grandmother, who had improved considerably from the night before, had told him that she could go in peace knowing that he would take care of her granddaughter.

Nina had rolled her eyes and told her grandmother to stop being such a drama queen. But he'd felt like a class-A heel anyway, knowing all they'd promised each other was six months, not forever.

He wouldn't have expected to feel so guilty at deceiving people who had been good to him. But most of all, guilt because he could offer Nina nothing of what she wanted while she gave him everything that mattered to him. And worse, he'd tried to rush a more substantial commitment out of her with his proposal. He should have known she wasn't ready for that yet, if she ever would be. He didn't know why he'd done it, except maybe to try to convince her that even if his great-aunt's will weren't hanging over his head, it wouldn't have changed anything. The timing might have been different, but he would still have wanted her for his wife.

Once they reached her door, he unlocked it, as usual, but for the first time in many days he waited on the threshold for her to notice he didn't follow.

After a moment she turned to face him with her hands on her hips. "What now?"

He chuckled at the exasperation in her voice. He crooked a finger at her. "Come here."

She walked toward him with that slinky way she had, teasing him. Promising him things he couldn't afford to take. Yet. He almost changed his mind, shut the door, and leaped on her. Almost.

She stopped a few inches from him and leaned her hand on the doorknob. "What can I do for you, Matthew?"

He swallowed down an inappropriate answer. "You can kiss me good-bye. I'm going up to my parents' house for dinner tonight. I figure I should tell them the news in person."

"We could do that together."

He shook his head. His parents would see right through the facade he and Nina had created. And, just in case his mother objected to his choice of a daughter-in-law for her, he didn't want Nina around to hear what she might say. "I was planning to go up anyway to discuss some family business. I'll kill two birds with one stone." It was the first real lie he'd ever told her and it left a bitter taste, like acid, in his mouth.

"If that's what you want."

Matthew inhaled and let the breath out slowly. That was the trouble: he'd gotten what he wanted but not the way he'd wanted it. He stepped toward her and placed his hands on her waist. "About that kiss . . ."

Bracing her hands on his shoulders, she went up on tiptoe to cover his mouth with hers. He tried to hold back from her, tried to maintain a small grip on his sanity, but she wasn't having that. Her arms slid around his neck and she pressed her soft body to his. Her tongue flicked against his—hot, tantalizing, and so erotic that he groaned and his body hardened from the pleasure of it. Obviously, she intended to make him regret leaving her, and she was doing a damn fine job of it.

He set her away from him before she did any more damage. "I'm leaving."

"Why?"

"We've already discussed my lack of self-control around you."

"Matthew," she said in a patient tone, "we're getting married in three weeks. You're the one who insisted on a real marriage, as you put it. Don't you think it's time we tested the equipment to make sure it works properly?"

"Mine is working just fine."

"You know what I mean. What if we're not compatible?"

He traced a finger down her breastbone to trail between her cleavage. She sucked in her breath, and her neck arched. "We're compatible."

She focused on his face, her eyes scanning his. "I don't understand you."

He rubbed his hands over her arms. "I know. But do this for me, Nina. Promise me to wait until we're married."

She made an exasperated sound and stepped back from him. "If you want to go, go. Lord knows, I've never had to beg a man to make love to me and I'm not going to start now."

Matthew gritted his teeth. He didn't doubt that. Under normal circumstances, he'd have gladly let her take him to her bed and make him the happiest man in North America. But these weren't normal circumstances, and the oddity of them was all his own doing.

He stroked his thumb over her cheek. "I'll call you tomorrow." He left before he was tempted to stay, despite his intentions. But as he waited for the elevator to come, he realized she'd never promised him anything.

That evening, as Matthew got ready to leave for his parents' house, he opened his apartment door to find Nina's brother on the other side. He carried a Louisville Slugger over his shoulder. The letters M-A-T-T-H-E-W had been written down the side. It took him a moment to realize they spelled his own name.

His mouth quirked into a sardonic smile. Nathan had told him how Daphne's brother Michael had shown up at his door in a similar fashion to inquire as to what Nathan's intentions were. Matthew supposed it was his turn. "To what do I owe the honor of this unexpected visit?"

"Why the hell are you marrying my sister?"

He figured as much. "You want the simple answer or the complicated one?"

"Both."

Matthew laughed. "Come on in, but I warn you my sister is in the other room, and if you try to use that thing on me, she will avenge me."

Nathan sauntered past him. "She'll have to catch me first."

Matthew followed Nathan into the living room and sat in the leather chair across from the sofa Nathan chose.

"As to the simple reason, I'm in love with her."

"Then what's the big rush?" Nathan fastened a narrow-eyed glare on him. "She's not pregnant, is she?"

"Not that it's any of your business, but no." He almost laughed wondering what Nathan would think if he knew they'd never been together. Probably suggest he needed testosterone replacement therapy. But he couldn't. To him that signaled the point of no return. He had to leave Nina the option of backing out if she wanted to, and he knew she wouldn't if she'd given herself to him.

But he did owe Nathan some sort of explanation. Or at least someone in her family that might talk some sense into her. Matthew leaned forward with his elbows on his knees. "As to the complicated reason." He huffed out a breath. "She's not in love with me, Nathan. She wants to help me get the five-million-dollar inheritance willed to me by my great-aunt if I get married by my fortieth birthday in a month and a half."

Nathan stared at him, then blinked; then he threw back his head and laughed. He laughed until tears ran from his eyes. "That's what she told you?"

He glared at Nathan, not finding anything humorous in what he'd said. "Not in those exact words, but that was the gist of it."

"Okay, man. I believe you. Who am I to argue?"

He was Nina's older brother, a man she listened to and respected. "Then you agree with me that she's making a mistake."

"Hey, I never said that. Anybody with two brain cells knows she's got more sense than I do. If she's decided she wants to marry you, I wouldn't stand in her way. But why did you agree to it, if you don't want to do it?"

He answered in the simplest way he knew how. "How do you walk away from the woman you've been waiting for all of your life?"

Nathan sobered. "I don't know, man. I couldn't do it. I came back into Daphne's life at a point when all I could bring her was trouble. I knew it, and I still couldn't stay away. I consider it a miracle things have turned out as well as they have."

Matthew sighed. It would take a true miracle for him and Nina to wind up with the happy ending Nathan shared with his wife. He assumed if Nathan knew about the wedding, he also knew about the conditions each had placed on it. "So are you going to sell me your apartment?"

"I'm planning on gouging you, too. As for the wedding, I'm willing to go half and half. My grandmother would never let me hear the end of it if she found out the bride's family wasn't footing at least some of the bill."

"It's a deal."

"How are you fixed for a best man?"

"I'll ask Garrett. I'm sure he'll agree."

Nathan nodded. "Honeymoon?"

He hadn't thought of that. "Got any suggestions?"

"I know a place." Nathan stood and extended his hand. "Welcome to the family."

Matthew stood and shook it. "Thanks." They started to walk toward the door.

"Be forewarned, my wife plans to throw you guys an engagement party this Friday night at our place. Invite your parents."

Matthew nodded. He'd invite them tonight after whatever scene played out when he told his parents he and Nina were getting married. He knew his father would be pleased for him. His mother was another story. Matthew opened the door and leaned his hand against the knob. "Anything else?"

"Don't hurt her." Nathan swung the bat up to his shoulder. "Because that time, when I come back, it'll be for real." Nathan winked at him, then headed down the hallway toward the elevator.

Eleven

"You did *what*?"

Matthew ground his teeth together. He had expected his mother to have some adverse reaction to the news that he and Nina planned to marry, and she didn't disappoint. He'd waited until after dinner to spring the news on them. The three of them sat in the great room, his father and mother on the settee, he in a chair on the other side of the coffee table. "Nina and I got engaged last night."

"I heard what you said. I just can't believe it."

"I can." Peter extended his hand toward his wife. "Pay up, Margaret."

Frowning, she reached into her pocket and pulled out a bill, which she slapped into his waiting hand. "You don't have to gloat."

"What is going on here?"

Margaret huffed. "Apparently your father knows you better than I do. When you called saying that you wanted to speak to both of us, he was convinced it was to tell us you'd changed your mind about the inheritance."

"And you two bet on that?"

"Unfortunately, only ten dollars," his father interjected.

After casting a disgruntled look at her husband, Matthew's mother focused her gaze on him. "Are you sure this is what you want, Matthew? You've been dead set against collecting that inheritance for years."

He wondered how much of his mother's apprehension was caused by concern for him and how much had to do with his choice of a daughter-in-law for her. "And those same years you have been doing everything possible to get me to accept it. Why the about-face now?"

"I haven't changed my mind. All I've ever wanted is for you to be happy."

"And you don't think I can be with Nina? Would you prefer to see me with one of your friends' daughters who couldn't give a damn about me as long as she had access to my bank account?"

"That's not fair. What kind of mother would I be if I didn't try to get my bachelor son to settle down with some type of decent woman? And if you'll remember, the night of the auction I was looking for you to introduce you to Nina, so how could I have any objection to her? From what I've seen, she's a lovely young woman."

"Then why are you so surprised I'd ask her to marry me?"

"Let me ask you a question instead. If you had to give one of them up, either Nina or the money, which one would you keep?"

"Nina, of course. I suppose I should have mentioned it before, but I'm in love with her."

His mother leaned forward in her chair, extending her hand toward her husband. "Your turn to pay up."

Matthew looked from one to the other. "What exactly was this bet?"

"Your mother said she doubted you'd be so mercenary as to marry purely for the money. And she was right." He reached in his pocket and extracted the ten-dollar bill. He laid it in his wife's hand, and stood. "I'm happy for you, son."

Matthew rose to accept his father's embrace. His mother followed, hugging him warmly. She stepped back, tears glistening in her eyes. "I think this calls for a toast." She glanced toward her husband.

"I'm on it," Peter said. He went over to the bar cart in the corner and produced a bottle of champagne. "We brought it up just in case."

Matthew chuckled as he and his mother retook their seats. "What did you two have planned if I'd come to tell you I was not taking the money?"

"The same. It's always been your choice, Matthew. But now that it's all over, would you mind explaining why you were so dead set against it? I admit your great-aunt's conditions were a bit odd."

"Odd? They're medieval. And considering what a miserable old woman she was when she was alive, I preferred not to indulge her controlling whims after death."

His mother shook her head. "You never could tolerate being made to do something you didn't see the logic of yourself. Constance didn't start out cruel, she became jealous of my mother's happiness. The only reason she had any money to hang over your head is that they paid her off to leave them alone."

"They who?"

"Your grandmother and DeWitt. She blackmailed them, actually, threatening to go public with what she knew about them."

"Which was?"

His mother's brow furrowed; then she smiled and shook her head. "For heaven's sake, Matthew. You're a grown man. Haven't you figured it out yet? Your grandmother wasn't his nurse, she was his lover."

Matthew blinked and sputtered, but no words came out. His father pressed a glass in his hand and he gratefully took it, glad to have something to hang on to. The sweet old lady he remembered was the mistress of one of the most notorious robber barons America had ever seen? Incredible! "When did this happen?"

"Actually, your grandmother came to this house as a maid. She caught the old man's eye." She shrugged. "That's how I always thought of him— the old man—though he couldn't have been any older than your father is now. Everyone thought he'd become a recluse due to failing health; hence the nurse story."

"Why all the deception?"

"It was the forties. Such things weren't done in

those days. They wanted to live a quiet life, away from scandal. Even today, there are many people, both black and white, who consider interracial couples unnatural."

"I meant why didn't you tell me?"

"Was I supposed to tell a child his grandmother was the lover of the former owner of the house? And as I said, I'd thought you'd figured it out. Especially since you knew he died from breaking his neck after his horse threw him. Any man sick enough to need a nurse is not out jumping fences."

Laughing, Matthew shook his head. "I suppose not." And he supposed he'd let his dislike of his family's fortune blind him to any hidden truths in his family's history.

"I know you have always thought of me as a snob, Matthew. Maybe I am. I don't know. But I can tell you one thing: I've been rich and I've been poor, and I'll take rich. I can remember visiting this house when I was only the daughter of the upstairs maid, a specter to be neither seen nor heard. And I remember living here as the daughter of the mistress of the house, and being sent to the best schools possible and having the servants call me Miss. Even though it provided me with little else, money gave me the power to be and do whatever I wanted."

"What do you mean money provided little else?"

"Your grandmother and DeWitt were in love. They were sufficient unto themselves. They didn't know the rest of us existed."

Which meant his mother had lost her mother's

love when the older woman fell in love. "Who raised you?"

His mother grinned. "I used to call him Uncle Andy when I was a girl."

"*Anderson?*"

She nodded. "I terrified all the female nannies they hired. At twelve, when I came to live here, I was a hellion, much like your sister. Anderson was the only one I would listen to. He told me I was going to behave like a young lady, even if he had to beat it into me, which it nearly came to a couple of times."

Margaret sipped from her glass. "And for your information, I tried to get him to retire years ago, but he won't have it. He says the day he can't work we are to put him out in the street, because he'll be of no use to anybody. He's a proud man and I respect that, but he never married, he never had children. Where would he go?"

Matthew shook his head. He'd had as much true confessions as he could stand for one night. Since he was driving, he set his untouched glass of champagne on the coffee table. "I'd better be going before it gets too late." He stood. "And by the way, Nina's brother, Nathan, and his wife are throwing us an engagement party this Friday night at their place. I'll call you when I know more details."

Rising, his mother nodded. "How's your sister?"

Matthew shrugged. "All right for someone who never gets out of her bathrobe. Do you know why she doesn't want to go back to Atlanta?"

His father, now on his feet, shook his head.

His mother said, "You know she doesn't talk to me."

Noting the pained expression on his mother's face, Matthew resolved to see what he could do about ending this feud between mother and daughter. He'd always taken a position of neutrality, but it was obvious to him that each of them suffered in their own way because of it.

He embraced each of his parents and left, hoping his sister might still be up when he got home.

Friday night, Nina arrived at her brother's house early. Although she'd spoken to Matthew on the phone, she hadn't seen him since he'd walked out of her apartment after refusing to make love to her. He claimed to be busy with work and his sister, but she got the feeling he was avoiding her, though she couldn't figure out why. She'd come here to speak with Daphne, someone mature enough to understand and sensitive enough not to judge.

Her brother opened the door to their East Side town house to her. He grinned. "If it isn't the bride-to-be herself. Where's your worse half?"

"He's coming later with his sister. Speaking of other halves, where's your better one?"

"Inside with the kids. May I take your wrap?"

"If you insist." She unwound the scarlet shawl from her shoulders to uncover a revealing black cocktail dress.

Nathan's eyebrows rose. "Who exactly are you

trying to impress with that dress? You've got the guy already, haven't you?"

Nina pressed her lips together. She'd thought the dress might have been too much for a family gathering, and Nathan confirmed it. But she hadn't worn the dress to impress her brother; she wanted to tempt Matthew. He claimed to have little self-control where she was concerned, and she aimed to test it tonight.

"I'm going to see Daphne," she said. She pushed through the door that led to the family rooms, the place where her first real interaction with Matthew had taken place.

Daphne was in the living room, lying on the floor. The two kids were doing their best to tickle their mother. When Daphne saw her, she sat up halfway. "Don't you look killer tonight?"

"I try." Nina sat on the sofa facing her sister-in-law. "I see the babies are keeping you busy."

Grasping the little one in her arms, she sat up. "Not too. If there's something you want to talk to me about, Nathan can take over."

Nina sighed, wondering when she'd become so transparent. "I do need some female advice, someone over the age of twenty-five who thinks with something other than her gonads."

Daphne laughed. "I'm your girl then. Let me get my husband in here. Then we can go upstairs for our girl talk. I'd love to know what you think of this punch I made."

"It's a deal."

Ten minutes later, when each of them had a cup

of champagne punch in her hand, Nina sipped from hers. The cool liquid slid down her throat, though its alcohol contents warmed her insides. "Not bad. What's in it?"

"Basically, it's a giant mimosa with a couple of other ingredients thrown in to liven it up."

"Don't let the kids get near it. They're liable to think it's plain orange juice."

"Tonight's soiree is an adults-only affair. I finally convinced your brother that hiring a nanny didn't make us horrible parents."

Nina's eyebrows lifted. "How did you do that?"

Daphne grinned. "I made him an offer he couldn't refuse." She set down her cup. "But I'm sure you didn't come here to talk about our domestic arrangements. What's Matthew done?"

"Nothing. It's not him, it's me." Nina sighed. On the cab ride down here, she'd rehearsed what she planned to say—words that would explain her dilemma, but wouldn't divulge the true reason that she and Matthew were marrying. But sitting here with Daphne, she wanted to tell someone the truth, someone who could reassure her that she hadn't talked Matthew into a big mistake. "I don't know if you know this, but Matthew's family is very wealthy."

Daphne shrugged. "I'd heard something about that."

"Well, he stands to inherit a lot of money if he marries before he turns forty next month."

Nina sipped from her cup, feeling Daphne's shrewd eyes studying her. "Is that why you two are getting married in such a hurry?"

Nina nodded. "I asked him to. He was dead set against marrying to claim the inheritance, but I talked him into it."

Daphne laughed. *"You* talked *him* into it?"

"Why does that surprise you?"

"Because I've never known Matthew Peterson to do anything he didn't want to. If you talked him into it, he was ready to listen."

Nina shook her head. "Maybe you're right." She sighed. "The day after we decided to get married, he took me up to the Empire State Building and proposed. At first, I thought it was just a sweet gesture, but then I thought maybe he was asking me for something more, a real commitment. I don't know."

"What did you say?"

"I didn't say anything. I didn't know what to say, and he sort of gave up."

"It sounds to me like he was asking for something more."

"Then maybe you can explain to me why the man refuses to touch me. And the last few days, I haven't even seen him."

Daphne's eyebrows lifted. "Never?"

"Not once. He says he wants to wait until after we're married. I sort of agreed to that."

"Now I know what your problem is, pure, un-adulterated sexual frustration."

"Tell me about it." Nina shook her head. "I don't understand him. If he doesn't want me, sex, or the money, what the hell is this all about?"

"The more important question is, what do you want? I've never known you not to know exactly what you wanted and go after it. It's a Ward family trait. Why don't you just ask him what he feels for you?"

"Because for the first time in my life, I'm afraid of the answer. Even if he were to say that he was madly in love with me and the inheritance was only an excuse to marry me, what then? What happens if he turns around and asks me the same question? The only answer I could give him is 'I don't know.' "

Nina looked down at her lap. That wasn't quite true. She knew that she was falling for him. The only thing that kept it from being a free fall instead of a terror-filled ride was the crash that she suspected awaited her at the bottom, where he broke her heart and abandoned her in one way or another.

"So you wore that dress tonight to tempt him, is that it?"

Nina touched her nose. "Bingo."

Daphne bit her lip. "He's not going to be happy about that."

"No, I don't suppose he will."

"I could lend you one of my skinny dresses from back before I had children."

Nina smiled. "That won't be necessary. I admit it was a dumb thing to do. But I'm a big girl, old enough to take my medicine."

"If that's how you want it. But since you asked for my advice, here it is. Level with him. Marriage is too difficult an undertaking to go into it without knowing what you're doing or how your partner feels—even if that relationship is only for six months."

As Nina nodded, the doorbell chimed.

"That had better be the caterer," Daphne said, rising. "It'll be okay," Daphne said, patting Nina's shoulder on her way out of the kitchen.

Nina nodded for her sister-in-law's sake, but suddenly she was not looking forward to this evening at all.

The guests had already started to arrive when Nina looked up and noticed Matthew standing across the room from her. She sighed as her gaze traveled over his smiling face, his tall, rangy frame, clad in a navy blue suit. The color suited him. Or maybe she was like every other woman whose man got more attractive every time she saw him.

That thought jolted her, spurred her to her feet from her place on the sofa. She went to him, noting the moment he saw her, because the smile fell away from his face to be replaced shortly by a plastic one that left his gaze on her cold. And he'd only seen the front of the dress. The back was nearly nonexistent. She bit her lip. Maybe she should have taken Daphne's offer, but it was too late for that now.

Only when she was almost upon him did she notice his sister at his side. She wasn't surprised considering that Frankie, sans baseball cap, sported hair nearly down to her waist and she actually had on a dress. She wondered fleetingly what Matthew must have done to get her to put one on.

Fearing the inevitable, Nina went to Frankie first and embraced her. "I'm so glad you could come."

"I wouldn't have missed it." Frankie stepped back. "Great dress."

Nina slid a glance at Matthew to find him stony-eyed, staring back at her. "Thank you," she said to Frankie, "same to you."

"Thanks." -

Nina turned to Matthew, unable to put it off any longer. With her hands gripped together behind her back, she said, "Hi, stranger. Did you miss me?"

"There's not much of you to miss at the moment."

She started to explain. "Matthew, I—"

He cut her off by pulling her close and pressing his lips to hers. His hands explored her back, not in a sensual way, probably assessing exactly how bare the dress left her.

"We will discuss this later," he whispered against her ear. "In private. Right now we have a room full of people staring at us." He released her and took her hand. "Maybe you ought to introduce me to the rest of your family."

For the next few hours, Nina talked and laughed, ate and drank champagne with Matthew by her side. Probably no one else in the room noticed the tension in him, but she felt it. She wanted to kill whoever invented the custom of clinking a fork against a glass, because the few times the guests started in with that, she'd felt the anger in him, simmering just below the surface. But to the eyes of everyone else, he appeared the devoted fiancé. She supposed she should be grateful he didn't embarrass her in front of both families, but the pretense, the pretense of all of it weighed on her.

After cutting the cake, they opened the presents.

Matthew sat beside her on the sofa, his arm around her shoulders as she opened the gifts, many of which were of a ribald or risqué nature. The last gift she opened was the one from Matthew's parents. She opened the lid of a rectangular jewelry case to reveal an exquisite diamond and sapphire necklace. Shocked, she gazed up at Matthew.

He touched the tip of his index finger to one of the stones. "That's *the* necklace. The one the girl stole from my mother. Needless to say that particular girl was banned from the house after that event. My mother knows you know about that story. It's her way of welcoming you to the family."

She pressed her lips together, not knowing what to say. She must have been crazy when she started down this path. She glanced around the room at all the faces smiling back at her. People who wished her and Matthew well, who invested their emotions in hoping that they succeeded as a couple. She'd forgotten that—how much family invested in a loved one's wedding. Matthew's mother beamed at her, but how would she feel in six months if Nina had to give her the necklace back?

She looked up at Matthew. As much as she dreaded facing him, she wanted to go home. Yet fifteen minutes later, as she rode in the backseat of the car Matthew had rented, with him sitting beside her grim and silent, she wished she hadn't been so eager to leave.

When the car pulled up to the curb in front of Nina's building, Matthew got out of the driver's side, tipped the driver, and went around to the passenger side to collect Nina. He hadn't said two words to her during the trip across town, trying to let his emotions cool, but all he had to do was look at that damn dress to get heated up again.

He'd spent the last few days missing her terribly. But he'd stayed close to home the last few nights, worried about his sister. At first, he'd assumed some man had broken her heart, but now he wasn't so sure. Until tonight she had seemed to be sinking into some sort of depression. Just as he'd thought he'd have to cajole her into coming tonight, he'd gotten home from work to find her dressed in an actual dress, making him regret the time he'd spent away from Nina.

On top of that, she'd spent the evening in the corner talking to Nina's cousin, Nelson, about what, he hadn't a clue. When the other man agreed to see Frankie home, that left Matthew free to take Nina home without having to be concerned about his sister.

But he didn't know what to say to Nina now. He'd been looking forward to seeing her with an anticipation he'd felt for few things in his life. He'd seen her and immediately known the purpose of her dress. A seduction dress.

She'd expected him to see her and salivate like one of Pavlov's dogs, and he had. His first impulse had been to drag her to one of the upstairs bedrooms and not give a hang what the relatives thought.

Although he wanted her with a ferocity that defied description, he'd long since passed being a teenager who couldn't control his testosterone. The sustenance he needed from her was emotional, not physical. But that obviously wasn't what she needed from him. And while he found it mildly ridiculous to be upset with a woman who made it clear she waned to sleep with him, like some sort of bizarre role reversal, he was. That dress told him he'd fallen for a woman who could never love him back the way he needed to be loved by her.

Matthew sighed. He doubted any other man in his position would be quite so circumspect. They'd jump into bed with her and worry about the consequences later, but he couldn't. Especially after seeing her tonight. He recognized the guilty expression on her face because he'd seen it on his own, remorse at deceiving people who didn't deserve it. That expression hardened his resolve rather than weakened it.

He let them into the apartment, as usual. This time she stood by the door, her hand on the knob, waiting for him to enter. When he did, she shut the door and leaned her back against it. She looked up at him with a plaintive expression. "Would you please say something to me, Matthew?"

He closed the distance between them, sandwiching her against the door. "Is that what you want from me, Nina? Talk? Somehow I got the impression you had something else on your mind for tonight."

She wrapped her arms around his neck and pressed her soft body to his, whether to soothe him or entice him, he wasn't sure. "I'm sorry, Matthew," she whispered against his ear.

He pulled her arms from around his neck and

pressed her back against the door. "Are you really? Or is this all you really want from me?" With one finger he traced the neckline of her dress that dipped low between her breasts. His gaze followed the movement of his hand, as it traveled over her soft skin.

He inhaled, breathing in the aroma of her perfume mingled with the natural scent of her arousal. His hand settled on her breast, molding the tender flesh in his palm. Her back arched and her fingers gripped his biceps. A tiny moan escaped her lips, egging him on.

He hadn't intended to touch her, not like this. But now that he had, he couldn't get enough of her. His mouth crushed down on hers. His tongue swept past her parted lips to claim the sweetness there. His hands moved over her body, rough, possessive, as wild as the erotic kiss they shared. His eyes squeezed shut, as she rubbed herself against his erection, sending a shock wave of pleasure to his groin.

He hadn't intended to touch her, but somehow his fingers found their way to the clasp holding the top of her dress in place. He undid it and watched the fabric slither down to bare her breasts to him. Lord, she was beautiful, more perfect than he'd imagined. Palming one breast in his hand, he lifted it, positioning the peak to take it into his mouth. He flicked his tongue against her nipple and was rewarded with a throaty moan from her.

When she pushed at the lapels of his jacket, he shrugged out of it and let it fall to the floor. When he put his hands on her again, one covered her breast and the other pushed up her skirt to explore the firm, rounded globes of her buttocks, first over the cover of her panties, then beneath. His mouth clamped down on hers and she welcomed him, drawing his tongue into her mouth and sucking on it.

He shifted so that his hand slid between her legs from behind. She jerked as his fingers explored the moist heat between her thighs. His first thought was that she was ready for him. His second thought was that he was three seconds away from taking Nina against the door to her apartment.

That thought sobered him, like a splash of cold water in the face. This was not how he had envisioned his first time with Nina to be. She deserved better than that from him. He withdrew his hand and straightened the damage he'd done to the lower part of her outfit as best he could. Wrapping his arms around her, he buried his face against her throat. "I'm sorry, baby," he whispered against her ear.

For a long moment, they clung to each other, each breathing heavily. "Why did you stop?" she asked him finally.

He lifted his head to look down at her. If anything, he would have expected her to wonder why he'd started this madness in the first place. A wiser man wouldn't have put his hands on her in the first place. Clearly, she anticipated his ardor but not his restraint.

Brushing a strand of hair from her face, he said, "Is this all you think I really want from you?"

She crossed her arms over her breasts, but didn't

do a good job of hiding anything. She looked up at him with a touch of defiance and another emotion he didn't understand. "It's all any man I've ever known *really* wanted from me."

What was he supposed to make of that admission? She'd told him once that she was used to being with a different kind of man, but the implications hadn't registered. She was used to the kind of man who used her or perhaps let her use him. She'd told him once that she didn't know how to deal with him. Maybe that was because for once a relationship for her didn't revolve solely around sex. Maybe she sought the familiar. Or maybe she thought that's all she had to offer him.

He retrieved his jacket from the floor and draped it over her shoulders to cover her. He cradled her face in his hands, forcing her to look at him. "Those men were fools."

"I won't argue with that. But tell me one thing. If you want me and I want you, why do you insist on torturing both of us?"

Because it wasn't all he wanted from her. "Because I want you to be free to change your mind about this marriage arrangement of ours if you want to."

"I'm not going to change my mind."

"How can you be so sure? I saw your face tonight when we were opening gifts. I watched you turn paler and paler with every gift you opened. Tell me you weren't sitting there wondering if you'd made a mistake."

She lowered her head. "I can't, but not because of you. I wished we would have run away to Vegas or something, or maybe that we'd leveled with everyone from the beginning . . . something. I felt terrible leading everyone to believe we were madly in love rather than simply fulfilling the obligations of your aunt's will."

"Don't worry. My family knows the truth, and only the female half of the family thinks we're in love. The male half thinks I knocked you up."

Her mouth dropped open and she shook her head. "They do not, and what a delicate way you have of putting things."

"Your brother did, until I set him straight."

Her mouth dropped open again. "He asked you that?"

"Yup, and threatened to pulverize me a couple of times."

"You wait until I get my hands on that man."

"Not to worry. He backed off when I told him Frankie would avenge me."

A smile tilted the corners of her mouth. "Now there's a scary prospect." She sighed and leaned into him, resting her cheek on his shoulder. "Are you sorry we ever agreed to this marriage?"

He rubbed his hands over her back, hoping to reassure her. "No, sweetheart, I'm not. But if you are, all you have to do is tell me. Up until the moment you walk down that aisle you can change your mind. But once you say, 'I do,' you're mine. Do you understand me?"

"Yes."

He didn't think she did, but she'd find out. Once she became his wife he didn't have any intention of letting her go.

Twelve

"Hold still, will you?"

Nina settled her hands on her waist as Yasmin set about fastening the million tiny buttons on the wedding dress she'd designed, using something that looked like an old-fashioned buttonhook. "Let me ask you something. If it takes all this time and *tools* to get this dress closed, how the heck am I supposed to get it off?"

Yasmin grinned up at her. "Brute force is always an option."

Nina made a face at her cousin. After that night in her apartment a couple of weeks ago, she could certainly imagine Matthew ripping the dress off her body. Not that she'd want him to. The gown was exquisite, a sleeveless sheath that molded to her body, decorated with delicate crystal beading on the bodice and at the hem. She could imagine passing such a gown down to her daughter if she ever had one, or maybe one of Daphne's girls would want to wear it. They, like her, were likely to be tall.

Nina glanced at the mirror in front of her, surveying the women assembled behind her: her grandmother and aunts, Daphne and her sister Elise, whose son Andrew served as ring bearer. All these women had crammed into her grandmother's bedroom to help her prepare for the big moment when she would walk down the aisle to meet Matthew. Daphne, who would serve as matron of honor, and Yasmin, who would serve as *la dama preferida,* wore almost identical dresses in the same shade of lavender. Her grandmother, who had made a miraculous recovery from the stroke, wore blue, while her aunts wore various shades of pink. They all looked festive, and for the first time in a long while, happy.

Once Yasmin finished with the dress, Nina turned to the assembled group. "How do I look?"

The question brought whoops and applause and laughter from the women. But the reaction that got to her most was her grandmother's *"Como una princesa, mijita,"* like a princess, she whispered while tears shimmered in her eyes.

Luz stood and ushered the other women from the room, saying she wanted to talk to Nina alone. When the other women were gone, Luz retook her seat on the bed and patted the spot next to her.

Gingerly, Nina walked to the bed and sat. "Is this the part where you give me the talk about sex?" she teased.

Luz's right eyebrow flexed. "If at this late date I had to tell you about sex, I'd really be worried. No, I just wanted a moment alone with you. My graydar tells me something is not right between you and Matthew."

"What makes you say that?"

"I haven't said anything before now, but it worries me, the haste with which you two decided to get married. I told you I thought he was your match, but I didn't expect you to strike it so soon."

Nina sighed. She should have known her grandmother was just playing possum, going along with what happened without question. But her grandmother was the last person she'd tell the real motive for the marriage. "I know. We wanted to be together and Matthew is sort of old-fashioned . . ." She let her words hang there and let her grandmother draw the obvious, if untruthful, conclusion.

However she didn't expect her grandmother's reaction to be uproarious laughter, either.

Luz swiped at her eyes. *"Pobrecita,* now I know why you are so jumpy today. I thought perhaps you were having cold feet. I see now you're anxious for the man to warm them up."

"Abuela," Nina protested, "you're supposed to be an old lady, not Dr. Ruth."

"And I was a young lady once, and I remember getting all hot and bothered when your grandfather touched me. How do you think your mother and your aunts got here? It wasn't immaculate conception, I can assure you of *that.*"

"Honestly, I never thought about it." The only thing she'd thought about regarding her grandparents' marriage was that it must have been rough for them considering the times and the fact that she was a fair-skinned Puerto Rican woman married to a black man. Since her grandfather had died before she was born, she'd never thought about the kind of love they must have shared to risk such a marriage in the first place.

Her grandmother patted her knee. "He's a good man, *mijita*. He'll make you happy if you let him."

Nina smiled. She couldn't argue with her grandmother's first statement. Matthew was a good man, but no one could make you happy. You had to do that yourself. "I know, *Abuela*. And I will try to make him happy, too."

"He better be happy. He's marrying my granddaughter. And speaking of which, we'd better get going. If we're late to the church they charge an extra fifty dollars."

Nina looked heavenward. With the combined wealth of her family and Matthew's, she knew fifty dollars was not her grandmother's true concern. To be late would show disrespect for the church, and her grandmother would never suffer that.

As Nina rose, the sound of a commotion in the hallway drew her attention. She heard raised women's voices and a deeper male one. She exchanged a look with her grandmother. It could not be. Matthew could not be here now of all times. Aside from the rehearsal at the church and the dinner afterward two nights ago, they'd barely seen each other in the past two weeks. And he had to show up now?

But the door opened and Matthew poked his head in. She followed his gaze as it traveled over her, a purely male gaze that left her feeling hot and flushed. Finally, he turned to her grandmother and said, "Would you mind if I spoke with your granddaughter for a moment?"

Luz turned to her, a mischievous grin on her face. "He's eager, this one."

Nina rolled her eyes as her grandmother left and Matthew shut the door behind her. For a moment, they simply stared at each other. Yasmin had insisted on designing him a new tux for the occasion and he looked even more handsome in this one.

He took a step toward her. "You look . . . incredible."

"Right back at you. But if you wanted to see my dress, you could have waited a few more minutes. I'd have shown you."

"I needed to see you before then. You remember I told you that you could change your mind up until the moment you walked down the aisle."

"Of course."

"So, what's it going to be, Nina? Are we on or off?"

Hands on hips, she stared at him as if he were a madman. "You come in here, where you are not supposed to be, see me in my wedding dress, which you are not supposed to see. Everyone knows the groom is not supposed to see the bride on the day of the wedding until she walks down the aisle. Yet, here you are asking me if I want to go through with it? What do you think?"

He closed the gap between them and cupped his palms over her shoulders. "I don't care about tradition or how it looks or anything else. All I care about is you. What do you want to do, Nina? I need to hear it from your own lips."

Closing her eyes, she lowered her head, mostly so he wouldn't see the tears that suddenly sprang to her eyes. She didn't understand it. Maybe it was simply the emotion of the day, but she felt something inside her soften at his impassioned words. *All I care about is you.* Maybe he did have some deeper feelings for her, feelings that went beyond the lust he'd shown her or the simple affection he exhibited. Maybe there was a chance for them to find true happiness.

That was the scariest thought that had ever entered her brain, but she lifted her head and looked at him levelly. "I want to marry you, Matthew."

He exhaled, his relief so palpable as to be comic. "I was hoping you'd say that."

She smiled. "Maybe now you can get out of here before my aunts string you up for flouting tradition. They're a superstitious bunch when it comes to things like this."

"I will, but I have two things for you first." He reached inside his jacket and pulled out a jewelry case. "I thought you might want to wear these."

She took the case from him and opened it. Inside lay a pair of diamond and pearl earrings. She looked up at him, surprised.

"It's traditional for the groom to give the bride a present. You're aunts should approve."

She'd forgotten about that custom and its reverse. "I didn't get you anything."

He winked at her. "You're giving me you. That's enough."

She pulled him closer by his jacket lapels. "You'd better watch it, bub. There's that macho again and I've sworn off macho guys."

"All of them but me."

She laughed. "What else did you want to give me?"

"Just this." He lowered his mouth to hers for a brief and tender kiss. "See you at the church."

"I'll be the one wearing white."

He winked at her. "But hopefully not for long."

As he sauntered from the room, Nina wondered exactly how early a couple could slip out of their own reception without being impolite.

Sitting beside Nina in the antique Rolls Royce that had been hired to take them from the church to the reception, Matthew sighed. The ceremony had gone off perfectly, though he had to admit he'd held his breath for a second when it came time for Nina to say, "I do." And when the priest said, "You may now kiss the bride," she'd come into his arms and kissed him as if she belonged there.

He took the glass of champagne Nina offered him, linked his arms, and sipped, feeling both contentment and anticipation wash through him. Nina was his, finally, and tonight would be their night, finally. He couldn't wait, except they had to make it through the damn reception first. Their small family celebration had somehow blossomed into a full-scale event, which included 250 guests. He wouldn't have thought so many people would be available on such short notice, but each and every invitee had responded in the affirmative.

"Why are you so quiet over there?" he asked her.

She lifted her shoulders and let them fall with a

sigh. "I don't know. It all seems a little surreal, I guess. A few words from a man in a robe and we're married."

"That's usually how it's done."

She shrugged again. "I know. It just seems like for such a momentous, life-changing event, you should have to do something more than say a few words."

He scanned her face and saw no trace of regret, but asked her anyway. "Are you sorry you went through with it?"

She shook her head. "Not at all." She drained her glass and set it in one of the holders in the door. She took his glass, too, although it wasn't empty.

"I wasn't finished with that."

"Yes, you were. From what I hear, you had your quota last night."

His eyebrows lifted. Her brother, Garrett, and a few of her other male relatives had shown up at his place the night before and dragged him out for an impromptu bachelor party. They'd shared a few drinks, a few stories, a few laughs, but Matthew had been in bed by midnight. "You know about that?"

"Of course. Nathan asked my permission first. He said he had no intention of walking me down the aisle sporting the black eye I would have given him if he hadn't."

"I've married into a vicious family."

She laughed. "So did you enjoy your last night of freedom?"

"I'm more interested in my first night of captivity." He reached for her. "Come here and kiss me."

She smacked his hands away. "You'll ruin my makeup."

"Pray that's all I mess up." He pulled her to him and his mouth found hers. His tongue plunged into her mouth and his hands moved over her body. She made that little sound in her throat he liked so much, not quite a moan, but not quite a whimper.

After a moment, he pulled away from her, knowing how quickly things between them tended to get out of control. "We're leaving tonight the moment we cut the cake."

She giggled. "My grandmother is right about you. You are eager."

Eager? He'd be champing at his bit if he had one. "We're almost there. Kiss me, again. I need another fix to make it through the next few hours." Laughing, her eyes twinkling, she did as he asked.

When he pulled away, she said, "Do you think they could manage to cut the cake without us?"

Hours later, after the toasts had been made, the food eaten, and the cake cut, Matthew pulled Nina onto the dance floor for a final dance. She came into his arms and rested her cheek against his shoulder. He rubbed his hand over her back in a gentle motion. "How are you doing?"

She lifted her head and gazed up at him. "Everything turned out beautifully, don't you think?"

He nodded, but the only beautiful thing that concerned him at the moment was her. "What were you and my father talking about before?" Although Nathan had escorted her down the aisle, his father had asked to be her partner for the traditional father-daughter dance, and Nina had agreed.

A teasing smile lit her face. "He told me several amusing stories about you growing up."

He grinned. "All lies, I'm sure."

"He says he's got pictures."

"He would." Although he was glad his family had accepted Nina so readily, but he had other things on his mind at the moment. "What do you say we get out of here and head upstairs to our room?"

Something akin to panic flashed in her eyes, but she said, "All right."

As they made their good-byes, he watched her. For the first time that day she seemed jumpy and nervous. She'd been calm and in control as she'd walked down the aisle to him; and when she'd joined him at the altar, she'd squeezed his hand, offering him reassurance. As he led her from the room he wondered, why now, when she was about to get what she'd seemed to want all along, did she suddenly seem ill-at-ease?

When they got to the door of the hotel room, five floors up from the reception room below, Matthew opened it and turned to her. "I hope you don't mind if I observe a little tradition."

"What's that?"

He shot her a droll look, as if she should know

what he meant, and she did, but the more she learned about him, the more she understood what an unconventional man he was. His desire to adhere to the customary surprised her. "Suit yourself," she said.

And he did. He picked her up as if she weighed nothing at all and carried her over the threshold and into the bedroom. He set her down beside the bed where a bottle of champagne chilled in a stand. Two glasses sat on the nightstand. "Would you like some champagne?" he asked.

"Please." Anything to quell the sudden attack of nerves that had seized her the moment Matthew had suggested they come up here. It had been years since she'd been a blushing virgin. Hell, she'd never been a blushing virgin. During her first sexual experience, her curiosity had overridden her apprehension. She hadn't been one-eighth as anxious as she felt right now.

Matthew popped the cork and filled each of the glasses halfway. With unsteady fingers, she accepted the one he handed to her, and downed most of the contents of the glass in one gulp.

He took the glass from her. "Easy, baby. I'm not trying to get you drunk."

"Why not?"

His gaze, hot and intense, met hers. "Because I want you to remember all the wild and wicked things I'm going to do to you tonight."

A shock of something, either fear or maybe desire, made her shiver.

"Or not." He sighed. "We don't have to make love tonight if you don't want to."

"I suppose I don't have to die, stay black, or pay taxes, either."

He ran his index finger down her cheek. "Understand something, Nina. I would never try to force you into something you're not ready for, not even tonight."

But he wouldn't understand. She didn't understand it herself. The only thing to do was to level with him. "I want to be with you, Matthew. I'm scared."

His thumb stroked her cheek. "Scared of what, baby?"

She didn't know how to put it into words. She only knew her fear had nothing to do with the physical act itself. Any of the other times they'd been together, she would have willingly taken him to her bed. That night two weeks ago had left her so stirred up she could have chewed through her front door in frustration. But all those times, the two of them had simply gotten caught up in the moment. Making love now was a conscious, deliberate act, an admission that she cared enough about him to give herself to him freely. A choice rather than simple surrender.

And more than that, she sensed that after this, there would be no turning back for her. She was three-quarters of the way in love with him already. Sex would push her over the edge, into scary uncharted territory. Looking up at his handsome, concerned face, she knew that's what really spooked her, the knowledge that she, of her own volition, was about to put herself in the one place she didn't want to be—in a position to be hurt.

Well, twenty-nine years of age was no time to start being a coward. Whatever came, she would deal with it. For now, all she could think of was him. She went on tiptoe, slid her arms around Matthew's neck, and pressed her open mouth to his.

Thirteen

Matthew's arms closed around her, binding her to him as her tongue swept into his mouth seeking his. If she'd been reticent a moment ago, now she was the opposite, bold, aggressive, the tigress on the loose. Despite all her talk about being with dominating men, he'd always sensed she was used to controlling things, having her way. Not this time. He wanted her to understand that he was not going to be like the other men in her life: quickly used and quickly discarded.

He broke the kiss and set her away from him a little, which clearly surprised her. She looked up at him with wide, questioning eyes. He didn't answer any of her questions, not with words, anyway. Cradling her face in his palms, he kissed one cheek, then the other, her forehead, the tip of her nose, and finally her mouth, a slow, sweet kiss that fired an even keener desire for her. His groin tightened, but he would not rush this first time with her, not if he could help it.

He pulled away from her, pleased by the closed-lidded expression of bemusement on her face. He took her mouth again, this time letting a bit of his desire show. She responded in kind, winding her arms around him and pressing herself against him. He pulled away from her again, this time more slowly because it was more difficult.

She glared up at him, an expression of impatience on her face. "You're torturing me again."

From somewhere he found a smile. "No, baby, I'm not. I just want to take things slowly with you. Hasn't any man ever taken his time just to please you?" She bit her lip, but didn't give him an answer, not that he needed one. "Let me love you in my own way," he whispered against her ear.

"As long as you hurry up."

His lips touched down on the side of her throat as his fingers found and unfastened the buttons at the back of her gown. He wasn't rushing, but he wanted to see her, wanted to see in the flesh what had haunted his dreams and disturbed his waking hours. He wanted to see all of her, and if there was a God in heaven, not pounce on her and forget his resolve when he did.

In a few minutes, she was free. He lifted his head to watch the dress fall from her body. Beneath that she wore a white satin bustier, a garter belt, and stockings atop a pair of four-inch white pumps. Both naughty and virginal at the same time. He squeezed his eyes shut for a moment, silently pray-

ing for strength; then he lifted her out of the circle
of her dress and laid her on the bed.

"My shoes," she protested

"Leave them on."

"Why?"

"Because I said so."

She laughed a wicked little laugh, because she
knew she got to him. He didn't mind. He shrugged
out of his jacket and tossed it on a chair. He took
off his cuff links and placed them on the nightstand. That was as far as he intended to go, but
seeing the expression on her face as she watched
him, curious, avid, intense, he continued, enjoying the knowledge that he got to her, too.

Nude, he joined her on the bed and pulled her
to him, so that they lay on their sides facing each
other. "Is that better?"

She eyed him with a seductive, narrow-eyed glare.
"I see what you mean about the equipment func-
tioning properly."

Her hand moved over his body, from his shoulder, down his arm, to his hip. Knowing where she
was heading, he grasped her wrist and pushed her
back against the mattress. Having her touch him
there now would surely be his undoing.

He covered her upper body with his as his mouth
sought hers and his hand roved lower to squeeze
her derriere in his palm. She writhed beneath him
and her legs twined with his. The soft silk of her
stockings and the even softer silk of her skin against
his bare flesh drove him crazy. He lifted himself on
one elbow and looked down at her. She smiled up

at him, a siren's smile, the smile of a woman who knows exactly what she is doing to her man.

Two could play that game, he decided. Her bustier opened in the front. He undid the clasp and pushed the material away. His hand roved over her breasts. He took one nipple in his mouth as his hand roved lower to slide her panties from her hips. She obliged him by lifting her hips so he could slide the lacy material from her body. He drew his hand upward again, this time on the inside of her thighs, skimming over, enough to tease but not satisfy.

Her back arched and she pressed herself against his hand, seeking more substantial contact. She called his name, her frustration evident in her voice. He drew her other nipple into his mouth and sucked hard as he gave her what she wanted. His fingers pressed inward, circling over her soft, slick flesh. She exhaled, a long, desire-laden sigh. He groaned, too, taking pleasure in pleasuring her.

Almost immediately, he felt the tension coiling in her, poised to explode. When she moaned his name in a breathless wail, he knew he couldn't wait any longer. He positioned himself above her and thrust into her, the most exquisite sensation he'd ever known. His entire body shuddered as she enveloped him. Perspired, breathing heavily, he withdrew, to thrust into her again and again, his control gone, his resolve shattered.

She locked her legs around him, meeting his rhythm. Her back arched and her breathing came in erotic gasps and sighs that drove him further over the edge. He leaned down and took her nipple into his mouth and she convulsed beneath him. Her nails scored his back and she called his name. He squeezed his eyes shut as his climax overtook him, arching his back and drawing a rumbling groan of pleasure from somewhere deep in his throat.

He eased down on top of her and when he could breath again, somehow managed to get them, minus Nina's shoes, underneath the covers. Lying on his back against the pillows, he pulled her to him, inhaling deeply, his nostrils flaring as he breathed in the fresh scent of their lovemaking. Their bodies were still damp, but his body hardened again, just having her next to him. He scrubbed his hands over her back.

She stirred, lifting her head to gaze down at him, an impish grin lighting her face. Her hair, wild and tumbled, floated around her face. He tugged on a strand of her hair. Remembering her earlier reticence, he said, "That wasn't so bad, was it?"

"Don't tell me you want me to tell you how good you are after I just screamed your name at the top of my lungs."

He chuckled. "No. I just wanted to make sure you didn't have any regrets about making love."

"You know I don't." She lowered her head. "I don't know what got into me before."

He curved his palm around her nape and let his fingers tangle in her hair. "Maybe we should get some sleep. We have an early flight in the morning."

"I'm not tired." She dipped her head to stroke her tongue over his nipple.

"Nina," he said in warning, knowing that at present, it wouldn't take much to get him going again.

"Shh. You'll ruin my concentration." With her mouth and hands she explored his body, moving lower. This time he let her have her way. He nearly came off the bed when she took him in her mouth, and when she straddled him and took him into her body, he groaned out his pleasure on a long sigh.

As she began to move over him, she smiled down at him, a smug grin that said she delighted in the potency of her female powers. He wasn't complaining either. "You like having me at your mercy, don't you?"

"Yes," she admitted unabashedly.

The urge seized him to flip her over and turn the tables on her, but he sensed in her the need for the control that he'd wrested from her earlier. Instead, he sat up, wrapped his arms around her, and buried his face against her neck. She wound her legs around him, and they both groaned from the deeper contact.

He pulled back enough to see her face. She regarded him through half-closed lids with eyes that had darkened to the most incredible olive color. With his hands underneath her buttocks he lifted her and thrust into her. Her eyes squeezed shut and her back arched, bringing her breasts in line with his face. He turned his head and pulled one engorged nipple into his mouth. She gasped and shivered. Her nails dug into his shoulders, but he didn't care. She was nearly there, at the brink, waiting to topple over. He wasn't far from it himself.

He dragged in a ragged breath and lifted his head to whisper in her ear. "That's it, baby. Come for me."

And she did. Her legs tightened around him and her body shook as she cried out her release against his neck. And he lost it. He squeezed her to him as his own orgasm overtook him, making him tremble with its potency.

For a long time, they clung to each other, waiting for their breathing to even out and their heartbeats to slow. Matthew recovered first. He kissed her temple, her cheek, and finally, when she lifted her head, her mouth. It was a lazy, sigh-filled kiss since both of them were too tired for more.

When he pulled away from her he stroked her damp hair from her face. "If I'd have known it would be like this between us, I might have given in sooner."

She offered him a lazy smile. "Liar. You and I both knew it would be like this. And you know you wouldn't have given in."

He chuckled. No, he wouldn't have given in, and now more than ever he was glad he hadn't. He would always have the knowledge that she'd come to him freely, without sex confusing the issue or clouding her judgment. He also knew she had to feel something for him to follow the marriage through and make love to him so uninhibitedly.

A niggling voice in the back of his mind urged him to tell her the truth about his feelings, but it was too soon. Considering her bout of cold feet at making love, she'd probably bolt if she suspected the depth of what he felt for her. He'd bet part of what made this marriage acceptable to her was the belief that neither of them had invested too much of themselves in it. He'd wait, but not much longer.

He ran his finger down the bridge of her nose. "Now I really think we ought to get some shut-eye."

"That's a prescription I can live with, but first I need to get out of this." She snapped one of the lines on her garter.

"Allow me." He laid her on the bed beside him. In a few seconds he had the belt unhooked, and took his time rolling off the stockings. When he stretched out beside her, she rolled in to him. He lay on his back and pulled her to his side. With his arms around her and her cheek resting on his shoulder, he fell asleep, contented for the moment, at least.

Nina awoke early the following morning and rose from the king-size bed she shared with Matthew. She'd never bothered to put on the peignoir set she'd bought to entice him, so she settled for his discarded shirt as a cover-up. She padded to the adjoining bathroom, washed her hands, and splashed water on her face. After blotting her skin with a towel, she surveyed her image in the mirror.

There were times in a woman's life—when she got her first period, when she lost her virginity, when she fell in love for the first time—that she expected to look in the mirror and find something different in her reflection, some infinitesimal change that marked the passing of a major life event. Nina scanned her face, finding nothing out of the ordinary, save the remnants of the day's makeup she'd never scrubbed off.

Yet, in one day, she'd married and fallen in love, or rather, she'd given herself permission to love him and shown him in the only way she knew how—with her body. Nina sighed. For the first time in her life she was in love. In love with a man arranged to be a temporary one. The irony of that didn't escape her. Here was her worst nightmare come to life, and she had no one to blame for that save herself. Even so, she wouldn't trade one minute she'd spent with him, either last night or any other time.

Nina sighed. Last night, Matthew had proved to her what she'd already suspected about him. The man was an incredible lover: sweet and gentle when it was called for, hot and wild when it was not. She'd fallen asleep in his arms, when usually all she wanted to do after sex was to roll over and be left alone.

"What are you doing up?"

She twisted around to see a sleepy-looking Matthew standing in the doorway, still nude, still erect, and her heartbeat quickened. She'd been so lost in her own thoughts she hadn't heard him approach. She tilted her head to one side, glancing downward. "I could ask you the same question."

He stepped farther into the room and wrapped his arms around her waist from behind. "I could give you an answer, but I think you probably know what it is." He undid one of the buttons and slipped his hand under the shirt. His hand settled on her breast. "Mmm, look what I found."

She drew in her breath as his thumb crazed her nipple. "I've got another one just like it."

He laughed and nuzzled her neck. "As much as I'd like to play, we do have a plane to catch."

"So you keep telling me, though you haven't told me where we're going." All he'd said in reference to their honeymoon destination was to pack for a tropical climate. This time of year that could cover a lot of places.

"A man can't tell all his secrets."

She turned to face him, dislodging his hand. "Not even a hint?"

"No. Now I suggest you get in the shower, because you know how long you women take to get ready for anything."

"Only if you come with me."

He kissed her nose. "You've got a deal."

They took turns lathering and rinsing each other under the warm spray of the shower. Then they made love against the shower wall and had to do it all over again. After a quick breakfast of eggs and toast, they checked out of the hotel and caught a taxi to the airport.

Snuggled next to Matthew in the car, she grinned up at him. "You're sure you won't give me a hint?"

"Nope."

"You do realize that as soon as we get on the airplane I'm going to know where we're going."

"If you say so."

She gritted her teeth, seeing the smug expression on his face. "Fine, don't tell me."

"I won't."

When they reached their gate and she saw the flight was headed to Puerto Rico, she turned to him. "Why couldn't you tell me we're going to PR? Don't tell me you've got a whole delegation of my relatives waiting to meet us at the gate?" Although her grandmother lived in New York, two of her great-aunts and their families still lived on the island.

"No, nothing like that."

She made an exasperated sound in her throat. "You really enjoy being mysterious, don't you?"

"One of life's great pleasures is being able to surprise the woman you . . . marry."

That little hesitation in his voice before he said marry didn't go unnoticed. Nina settled into her window seat aboard the plane, wondering what, if anything, he might have said instead and changed his mind.

When the plane touched down in Puerto Rico, he turned to her. "Ready for another plane ride?"

"This isn't going to be one of those things where we fly around for a couple of days and end up in Disneyworld or something? If so, I'm staying here."

"No. Just one more short flight."

"I guess I'm game."

That's what she said, but when she saw the tiny jet waiting for them, she balked. "You're kidding, right? I barely held on to my stomach on the big bird."

"That's why we didn't take this one all the way down."

Her eyebrows lifted. "Now there's a scary thought."

"Come on," he urged. "The flight is less than an hour."

Forty-five minutes later, their final destination came into view. Tiny Isla de los Milagros, commonly known as Milagro Island, sat in the middle of the Caribbean. Know for its year-round sunny weather, exotic teas, and tropical fruits, the island was also owned by Nina's brother and his wife.

Looking out the window, Nina chuckled. "Don't ask me why I didn't suspect you were bringing me here. I've always wanted to see this place."

"Nathan told me." Nathan also told him that Garrett and his wife had come here one Christmas and it had saved their marriage. Matthew only hoped it was the perfect place to start theirs.

Fourteen

As the plane made its descent onto the island's tiny runway, Nina turned to him. "They could have used this place for the opening shot of *Fantasy Island*. The island is gorgeous."

Matthew leaned over Nina to get a better look of the island outside her window. From this vantage point, he could see lush, green foliage, colorful flowers, and a waterfall that flowed into a large pool at the side of the mountain. A large villa, their destination, sat at the island's peak, though smaller houses, most of them no bigger than small huts, dotted the hillside. The far side of the island boasted a resort community. Nathan hadn't been kidding when he said he knew a perfect spot.

When they debarked from the plane, a young man was waiting for them beside a gray van. *"Bienvenido,"* he said as they approached. "Welcome. I'm Lucius. The Tremaines sent me to pick you up."

"Where are they?" Matthew asked. He was looking forward to meeting the elderly couple Nathan had described as real characters. They had owned the island until a couple of years ago when they sold it to Nathan and continued to serve as its caretakers.

"They were called off the island, but they should be back this evening."

Matthew helped Nina into the van while Lucius loaded their luggage into the back of the van. The three of them set off on a road that was barely more than a dirt path through dense foliage. If the island had seemed beautiful from the air, its lush plants and flowers were breathtaking up close. He squeezed Nina's hand, drawing her attention. He didn't know why he'd made the gesture, but he was rewarded with a beatific smile from her, one full of excitement and expectation. Maybe he wasn't the only one who saw this trip as a means of setting their marriage off on the right foot.

Lucius pulled the van into a circular drive that boasted an ornate fountain at its center. The house that loomed before them had been built in the Spanish style with a beige stucco exterior and a tiled roof.

"Here we are," Lucius said as he drew the van to a halt. "If you give me a minute to take your bags upstairs, I'll give you a tour."

Lucius got out of the van. While the younger man retrieved their luggage, Matthew helped Nina out. "This is some spread," Nina said, surveying the house.

"Hmm," Matthew agreed, but the interior of the

house was more impressive. He was no connoisseur of art, but he suspected the wealth of pre- and post-Colombian works that graced the house was both authentic and quite expensive.

Lucius led them to a set of rooms on the east wing of the second floor and deposited their bags on the carpet. "If you need anything, I'll be in the garden."

"Thank you," Matthew said, but when he tried to tip the young man for his troubles, Lucius held up both hands and looked at him as if he were crazy.

"I'll be in the garden," Lucius repeated, then left, closing the door behind him.

Matthew shrugged and put his money back in his pocket. He focused on Nina, who had stepped farther into the room, surveying her surroundings. "What do you think?" he asked.

"If there was any doubt in my mind why they called this the red suite . . ." Nina let her voice trail off as she looked around the room. Although the walls were painted white, every accent in the room was colored some shade of red. Even the paintings on the walls were rendered in the same colors and featured provocative poses of men and women.

Matthew opened the door to the bedroom and started laughing. Nina went to his side, peeked in, and gasped. An enormous heart-shaped bed with a scarlet coverlet dominated the room.

Matthew chuckled. "I think we've discovered the Mount Airy Lodge of the Caribbean."

"If there's one of those giant champagne glasses in the other room, I'm leaving."

With an arm around her waist, Matthew pulled him in front of her and nuzzled her neck. "It's not that bad, is it?"

"Ten bucks says my brother fixed this all up as some sort of practical joke."

"What makes you say that?"

"The rest of the house is so, so . . . tasteful. If I didn't know better, I'd swear I wandered into somebody's love den from the seventies. All we'd need is a bong and a lava lamp to complete the picture."

He wrapped his arms around her from behind and nuzzled her ear. "I'll bet you another ten bucks that's a water bed under that hideous cover."

She glanced at him over her shoulder. "Why do you sound so hopeful when you say that?"

"I can be as hedonistic as the next guy. Let's find out." He lifted her in his arms and carried her to the bed. As he sat down with her on his lap the bed beneath them sloshed. He ran a finger along the square neckline of her dress. "Looks like someone owes me ten dollars."

"So it does. But I left my purse in the other room. You'll have to take it out in trade."

"I intend to." He cradled her face in his palms and brought her mouth down to his for a series of soft, sweet kisses that left her breathless.

When he pulled back, he grinned up at her, his gaze both hot and playful. His hand settled on her thigh, roving upward and back. "So what do you want to do now?"

Her heartbeat revved in response to his husky entreaty, anticipating what was to come. "You know very well what I want to do now."

"Do I? Maybe you'd better give me a hint."

She pushed at his shoulders and he obliged her by falling back on the bed in feigned helplessness. She turned, kicking off her sandals, and came over him with her knees between his parted legs and her hands braced against the mattress. "Does this give you a clue?"

His hands rose to cover her breasts, which threatened to pop out of her dress in this position. He quickly freed her. "Then let it all hang out, baby."

She laughed, but as his mouth closed over one of her nipples, her breathing hitched. "You're really enjoying this seventies stuff, aren't you?"

His tongue flicked against her nipple. "Unlike some people here, I actually remember them."

"I remember them too. I wore diapers then."

"Ouch," he protested, lying back and regarding her with playful, narrowed eyes. "Are you trying to call me old?"

"If the dashiki fits . . ."

He tickled her and, squeezing her eyes shut, she collapsed on top of him. He rolled her over so that she lay on her back with him on his side facing her. As her laughter subsided, she smiled up at him, her hand stroking the side of his face. How this man pleased her. What other man did she know secure enough in himself to be able to joke with her at such an intimate moment?

He turned his head and kissed her palm, and suddenly the humor between them had fled. She watched his head lower toward hers, but a movement above caused her to look upward. At the last moment, she turned her head so that his kiss landed on her ear. "Are you aware there's a mirror on the ceiling?"

His lips nuzzled her neck as his hand roved over her body. "You just noticed that?"

She shrugged. Her attention had been so focused on him she hadn't paid attention to anything else. But now that she'd noticed it, she couldn't seem to look away, fascinated by the way his hands, his lips moved over her body. Her fingers went to the back of his shirt, freeing it from his pants. Her fingers slid under the fabric to touch his bare muscled back.

His response was to yank the shirt over his head and toss it to the floor. He didn't stop until he'd divested them both of their clothing. And then he joined her again, his mouth at her breast, his fingers exploring the soft flesh between her parted thighs. Her gaze locked to the image of the two of them that hung above her.

He lifted his head and looked down at her with hooded, darkened eyes. "Are you watching us, baby?" he asked. "Are you watching what I'm doing to you?"

"Yes." She moaned and her back arched as his lips touched down on the sensitive valley between her breasts.

"And now?"

"Yes."

His lips moved lower, skimming over her rib

cage and lower. She jerked as his tongue, hot and moist, delved into her navel. "And now?"

He brought his mouth down on that most sensitive part of her, exploring her slick flesh with his tongue. Her fingers flexed, bunching the comforter in her hands, and she arched against him. Tiny shivers racked her legs as his tongue delved inside her. She gasped for air, enough to utter one syllable. "Yes."

She felt it almost immediately, the ache in the feminine places on her body, the tightening in her womb. She called his name, wanting him to be inside her when she came, but she couldn't hold it back. Pleasure exploded in her body and flooded her brain, making her cry out, contracting her body around him. He joined her then, thrusting deeply, and it started all over again, the exquisite tension followed by the ecstatic release.

She clung to him, her entire body perspired and trembling. She wrapped her legs around him and held him as his body shuddered with its own release. She welcomed his weight on her as they lay together, as their bodies cooled and their heartbeats steadied. Her eyes drifted shut, and for a brief moment she contemplated telling him she loved him. She felt it with every pore of her being, but she canceled that thought almost immediately. Simply loving him left her vulnerable enough without the added risk of confessing her feelings to him when she didn't know how he felt.

If he loved her, wouldn't he have said something before now? She thought of their time atop the Empire State Building. At that moment, she'd thought he was asking for something more from her, but he hadn't mentioned it since. Maybe she'd misread his intentions. Maybe he wanted less rather than more. Maybe when he'd shown up at her grandmother's house he'd done so hoping she'd back out and let him save some face.

But her body still tingled from his lovemaking. Could he arouse her that way, touch her that way, and still feel nothing for her? She supposed millions of men did it every day. Some had done it for her. Maybe, when all was said and done, all he really did want from her was sex—mind-blowing, earth-shattering sex, but just sex just the same.

It occurred to her that she should ask him what he felt for her. He'd been honest with her about everything else. She doubted he'd dissemble and try to tell her what he thought she expected. But that was the problem. Could she handle the truth if it wasn't what she wanted to hear?

Why Matthew chose that moment to lift his head to gaze down at her, she didn't know. She only knew he watched her. She kept her eyes closed, fearing he'd read her emotions in her eyes. With a gentle touch he stroked her hair from her face before lowering his mouth to hers for a brief kiss.

When he pulled back, his fingertips grazed her cheek. "Nina, look at me."

She complied and instantly she knew he sensed the turmoil of her emotions.

"What's the matter baby?" he asked.

She tried to inject a note of levity into her voice. "Other than you crushing my spleen? Nothing."

Judging from the lack of change in his expression, her attempt at humor failed completely, but he did move off her, rolling onto his side. She turned in the opposite direction, wanting a moment to collect herself.

But he followed, snuggling behind her, spoon fashion, and bringing the blanket to cover them both. He kissed her shoulder. "Nina, don't shut me out. Tell me what's bothering you."

Don't shut him out? That was the problem. She'd let him too far in already. But she could imagine how he interpreted her closing in on herself, especially after the powerful bout of lovemaking they'd just shared. She turned to look at him over her shoulder. "I'm not trying to shut you out."

His hand stroked her waist. "Then what would you call it?"

Having no answer for that, and not wanting to confess her concerns to him, she decided to take another tack. She shifted onto her back to look up at him. "Promise me something, Matthew. Promise me that for the time we're here we'll forget about everything else and just enjoy being together."

Under his intense gaze, she worried he'd say no, or worse, ask her what she considered everything else to be. But his expression softened and he stroked her cheek with the back of his fingers. "If that's what you want."

In an unspoken thank-you she brought his mouth down to hers for a brief kiss. One kiss turned to many and Nina was content to lose herself and her worries in the haven of Matthew's arms.

Later, the rumblings of Matthew's stomach woke him from the sleep that claimed him after the second time they'd made love. He flexed his hands, relieved to feel Nina's soft skin beneath his fingertips. How had it happened so soon that his first thought upon waking was to check to see if she was with him? His arms tightened around her. In response she burrowed closer to him.

At least in her sleep she turned to him. He lowered his head and kissed her temple. The way things were, he could almost be content. He knew that she had feelings for him. Given time, they might eventually turn to love. But every time she had the opportunity to let him in, she chose to keep him out. She didn't trust him. He didn't know what to attribute her distrust to, or whether it extended to the entire male half of the population or just him.

He'd promised her that they would put aside any concerns and enjoy being together. He intended to keep that promise, but her aloofness ate at him, because no matter how much she might care for him, if he didn't have her trust, he really didn't have anything at all.

Fifteen

Nina blinked her eyes open, her gaze settling on Matthew's smiling face. She smiled back, a lazy, contented expression. "Hi."

"Hi yourself."

She brushed the hair from her eyes. "How long have you been up?"

"Just a little while."

"And you've just been lying there staring at me?"

He chuckled. "I guess you could put it that way." He ran a finger down her cheek. "It's a man's prerogative to stare at his wife."

His wife. It still seemed a bit surreal to her, this marriage of theirs. Especially, she guessed, since nothing had been settled between them. That was mostly her own fault, since she took the chicken's way out and refused to ask him point-blank what his feelings were. And, although she hadn't expected him to, he'd agreed to put off the big questions for now. Maybe he wasn't ready to face the tough stuff either. For the present, she'd keep it light. They would both have enough to deal with once they got back home to the real world.

She ran her foot up one of his legs. "And it's a wife's prerogative to demand that her husband feed her. What time is it, anyway?"

"About five-thirty."

"That late? They must think we died up here or something."

"Or they figure we're a honeymooning couple doing what comes naturally."

"And doing it, and doing it," she teased, running her hand over his chest. "But seriously, I do think we should at least introduce ourselves to our hosts."

"Whatever Nina wants . . ."

"Whatever I want? This could get dangerous."

"You're telling me. Now get out of this bed before I change my mind." He swatted her bottom for emphasis.

She laughed and threw off the covers and jumped out of bed a moment before Matthew would have grabbed her again. She hurried off to the bathroom, smiling. She liked him like this, playful and lustful, and in some indefinable way, different than he had been before.

She set the tap for the shower and stepped inside. The warm spray of the water felt heavenly on her skin, but she got out quickly, surprised Matthew hadn't followed her. She found him still in bed, apparently asleep. She shook his shoulder. "Matthew, you lazy thing, wake up."

His response was to grab her and pull her down to him so that she lay half on the pillows, half across him. He nuzzled her neck. "I love the smell of freshly bathed woman in the afternoon."

She giggled and hit him on the shoulder. "You'd better hurry up and get ready or it will be evening and I still won't have any food."

"Spoilsport." His hold on her eased. "All right, I'll behave myself." He extricated himself from her and stood. Nina lay on her side for a moment, watching him walk away from her. She sighed. If she followed the directions of her thoughts she'd never get any dinner. She rose and went into the other room to find her suitcase.

Fifteen minutes later, they headed down the stairs in search of Verity and Aristotle. They found one-half of the couple in the kitchen. Verity stood at the stove top built into the room's center island, stirring something in a large pot. The moment she saw them a broad grin broke out across her face.

"Well, if it isn't the dead risen from the grave. For a while there we thought we'd opened the house to a pair of ghosts." Verity waved them forward. "Come in here and let me get a look at the two of you."

She wiped her hands on the terry cloth apron around her waist and came around the island to embrace Nina. Stepping back, Verity planted her hands on her hips and tsked. "You look just like your brother. Too skinny, too. Don't worry, we'll fatten you up while you're here."

Nina blinked. No one had ever referred to her as skinny before. Then again, Verity topped her height by a good three inches and must have out-weighed her by fifty or sixty pounds.

Nina turned to Matthew, who had become the subject of Verity's interest. "You must be Dr. Peterson."

"Please, call me Matt."

"Well, Matt, you're a handsome thing, aren't you? And a doctor." She grinned at Nina. "Not bad."

She cast a wicked look at Matthew. "He'll do."

"Dinner is almost ready. I assume you two are hungry."

Nina patted her belly. "Starved, actually."

"Matt, would you see what that old man I'm married to is up to in the garden? He's taken to hiding out there whenever I have work for him to do." Before Matthew had a chance to agree, Verity ushered him out the door with the aplomb of a field general with a new recruit.

Nina suspected Verity's rushing Matthew out the door had less to do with concern for her husband than having a moment alone with her. Her suspicion was confirmed a moment later when Verity turned to her, a sheepish expression on her face. "I must apologize to you, Nina."

"For what?"

"For that knucklehead Lucius putting you in the wrong room. We had the master bedroom all set up for you. I swear that boy must sit on his brain, because he doesn't do anything else with it." Verity moved back to her pot on the stove and stirred vigorously.

"I admit I was a bit surprised at the, shall we say, decor?"

Verity snorted. "A few years back we had a friend of Aristotle's staying with us. An odd bird. He did up the room like that."

Hearing the disapproval in Verity's voice, she wondered why she hadn't redecorated. "Why didn't you change it?"

Verity lifted one shoulder and cocked her head to one side. "No need to. We have plenty of space otherwise." Verity shrugged again. "And every once in a while when the mister is feeling frisky . . ."

Nina stifled a smile. Somehow she couldn't imagine this woman, who had to be in her eighties, romping in that big bed with any man. "If you don't mind, we'd rather stay where we are."

Verity gave a wicked chuckle. "Suit yourselves. I have to warn you that we islanders have planned a little celebration for you."

"What kind of celebration?"

"An old-fashioned Milagran wedding ceremony. Actually, it's more of an excuse for everyone to meet you. We are all quite fond of your brother and his wife. I hope you don't mind."

Nina wanted to laugh, not with humor, but with irony. No matter what, they seemed to dig themselves in deeper and deeper with this marriage charade. "Sounds like fun."

The kitchen door opened and Matthew walked in with Aristotle following behind him. He greeted her with the same warm hug his wife had. "It's so good to finally meet you, my dear. What stories has this old hen been filling your head with?"

"Nothing you need to be worrying about, old man. Now supper is ready. You need to go wash up and you young people go out onto the lanai. Your dinner will be served there." Verity flicked her hands toward them. "Scoot."

Aristotle left the room grumbling about old, cantankerous women.

Laughing, Nina linked her arm with Matthew's and followed. "Have you got any idea where the lanai is?"

"Lucky for you, I do." He led her to a door that opened off of one of the sitting rooms. Nina stepped through the door onto a stone patio with a concrete overhang that protected diners from the elements. Wall sconces in the shape of burning torches lit the area. A small round table sat at the end of the path, set with white china and decorated with flowers and sweetly scented candles. Next to the table, a bottle of wine chilled in a bucket on a stand. Soft West Indian music wafted around them from overhead speakers.

Nina turned to Matthew. "It's lovely, isn't it?"

"No more lovely than the woman I'm sharing it with." He lifted her hand and kissed her wrist. Then he pulled her into his arms to dance with him.

Nina snuggled against him, enjoying the slow, steady rhythm, the warmth of his body, and the feel of his hands on her back. She buried her nose against his neck and inhaled the citrus of his cologne and the essence of the man himself.

She smiled as his mouth descended toward hers. But she sprang away from him a second later when she heard a coughing sound behind them. She turned to see Lucius, tray in hand, approaching them.

Matthew grinned, lacing his fingers with hers. "Since dinner is here, I guess we'll have to get back to dessert later."

Nina rolled her eyes at his attempt at humor and let him lead her to the table. Over a dinner of salad, fish stew, and glasses of fruity Milagran wine, they talked and laughed, shared stories from their work and their childhoods. As they lingered over black cake, she regarded Matthew, wondering how some things between them could be so easy while some things were so hard.

Well, part of that was her own fault. Her own need for self-protection created a wall between them she hadn't allowed him to breach. He wasn't the first man to fault her for not letting him in, but he was the first man she wanted to. The first man she wanted to trust, though she had no idea how to go about doing that. Maybe the next time he questioned her, she'd find a way to open up to him. How could he ever love her if he didn't know a thing about her?

When they got back to their room, Nina finally slipped into the peignoir set she'd bought. She opened the bathroom door and leaned against the frame dramatically. "What do you think?"

Matthew, already in bed, looked at her with a scorching gaze. "It's lovely; now come over here and let me take that off you."

"Such delicacy. No one would doubt you are a man of education and breeding."

"To hell with breeding. Come over here."

She did as he asked, sauntering over toward the bed while his hot gaze wandered over her. True to

his word, he divested her of the gown in about five
seconds flat and made such sweet love to her that
her climax brought the sting of tears to her eyes.
She blinked them back as she lay against him, her
cheek on his chest, waiting to recover.

"Are you okay, sweetheart?"

Hearing the concern in Matthew's voice, she
lifted her head. "I'm fine."

He brushed away the lone tear that made it past
her lashes with his thumb. "Then why does making
love to me make you cry?"

"It doesn't. I . . ." Not knowing what else to say,
she trailed off, burrowing her nose against his
neck.

Matthew held her to him, stroking his hands
over her back. Here they went again. Her shutting
down the moment he tried to dig beyond the su-
perficial. He'd promised her he'd back off, and he
would as far as their future was concerned. But he
needed to understand her, and that couldn't wait.

"How many men have there been before me?"

She lifted her head and stared at him with a
look that was part incredulous and part annoyed.
"Don't tell me you want to do that whole past
lovers postmortem thing now."

"No. I'm just trying to figure out who hurt you
so much that you shut me out over the simplest
things."

Her eyes narrowed and she shook her head.
"You men. You always think it has to do with you.
No man hurt me. I've never allowed any man to get
close enough *to* hurt me." She rolled away from
him, onto her stomach, pulling up the blanket to

cover herself. She turned to look at him, clearly angry now. "No, I take that back. There is one man who hurt me. My father."

Her gaze became belligerent, as if daring him to question her. Maybe he was treading where he shouldn't, but he knew he'd tread anyway. "What did he do?"

"He deserted my mother when I was two months old and died before I got up the nerve to ask him why he abandoned us. I was too young to know, but my grandmother says my mother never recovered from his leaving. These days we'd probably call it clinical depression, but then . . . " She sighed, shutting her eyes. "She died of a combination of alcohol and sleeping pills her doctor had prescribed for her. Everyone says it was an accident, but I don't know. I only remember her as a sort of sad woman who felt no joy in life, no love for anyone, especially not me"

She turned away from him, onto her side, and tucked her hands beneath her head. "Are you happy now? I shared."

He hadn't expected her to share that. But her confession explained a lot about her: her aloofness, her self-reliance, given that both her parents had abandoned her in one form or another. He understood, too, why her grandmother's illness had thrown her so much. Luz had probably been the only real parental influence in her life.

And due to his insecurities, he'd caused her to revisit all that. With his arm around her waist, he pulled her back against him. "I'm sorry, baby. I'm so sorry," he whispered against her ear. Then she surprised him by turning in his arms and snuggling against him. Her fingers stroked his arm, his back, wherever she could reach. After a moment, realization hit that she was trying to soothe him.

She gazed up at him, both the anger and hurt gone from her expression. "I shouldn't have gotten angry with you. You couldn't have known. I should have been more up front with you from the beginning about how screwed-up my life has been. I'm new at this laying-your-guts-out-on-the-table stuff."

"It's okay, sweetheart. I shouldn't have pressed you so hard, either." But he wondered how she could manage to stay dry-eyed while recounting that story, when making love made her weep. "At the risk of pressing my luck further, why were you crying before?"

She gritted her teeth, then huffed out a breath, but he could see the humor in her eyes. "For the last time, I wasn't crying. Do you really need me to say it? That last time was so incredible. I got a little emotional, okay?"

"You couldn't tell me that?"

"No. I don't want to end up with a man with an ego the size of Cleveland."

Relieved, he laughed and pulled her on top of him and hugged her to him. "And I was lying there wondering if I could ever have enough of you, Nina Ward. I'd just made love to you, and simply having you next to me, I wanted you all over again. I have the feeling I'll be lying on my deathbed one day and I'll be begging you for one more time before I go."

"You keep doing your job right and you won't have to beg."

He took her face in his hands and brought her mouth down to his. Her hands roved over his chest, but before anything else started between them, he wanted to share a bit of honesty with her himself. He owed her that for finally letting him in.

"Understand something, Nina. The money has nothing to do with why I agreed to this marriage. I care for you, more than any woman I've ever known. I wanted to know where things would go with us, and I thought you'd clear out, leaving me the option of gaining my inheritance with some-one else's help. That's the only reason."

"That's the reason I asked you to marry me, sort of in reverse. I knew you wanted the money and I would have felt horrible for you to lose it while we waited to see what developed between us."

That admission surprised him, not because he thought she didn't care for him, but because he knew she did. Yet, until now she'd done everything possible to protect her heart from him, to keep him from knowing how she felt about him. Even her disclosure about her parents wasn't the same as telling him flat out that she hadn't wanted to lose him.

He didn't know to what to attribute this change in her. Maybe it was the ring on her finger and the piece of paper they'd signed, but he doubted it. Maybe it was this place, an island in the middle of nowhere, that worked its magic on her. Maybe they didn't call it Island of Miracles for nothing.

Sixteen

Nina woke the next morning and stretched languidly. From somewhere above her she heard Matthew's voice.

"Well, if it isn't the dead come to life," he said in imitation of Verity's voice.

She opened her eyes and smiled at him. He sat on the bed beside her, already dressed in a T-shirt and jeans. "What time is it?"

"Almost nine o'clock."

"Why didn't you wake me?"

"I like watching you sleep."

"Voyeur," she accused.

"Only sometimes." His hand caressed her breast and his thumb strummed against her nipple. "You'd better get out of this bed or we'll never make it to our destination today."

Nina drew in a ragged breath. "Where are we going?"

"A little spot Aristotle told me about." His hand

drifted lower to swat her bottom. Now get out of this bed."

"All right, all right. Give me fifteen minutes to get ready."

"I'll be waiting for you downstairs." He kissed her cheek, then left her.

She threw off her covers and padded off to the shower, a smile on her face. Undoubtedly Matthew had picked a spot where they could be alone together. It only took her ten minutes to wash and dress in a pair of shorts and a T-shirt. She applied a minimum of makeup, pulled a brush through her hair, slid on a pair of low-heeled sandals, and declared herself ready.

When she got down to the kitchen, both Verity and Aristotle sat at the small kitchen table enjoying coffee and scones. After greeting them, she asked, "Where's Matthew?"

"Out back," came Aristotle's answer. "You two have a good time, but be back by nightfall."

"We will."

She pushed through the kitchen door and drew up short. Matthew was standing beside an ancient-looking motorcycle, securing one of the saddlebags.

"What are you doing with that thing?" she asked.

Grinning, Matthew straightened. "Getting ready to ride it. Lucius lent it to us for the day."

"Well, give it back. All the bolts will probably pop off that thing before we've gone ten feet."

He folded his arms in front of him, the expression in his eyes challenging. "Don't tell me you're afraid of a little motorcycle."

"No, I'm afraid of *riding* a little motorcycle. And shouldn't you know better? Don't you doctors call them *donor* cycles because of all the folks who end up brain-dead riding those things?"

"Those people don't wear helmets. I've got one for each of us."

She inhaled and breathed out an exasperated sigh. Obviously, he didn't intend to change his mind. "I will get on that thing under two conditions."

"Which are?"

"You refrain from giving me one of those ridiculous Motorcycle Mama pet names."

"I promise. What's the other condition?"

"No laughing when I scream my head off."

"Fair enough. Come on."

After putting on his helmet and hers, he slid on to the bike and helped her on behind him, explaining where to put her feet. He jumped on the starter and the engine roared to life beneath them. "Ready?" he asked.

"Aren't I supposed to hold on to you or something?"

"You can if you want to, but you won't fall off if you don't."

She slid her arms around his waist, clutching at him for dear life. Hearing him chuckle, she smacked him on the shoulder. "I thought you weren't going to laugh at me."

"I agreed not to laugh if you screamed." He rubbed a hand along her arm. "Relax, sweetheart. I know what I'm doing. I've owned a bike since I was sixteen."

"Okay." She squeezed her eyes shut and pressed her lips together. "Go ahead."

The bike pulled off, jarring her with its sudden burst of speed. But after a few moments of traveling the dirt road that led away from the house she opened her eyes and relaxed her grip on him. They weren't going very fast, maybe forty miles an hour, but she had to admit the ride was exhilarating. And the scenery was breathtaking. Lush tropical greenery grew on either side of the narrow road punctuated by colorful flowers of every hue. Before she knew it, Matthew was drawing to a halt beside a high waterfall that flowed into a wide pool surrounded by multicolored azaleas.

He put down the kickstand, pulled off his helmet, and looked back at her over his shoulder. "That wasn't so bad, was it?"

She pulled off her own helmet and shook out her hair. "Actually, it was kind of fun. What are we doing here?"

He took the helmet from her and helped her off the bike. "According to Aristotle, this waterfall flows from an ancient hot spring underground. Among the islanders, swimming in it is supposed to promote fertility."

"I take it you didn't bother to tell him that we have no use for the spring's powers."

He shrugged. "Do you honestly think swimming in some warm water promotes anyone's fecundity?"

"Spoken like a true doctor, but no."

"Then see it as I did: an opportunity to spend the day in a beautiful tropical spot all by ourselves."

"When you put it that way . . ."

Matthew bent and kissed her cheek. "Come help me spread the blanket."

Ten minutes later, they sat on the blanket, sharing the breakfast Verity had prepared for them: fresh fruit, scones, and coffee. Nina finished her last bit of scone, wiped her hands on a napkin, and lay down on the blanket. She closed her eyes and let the warm sunshine wash over her and the tropical breeze stir her hair. She inhaled and the mingled scents of exotic flowers filled her nostrils. She sighed contentedly. "I'm not moving from this spot. Ever."

Matthew's soft laugher reached her ears. "Not even for a swim?"

She turned her head to look at him. "I'd consider it, except someone here neglected to mention I'd need my suit."

"You won't. This is private land. No one around here but us."

"In that case . . ." She sat up and tugged off her T-shirt. "Last one in . . . well, you know the rest." She shed the rest of her clothing, while Matthew lay back watching her with a heated look in his eyes. She stuck her tongue out at him and headed toward the pool. The water at the edges was shallow, but toward the center it was over her head. Nina immersed herself in the warm water. When she came up, Matthew remained on the blanket, sitting up now, watching her.

"Do you plan to stay on that blanket the whole day?"

"Just a little while longer."

"Suit yourself," she called back, "but this water is

divine." She closed her eyes and floated on her back, enjoying the warmth of the water and the heat of the day. For the first time since she could remember, she felt carefree and happy and expectant in a good way. She wished Matthew would join her. She opened her eyes and scanned the glade, but saw no sign of him. An instant later, she felt him behind her, his arms enveloping her, pulling her back against him.

His breath fanned her cheek as he whispered in her ear, "You didn't think I'd let you have all the fun without me, did you?"

"I hoped not." Her breath caught as his hands moved over her body, over her breasts, and between her thighs. After a moment, he turned her to face him. His mouth claimed hers and his fingers gripped her hips, pulling her against him. She arched against him and clung to him with her arms around his neck and her legs around his waist. And then he was inside her, filling the length and breadth of her, moving with such exquisite slowness that it made her ache. Burying her face in the crook of his neck, she whimpered her frustration and her arousal.

One of his hands stroked her back in a soothing manner, while the other gripped her buttocks, holding her in place. "Shh, baby," he whispered. "We've got all the time in the world."

"You enjoy torturing me."

"Um-hmm," he admitted.

She wrapped her legs more tightly around him, drawing him deeper inside her. A smile of satisfaction turned up her lips as he groaned and his grip on her tightened. Suddenly, the tenor of their lovemaking shifted from slow and languorous to fast and impatient. Their mouths met and their tongues danced a wild tattoo. She hung on to him as pleasure, deep and all-consuming, washed over her. She buried her face against his neck as his own release claimed him.

Somehow he managed to get them both out of the water and onto the blanket. She lay on her back as the late morning sun beat down on them, feeling sated, enervated, and good for nothing more than doing exactly what she was doing— basking in the afterglow of her husband's love-making.

After a moment, she felt him shift beside her. She opened her eyes to find him looking down at her with his head propped up on his hand. "How are you doing?" he asked.

She smiled, partly in answer and partly out of humor. "Do you know, you ask me the same question every time?"

He stroked a lock of hair from her face. "I always want to know the answer."

"Bull. You want me to tell you how fabulous you were."

"Not true. But if you wanted to give, say, a thousand-word dissertation on the subject, I wouldn't stop you."

She laughed and smacked him on the shoulder. "Cut it out. You're no egomaniac."

"No? Then what am I?"

She touched her fingertips to his cheek, letting her gaze wander over his handsome, smiling face.

"You're sweet and sensitive and sexy as hell, and . . ." She trailed off, knowing the next words that would have come out of her mouth were *and I'm in love with you*. She didn't know whether she was ready to voice that sentiment just yet.

But he picked up on it anyway. He kissed her eyelids, her cheeks, and finally her mouth. When he finally drew away, he asked her, "Are you in love with me, Nina?"

She shook her head. "No fair, Doctor. You've asked me that question twice without answering it once yourself. Are you in love with me, Matthew?"

"Yes. I have been for some time now."

She had expected straightforwardness from him, but she hadn't really expected that response. She shook her head again, as if doing so would shake out the answer she wanted to hear and leave her with the truth.

"Why does that surprise you so much? I as much as told you the same thing last night."

"I know." But she hadn't really trusted his words. Men were bound to say all sorts of things they thought a woman needed to hear in order to keep her contented. Men were bound to promise all sorts of things they had no plans on delivering. But none of those men, the ones she'd known anyway, were anything remotely like Matthew. She wondered what it was inside her that didn't allow her to take him at his word.

From somewhere deep inside her she gathered up the courage to say the words she knew he waited for. "I love you, too, Matthew."

He closed his eyes and buried his face against her throat. "I didn't think I'd ever hear you say those words."

Her arms closed around him, stroking his back in a soothing motion. "Why not?" She'd assumed he must have some inkling as to what she felt for him.

He lifted his head and there was such a wistfulness in his eyes that it tore at her. "Because you don't need me, Nina. We both know that if I hadn't come into your life, you wouldn't have missed me. You were looking for something else and I happened along." He tugged on a strand of her hair. "Don't think I'm complaining, because I'm not. I'm not ashamed to admit I'll take you any way I can get you."

He winked at her and rolled away from her to stand and walk to where they'd left the motorcycle. "Hungry?" he asked, as if the previous conversation had never happened.

She shook her head, both as a refusal and because she didn't understand him. She turned onto her stomach and rested her cheek on her folded hands. If anything, he didn't need her, except as the means by which to gain his inheritance. And despite the earnestness of her words, he hadn't believed her, either, when she told him she loved him. God, what a pair they made.

She felt him settle beside her, but she didn't look at him. She concentrated on the heat of the sun on her back rather than the icy dread that pervaded her that the two of them would never get things on track.

Then the warmth of his body replaced the warmth of the sun. He lay beside her, half covering her. He tilted her toward him, giving him access to her body. His hand roved over her breasts, her belly, and lower. His lips feathered tiny kisses along her shoulder. And then he was inside her, firing a different kind of warmth deep within her. She clung to the arm banded around her waist and forgot for a few moments that no matter what they said, nothing had really changed between them.

The Milagrans, Matthew mused, as he stood beside Aristotle in the clearing, were an interesting group of people. Some tall, some dark, some fair, some short, some with blue eyes, others with green or gray or a brown so dark they appeared black. Aristotle described the people here as a combination of native Indian and runaway slave with a smattering of European blood to spice up the mixture. And every one of them seemed to be crammed into this little glade in the middle of the woods, waiting, like him, for the bride's arrival.

He did his best to stifle a yawn behind his hand. After a day spent swimming and making love au naturel, he was tired. Although Nina had fallen asleep in the heat of the afternoon sun, he'd remained awake, pondering the admission she'd made. She told him she loved him. Even now, thinking about it filled him with a combination of relief and foreboding. He hadn't lied to her when he said he thought he'd never hear those words. He'd figured that when the six months was over, she'd slip out of his life as effortlessly as she'd slid in. Part of him wished she would, because no matter what, he knew he'd been unfair to her in going through with this marriage. Unfair, because when it came down to it, he knew he couldn't give her what she really wanted.

Before he met her, he couldn't imagine ever regretting his decision. He couldn't imagine wanting to trace over old wounds, both literally and figuratively. Part of him wished he'd met her before he'd forsaken the chance to give her the children she wanted. As the day wore on, that part of him grew stronger, seeing the love that shone in her eyes when she finally came to meet him, the joy in her eyes as the Milagrans welcomed her with their most precious gifts, their children.

They flocked to her, and she loved them all, letting them sit on her lap, listening to their stories, accepting their hugs and watery kisses. At one point, her beaming gaze met his. She had a baby in her arms, a toddler in her lap, and several little ones around her feet. His throat lurched and his stomach cramped, knowing all that he deprived her of.

Aristotle elbowed him, jarring his attention away from Nina. "Maybe you'd better go rescue your missus if you intend to get out of here tonight."

"Maybe you're right." The Milagrans didn't show any signs of wanting to call it a night, and Nina didn't seem anxious to have them leave. He set the bottle of Red Stripe he'd been nursing on the table and walked toward her. "Are you ready to go?"

"Sure." She handed the tiny baby in her arms to

one of the women around her while the toddler scooted from her lap. She took the hand he extended toward her and rose from the chair, but it was another fifteen minutes before they managed to escape, as the Milagrans, child and adult, all wanted to wish them well.

When they got back to their room, they settled on the sofa in the living room part of the suite. "Did you have a good time?" he asked.

"You know I did. You're not mad at me for ignoring you in favor of the kids?"

"Of course not."

She shifted and licked her lips. "Did you see that baby I was holding? The little boy?"

"Yes," he answered hesitantly, wondering what she was leading to.

"The poor sweetie. He's not doing well."

"I know." Aristotle had already told him about the infant being born with tetralogy of fallot, a congenital heart defect that caused oxygenated and nonoxygenated blood to mix in the bloodstream. Without surgery, the boy would certainly die. Even with surgery, he would be at risk for heart failure and other conditions, as well as expect a shortened life span. "What about him?"

"Ironically, his name is Mateo, which is Spanish for Matthew. Both his parents are dead. They're looking for someone off the island to adopt him. There's no one here who can care for him. They don't have any doctors here."

She looked at him with such a hopeful expression that alarm raced along his nerve endings. "Don't look at me like that, Nina."

"Like what?"

"Like you want me to agree to adopt that baby."

"I admit I was thinking about it." She paused, running her tongue along the seam of her lips. "Would it be such a terrible idea?"

He stood and shoved his hands in his pockets. "We've been married four days. Nothing is settled between us. I haven't even moved my things into your apartment. And you want to bring a baby into that?"

"Who better than a pediatrician to adopt a sick child."

"And what about you, Nina? A child that ill needs constant attention. Are you willing to give up your career, everything you've worked so hard for to care for it? Are you willing to spend your nights worrying if it will survive from one day to the next? Are you willing to do that for a child that's not even yours?"

"He *would* be mine if we adopted him." Her eyes narrowed and she regarded him closely. "Matthew, you're a physician, you see sick children every day."

"Where I work. Not in my home."

"So only a healthy child will do? Is that really why you had the vasectomy? Life couldn't guarantee you a healthy child so you opted for none?" She shook her head. "I never would have expected that from you. As much of a snob as you claim your mother is, I couldn't imagine her turning her nose up at the prospect of a sick child. Maybe she's not the real snob in the Hairston family."

She stared up at him with a mixture of anger and disappointment. He couldn't blame her. Without explanation, his reaction to the baby must seem inexcusable. Worse yet, she'd hit close enough to home for her words to really sting.

But he didn't know what to tell her. He was no longer sure how he felt anymore or if it was possible for him to let go of a hurt that had claimed him since childhood. He only knew that at that moment, her happiness weighed more heavily on him than his own.

"Ask me anything else, Nina. Ask me anything else, and if I can give it to you I will. But not that." He turned and walked away from her, went to the balcony in their room, and stared out at the night sky, seeing nothing but clouds.

Seventeen

They spent the rest of their time on the island swimming, sunbathing, making love. To outward appearances, nothing between them had changed. Yet Matthew sensed Nina's profound disappointment in him. He didn't know what to do about that, because every time he brought up the subject of the baby, she changed it. Suddenly, rather than their growing closer, a widening chasm had opened between them. He didn't know how to reach her and she seemed unwilling to reach out to him.

The morning after they arrived home, he went to his apartment to retrieve the items he intended to move into Nina's apartment. His sister, dressed in a pair of decent blue jeans and a shirt that covered her navel, greeted him at the door with an enthusiastic hug.

"How was paradise?" she asked, stepping away from him.

"Beautiful. I'm glad to see you're giving that bathrobe of yours a break."

"I'm done with my pity party for one. Are you hungry? I'm just finishing up breakfast. That is, if the eggs didn't burn."

He lifted his eyebrows in a comical way. "You? Cooking breakfast? This I've got to see."

She shot him a droll look. "I can cook, at least well enough not to poison anybody—unintentionally, that is."

Once they were seated at the kitchen table with eggs, bacon, toast, and coffee in front of them, he asked her, "How much does Nina's cousin have to do with the end of bathrobe fever?"

"Who, Nelson? How big brotherly of you. I spend fifteen minutes talking to a man and you figure something hot and heavy is going on."

Matthew speared a piece of egg with his fork. "It was more than fifteen minutes and I wouldn't object if there was something going on."

"That's good to know. If I ever find myself getting turned on by muscle-bound Neanderthals, I'll give him a call."

"Then what were you two getting so cozy about during the engagement party?"

"That's none of your business."

He put down his fork and speared her with a look that said otherwise.

Frankie sighed. "He's a private investigator. I wanted him to investigate something for me. He said no, so that's the end of it."

"Does this have anything to do with why you won't go back to Atlanta?"

"Yes, but that's all I'll say about it. We should be talking about you. You're the one who just got back from his honeymoon. How was it?"

"Wonderful."

Frankie crossed her arms in front of her. "Okay, what did you do?"

"What makes you think I did anything?"

"You walked in the front door."

"I came here to get some things to take back to Nina's."

Frankie held up both hands as if weighing two things. "Spend the morning in bed with my new wife, get some clothes." The side for staying in bed won. "You wouldn't be here if everything was okay, so spill it."

He told her about Mateo and watched a look of horrified concern come over her face. In a quiet voice, she asked, "Why didn't you tell her the truth, Matt?"

"It would be nice if I knew what that was. Is it that thirty years ago I watched my kid sister die and I've never gotten over it? Or is it that I've taken the coward's way out, ensuring that I never have to deal with any of that again? I didn't tell her because what she wanted to know didn't concern that baby or any baby in particular. She wanted to know how shallow her husband is, and I didn't have an answer for her."

"Oh, Matt, you're not shallow at all. And you want to know something funny? Part of the reason Mom and I don't get along is Claire, and I wasn't even born when she was alive. I've always felt she was the daughter Mom wanted. I've seen pictures of her, the perfect little lady Mom has always tried to make me into. I've always felt that the only reason they had me was that Claire died, and I don't measure up."

"You're not being fair to yourself, Frankie. We all love you, navel ring and all. Besides, Mom confessed to me she was more like you as a young girl than she has led you to believe."

"Somehow my mind can't seem to wrap around that possibility. But I do know you aren't being fair to yourself, either. Nina loves you. You owe her some explanation of how you feel."

He agreed with Frankie on one point: Nina did deserve an explanation from him. But did she love him? Maybe she'd started to, but he wondered if he'd crushed her budding feelings by not leveling with her.

Matthew sighed and sat back in his chair. His appetite had fled and his disposition had worsened. He'd already packed what he wanted to take with him. "I'm going to get what I came for and get back uptown." He rose from the table and got ready to go.

As he stood at the door ready to leave, Frankie embraced him again. "Talk to Nina. I'm sure she'll understand."

He nodded, but a sense of hopelessness pervaded him. His dread increased when he got back uptown to find that Nina had left him a note saying she'd gone in to her office to check on a few things. He'd hoped she would have been there and they could have talked while he still had the nerve to do so.

Rather than remain in the empty apartment, he prowled around Manhattan, having no clear destination. The city had a different cadence during the weekend, still hectic, but less stressful. Suddenly, he found himself on Fifth Avenue, a block or so away from the Empire State Building. The day he had proposed to her seemed like a lifetime ago, when in reality it had only been a few weeks. He'd vowed to himself that morning he wouldn't let her get away, not if he could help it. But could he help it? The decision of whether or not to stay was in Nina's hands, not his. And his greatest fear was that she would find it easier to simply walk away.

Nina got back to her apartment early in the afternoon. She had expected to find Matthew waiting for her. Instead she found Yasmin ensconced on her sofa, talking on the phone and drinking a glass of the only bottle of wine Nina had in the house. "I gotta go," she told whoever was on the other end of the line, clicked off the phone, and tossed it onto the sofa. "Hey, cuz," Yasmin said, embracing her. "How was the honeymoon?"

"How did you get in here?" Nina stepped back from her cousin.

Yasmin shrugged in the dramatic way she had. "I bribed your doorman to let me in."

"I swear, that man makes out like a bandit with this family." Yasmin scooted over to accommodate

Nina sitting beside her on the sofa. "Okay, what are you doing here?"

"I came to hear all the juicy details and to see how you two were doing. Speaking of which, where's your other half?"

"Good question." Nina set her handbag on the coffee table. "I thought he'd be here."

"Don't tell me there's miscommunication in paradise already? Aren't you folks supposed to wait a couple of years for that?"

"I wish I'd thought of that."

Yasmin folded her arms across her chest. "What did you do?"

"We had a fight, sort of. Or a disagreement. I don't know what you'd call it. I want children and he doesn't."

"You're kidding. Dr. Miracle doesn't want kids?"

Nina almost laughed at the incredulous note in her cousin's voice. "No, he doesn't."

"Did you know that before you got married?"

Nina sighed. "I knew but I didn't know. I thought I'd change his mind."

"And you don't think you will now?"

"No."

She expected Yasmin to ask her why she'd changed her mind, but she didn't. In a quiet voice she asked, "Is that a deal breaker for you?"

"I don't know." The prospect of losing Matthew was untenable. So, too, was the idea of going through life without children. As things stood now, she faced one scenario or the other. "Why does everything in life have to be so hard?"

"If it weren't hard it wouldn't be life. It would be a fairy tale."

Nina snorted. "I hate it when you get profound. I'm supposed to be the older, wiser cousin."

Yasmin grinned. "Hey, everybody needs a little help now and then." Yasmin leaned her temple against Nina's shoulder. "You have to make up your mind what you want."

True, but before she did that, she needed to apologize to Matthew. She'd spent the last few days punishing him for having convictions she'd known about almost from the beginning. She'd accused him of vile things with only the tiniest provocation. He didn't deserve that from her. She planned to set that right between them when he got home tonight. She only wished she knew when that might be.

Nina was waiting for him in the kitchen when he finally returned that evening. She didn't ask him where he'd been or what he'd been thinking about, and in some ways he was grateful. He went to her and wrapped his arms around her from behind and kissed her ear. "I didn't expect you to fix anything. I thought we'd go out to eat tonight."

"It's my turn to cook."

He'd forgotten that long-ago conversation about taking turns in the kitchen. "I guess I'm on call for tomorrow night then."

"Yup, and if you think I'm eating Spaghetti-Os or tuna sandwiches you're out of your mind."

"I'll have to see what I can come up with. How about Spam? Everybody loves Spam."

She looked back at him over her shoulder, her eyes twinkling green in the fluorescent light. "I don't even allow Spam in my kitchen let alone my mouth."

He hugged her to him, enjoying her playfulness, sensing a subtle change in her that pleased him even if he didn't understand it. With a heavy, drama-filled sigh, he said, "Back to the drawing board."

"If you plan on eating tonight, you'd better wash up. Everything's almost ready."

"Yes, Mom." He released her to go to the hall bathroom to do what she asked. As he washed his hands, he surveyed himself in the mirror above the sink and called himself a coward. He'd come home with the intention of bridging the gap that had opened between them. More than anything, he'd been relieved to find Nina in a mood recep-tive to him and kept his mouth shut. He couldn't put it off much longer, though.

He tried again as they settled into bed for the night. He lay on his back and pulled her to his side. Surprisingly, she came to him eagerly, laying her cheek on his shoulder, while her fingers wove a tantalizing pattern on his chest.

He covered her hand to still it. "We need to talk, Nina. I want to tell you something, an explanation for why I reacted the way I did on the island."

She lifted her head to look down at him, a solemn expression in her eyes. "You don't have to explain yourself to me. You told me from the start that you didn't want children. I was foolish enough to believe I could change your mind."

"Nina—" he started, but she cut him off with a finger against his lips.

"No, let me finish. I want to tell you that I admire you for sticking to your convictions. I wish more people would realize they're not cut out to be parents and not have them rather than abusing the ones they have or neglecting them as punishment for being born, like my mother did to me. I'm sorry I said what I did, but if you don't mind, I don't want to talk about it anymore."

He sighed because he didn't know whether to press forward or let it be for the moment. She took the decision away from him by pressing her lips to his. When she pulled back, she said, "I'm going to church with my grandmother tomorrow."

"Okay," he said hesitantly, wondering what she was leading up to.

She laid her head against his chest. "Next weekend I'm scheduled to go to a writing conference in Dallas."

More confused now, he asked, "Why are you telling me this?"

"It's customary to let the person you're living with know where you are going to be. I figured you might notice if I didn't come home for a few days."

He laughed, not with humor, but at himself. She was telling him in her own way that he'd worried her by disappearing without telling her where he was going or when to expect him back. He threaded his fingers through her hair. "I'm sorry, baby. I'm not used to having to answer to anyone about my whereabouts. Even so, you have my beeper number if you need me."

"I hadn't thought of that."

"Remember it for next time."

"There better not be a next time." She lifted her head again. This time the expression in her eyes contained equal parts of desire and another emotion he couldn't read. "Make love to me, Matthew," she whispered.

She brought her mouth down to his. Despite her entreaty, she took the lead and he didn't try to wrest control from her. He let her have her way, let her set their pace. But afterward he gathered her against him, running his hands over her soft, lax body, contented that she fell asleep in his arms.

Yet, sleep evaded him for a long time. He didn't know what to make of this woman who lay in his arms. She'd forgiven him, even though he was the one who had done her an injustice, not the other way around. He forced her to make a choice. Had she given him her answer tonight? Would she give up the one thing she truly wanted just to be with him?

Maybe it was best he hadn't said anything to her. He needed to settle something within himself first. He'd do that first thing the next morning. Then he'd make things right with her, if he still could.

Nina awoke the next morning and instantly knew she was alone. She stretched and her arm bumped a piece of paper lying where Matthew's head had lain. She picked up the note, written in a doctor's

barely legible script. *Had to take care of something this
morning. Matthew.*

She exhaled. He left her no clue as to where
he'd gone or what he had to do, but he had taken
her hint last night and not gone out without telling
her something. Though she wondered what urgent business he might have before seven o'clock
on a Sunday morning, she didn't dwell on it too
long. No matter what happened between her and
Matthew, she had some business of her own to take
care of.

She dressed and called a taxi to take her to her
grandmother's house in Queens.

Eighteen

The first surprise awaited Nina as her taxi pulled up in front of her grandmother's house. The driveway and curb in front of the house were occupied by cars she recognized as belonging to her aunts. The Wicked Witches didn't usually show up anywhere together unless there was a family function. To Nina's knowledge, there wasn't anything going on today, which was why she'd come.

Letting herself in with her own key, she first noticed the sound of feminine voices and laughter. *"Mami,"* she called out, hoping to catch her grandmother's attention.

"Shoot, we've been found out," came a muffled voice, followed by more hushed laughter.

"We're in here," Luz called back. And then in a quiet voice, an admonition, "You girls behave yourselves."

Smiling, Nina made her way to the kitchen. Her imagination must be playing tricks with her. Her aunts and grandmother were seated around the kitchen table. Wine and snacks were laid out before them. Each of them raised her glass to her.

"If it isn't the new bride," her aunt Carla said. "What are you doing here?"

"I could ask the same question. I'd think all of you would be in church today."

"We're playing hooky today," Genie said.

"Hell, I haven't been to mass since the pope said women shouldn't use birth control," Jackie, Yasmin's mother, said. "Just like a man to try to tell women what to do with their bodies."

Carla, the oldest, shot her sister a warning look. "Let's not get started on that again." She stood. "Come, sit down. Tell us about your trip."

Marie, the youngest, teased, "Carla only wants to hear all the details so she can get a vicarious thrill."

"Are you trying to imply I need a man? Please, who wants one? They're big and smelly and nothing but trouble."

"They think they know everything. And they're bossy."

"They take up the whole bed and they snore."

"They think that penis of theirs is the Holy Grail. Who wants something dangling off them like that? They can have it."

"Find me one of them who can get it up these days without Viagra. I'm serious. Someone find me one, please," Jackie teased.

"Oh, you're as man crazy as your daughter," Luz protested.

"You got that right. She takes after her mama."

Nina looked from one woman to the next. These could not be the women she'd grown up with, who seemed discontented with everything in life. "Who are you people, and what have you done with the sisters Grimm that usually show up to family gatherings?"

"How else do you think we've kept you young people in line all these years?"

"I wanted my son, Nelson, more afraid of me than anything he'd find out there in the streets," Genie said.

"You think it's easy raising kids alone?" Carla asked. "At least with a man around, it's another set of eyes to see what the kids are doing, another pair of arms to hug them, another person to turn to when times are tough." She looked around the table. "Am I right, girls?"

The others nodded. "And look at you kids," Marie added. "You've all grown into fine adults, professional people. We didn't lose a single one of you to crime or drugs like so many other families we know."

"We hung together and hung tight—and nagged you folks into doing what was right."

"And, seriously," Marie said, "I don't want it to sound as if we are bashing men, here. We joke around, but that's all it is. I know I'd give anything to find a man half as decent as your uncle Arthur. I'd snap him up in a minute."

Jackie said, "Saint Arthur, you mean. You better start focusing on the mere mortals if you expect to find a man. Now, I admit my Victor was a piece of work and I'm glad to see him gone, but for whatever reason, none of us had great luck with the men we married, not that we didn't want to. It just didn't work out the way we planned."

Finally, Nina asked the question that had brought her here in the first place. "What about my mother? Why did my father leave her?"

Nina noted the looks of concern that passed between her aunts and her grandmother. Jackie stood. "Come on, ladies. I've got some pictures from my trip to Cancun I haven't shown you yet."

The others filed out, grumbling at the prospect of seeing any more of Jackie's pictures, trying unsuccessfully to give credence to the excuse to leave Nina alone with her grandmother.

After they left, Luz took the seat next to her. "I always figured you'd get around to asking me that question. But, *mijita,* you have to promise me you won't share with your brother what I'm about to tell you. He adored her and I don't want to see his memory of her ruined."

"I promise."

Luz sighed. "Your mother was always discontented, even as a little girl. She always wanted what she couldn't have and what she got she never wanted. It was that way with your father. She wanted him and she made sure she got pregnant to keep him."

Nina's eyebrows lifted. She'd always assumed Nathan's conception had been the proverbial accident, and it surprised her to find out it wasn't.

"Your mother got what she wanted, but she still wasn't happy. Your father was a musician, he traveled, he was out late at night, most times she had to fend for herself. Truthfully, I think the only reason they stayed married as long as they did was that they saw so little of each other.

"Your mother had decided to leave him when she found out she was pregnant with you. In those days, no self-respecting man would allow his pregnant wife to walk out on him. They fought through the entire pregnancy, but your father was so happy the day you were born. He and Nathan had never really bonded, your mother saw to that. But from the beginning, it was clear you preferred him to your mother. One night, you must have been about two months old, they fought again and she told him that you weren't his, that neither of you were."

"Why would she say such a thing?"

"Out of vindictiveness. To hurt him. And she succeeded. He packed his bags, saying that if neither of the children was his, there was no point in ever coming back. Realizing her mistake, she tried to tell him she lied. But there are some things said in anger or the heat of the moment you can't take back. Do you know what I mean?"

Nina nodded. She thought of the harsh words she'd spoken to Matthew on the island, and her own fear that he wouldn't forgive her for them. "That's why he left?"

"Mostly." Luz exhaled a heavy breath. "Your father came to me. We got along and we both commiserated over the fact that the only person your mother ever seemed to truly love was your brother. Don't ask me why that is, because I don't have an answer for you.

"He came to me to ask me if I believed what your mother said was true and I told him yes. Your mother had already called me, in tears, claiming that your father had left her to pursue a relationship with another woman. Prideful as she was, your mother didn't want to appear at fault for your father's disappearance. Frankly, it wouldn't have surprised me if it was true, nor would I really have blamed him for anything except not ending his marriage first.

"He came to me because he trusted me to tell him the truth as I knew it. When I said yes, I confirmed what she'd told him without knowing it. I'll always regret that I never asked him what he meant or never went after him once he walked away from me, looking shaken and defeated. I don't know why I didn't, but that's the last time I ever saw him.

"About a year later, she moved back in with me and confessed everything that happened. I felt sick about the part I'd played in that drama, even if it had been inadvertent. I tried to contact your father, but he wouldn't listen to me. There was no DNA testing then to prove conclusively that he was your father, and between the two of us, your mother and I had planted the seed of doubt so firmly, he wouldn't listen to reason."

"Is that why she hated me so much, I was the cause of her breakup with my father?"

"No. She didn't hate you. In her own way she loved you, but I think it finally caught up with her, all that she had lost due to her own dealings. I can only imagine her guilt at depriving you and your brother of your father."

"Looking back, I think she was probably depressed."

"Maybe. I'm no shrink. I do know she was having trouble sleeping. We had a party one night. I don't remember what for, probably someone's birthday. We had all had wine with dinner. Your mother hadn't been feeling well and wanted to lie down for a few minutes. She must have forgotten about the wine and taken one of her pills. She never woke up."

"Then she didn't intend to kill herself?"

"Oh, no. She had plans for you, both you and your brother. A few days before, she'd opened a bank account in your name. She was saving for your college education or your marriage, whichever came first. I added to it over the years. It was the money that sent you to Vassar. Your mother wanted to see you grow up. It was an accident that prevented her from doing that."

Nina closed her eyes and pressed her lips together, fighting back tears. How could the truth be so much different than she'd imagined it all these years? She'd always assumed neither of her parents had wanted her, but both of them had. She'd lost each of them in tragedies that had nothing to do with her. She hadn't been the cause of anything. Relief, as well as a host of other emotions, skitted through her, vying for attention.

She felt her grandmother's hand on her knee. "Are you okay, *Mijita?*"

She opened her eyes and focused on her grandmother's concerned face. "That's a lot to take in all at once."

"I know, but I wanted you to know the whole truth, nothing held back. That's what you wanted, wasn't it?"

She nodded. "I'm glad you told me, and I agree Nathan shouldn't hear a word of it."

Luz sighed. "Men and their mamas. One day when you have that little boy you'll know what I mean."

She shook her head, as resignation took its place at the fore. "I don't think that's going to happen. Matthew doesn't want children."

Luz seemed unfazed by her admission. "Trust me on this. He'll come around."

"Is that your graydar talking again?"

"No. What I say comes from knowing him. He's a good man, a sensitive man. As a pediatrician, he's seen tragedies that you and I can only guess about."

For some reason Nina suspected her grandmother wasn't telling her all she knew. "Do you know something I don't?"

"Yes, and I'm not going to tell you either. Ask him about it, he'll tell you."

Nina nodded. She knew he would. He was the most straightforward man she knew. But she also knew that whatever he told her wouldn't be pleasant.

Luz smiled, encouragingly. "Do you suppose we should let those busybodies back in the room now? I'm sure they listened to every word we said, anyway."

"We did not," came a protest from the other side of the wall.

Nina stood as her aunts filed back into the room. "I've got to be going anyway. I have a new husband who's probably waiting for me at home."

That comment incited several more ribald jokes. As Nina hugged each of them good-bye, she was glad she'd happened on their gathering and gotten to see these women through adult eyes rather than those of a child. But as she rode the subway home to the city she wondered what Matthew could possibly have to tell her.

Matthew arrived at Woodlawn Cemetery in the Bronx a little after two in the afternoon. He hadn't been here since his grandmother died when he was seven. At nine, he'd refused to go to Claire's funeral and his parents hadn't forced him. He'd grieved for her, but he'd never said good-bye to her, never let her go.

Finding the DeWitt mausoleum wasn't hard as it lay along a path that led to newer aboveground crypts near a pond populated by geese. He sat on the white stone bench in front of the mausoleum. He didn't know what he'd come here to say, or if at this point he had anything to say. He knew only the physical remains were buried here, not the mind, not the spirit, not the essence of the person who had passed on.

Now that he was here, it wasn't Claire's death that haunted him, but his own life. He'd loved his little sister, and felt the impotence of knowing he could do nothing for her. In his heart, he knew that experience had led him to pediatrics, the doctor's power to heal. But in many ways, that, too, was an illusion. Kids got sick and died every day, and the emergency room was no place to go if you expected to hear good news. He could no longer count the number of parents to whom he'd had to deliver bad news, but their faces were all the same. They all reacted the same: their features would seem to crumble, the tears, the grief. He'd been on the receiving end only once, and he never wanted to face that again.

He'd always considered himself a pragmatic man, able to look truth in the eye. But he'd been deluding himself. Nina had accused him of having the vasectomy because life couldn't offer him any guarantees, and he saw now that she was right. Life couldn't offer him any guarantees so he'd taken the option away. He'd made the decision because he was afraid some other man in a white coat would one day come to him and give him some dreaded news. Then he'd be the one whose face would mirror his grief, and his life would be the one forever changed.

He'd saved himself from his greatest fear, but at what cost? He'd denied himself the chance of fatherhood and risked losing the woman he loved because he couldn't allow her to give up her desire for children even if she agreed to it. Together, they would have to work something out, or he'd have to let her go. That was the only fair thing to do.

He stood and placed the single white rose he'd brought on the entrance to the mausoleum. It was time to go home to Nina and whatever the future held for them.

When she got home, Matthew wasn't there and there was no sign he'd ever come home from wherever he'd raced off to that morning. Nina prowled around the empty apartment, a feeling of unease gripping her. She fixed dinner but couldn't bring herself to eat any of it. She checked the clock for perhaps the fiftieth time since she'd been home. Almost ten o'clock, and still no word from him. Where could Matthew have gone that would keep him out all day?

She thought of the trip up to Scarsdale and dialed his parents' number. His mother told her they hadn't heard from him since the day they were married. Margaret was in a talkative mood, interested in discussing how well the wedding had gone off. Nina indulged her, partly because she didn't want to insult her mother-in-law, and partly because she didn't want to go back to worrying about Matthew without anything else to occupy her mind.

She tried his sister next. Frankie told her that he'd been there early in the morning to use the phone, mooch breakfast off her, and get his bike. But she hadn't seen or heard from him since he walked out the door.

She didn't know why, but she called her brother's house, hoping to talk to Daphne. Nina didn't know what she expected her sister-in-law to do, especially since she didn't intend to tell her that she didn't know where Matthew was. Maybe she simply wanted to hear a friendly, sympathetic voice.

Garrett answered the phone, surprising her. "What are you doing there?" she asked after they exchanged hellos.

"Unfortunately, finishing up a completely indigestible meal your brother cooked. Who did you want to talk to?"

She hesitated, hearing voices in the background and laughter. Obviously, the two couples were having a good time. They didn't need her dampening their good spirits when she wasn't sure anything was really wrong. "Just tell Daphne I'll call her tomorrow."

"Better yet, why don't you and Matt join us? We'll be here another hour at least. You can bore us with your honeymoon photos. What do you say?"

She opened her mouth to refuse, but other words rushed out instead. "I don't know where he is."

"What do you mean?"

Now that she'd opened her mouth, there was no turning back. "He went out this morning and he hasn't been back."

"Did you beep him?"

"No." Despite what he'd said last night, because he was a doctor she viewed beeping him as a desperate measure, a last resort in an emergency. Well, what did she have now, if not that? She'd disturbed both his family and hers, when the man probably didn't have enough sense to know when it was time to come home. "I'll try that now."

"Sweetheart, if you're worried, one of us can come and stay with you until he gets back."

"That's not necessary. We're both getting used to this letting-each-other-know-our-whereabouts thing." She tried to inject a note of humor into her voice. "If you hear any screams coming from the west side of town, that's me killing him for scaring me half to death."

"Call us here when he turns up. We'll come over and help."

"Will do." She disconnected the call and dialed Matthew's beeper number. She left her number and a message for him to call her. She paced the floor in front of the phone, waiting for him to call. But an hour passed and she didn't hear from him. Dread clutched at her, as she contemplated the only possible reasons for his lack of communication with her: he wouldn't call her back or he couldn't call her back.

She didn't know which possibility terrified her more. God only knew what could have happened to him riding that motorcycle. Horrible images of Matthew broken or bleeding or dead filled her consciousness. She pressed the heels of her hands to her eyes to banish those images.

If he was hurt or injured, wouldn't somebody call? Somebody always called. Someone from the hospital or morgue to tell you that they had your loved one. But the telephone hadn't rung since Matthew's mother called her back hours ago wanting to know if Matthew had turned up yet.

She remembered his hesitation before making love to her last night. And somehow the quality of their lovemaking had been different. She'd noticed it at the time, but had dismissed it. Maybe he hadn't really forgiven her for what she said to him. When she thought about it now, she realized he'd never said anything one way or the other, not that she'd given him the opportunity to do so.

No. The Matthew she knew wouldn't just disappear on her. He'd tell her flat out if he intended to leave her. Which meant he had to be in some sort of trouble somewhere, didn't it?

She turned things over and over in her mind, coming to no conclusion. About midnight, she tired of pacing the floor. She hadn't eaten, hadn't slept. She felt drained and exhausted and so worried, she didn't know where to put herself. She lay down on the bed in her darkened bedroom and tried to close her eyes. But the images came back, stark and horrifying.

"Where the hell are you?" she asked the empty room in frustration.

Despite everything she'd ever told herself about never falling apart over a man, she turned her head into her pillow and wept. Tears streamed from her eyes, but she made no effort to hold them in check. Tears stored from a lifetime of disappointments, fueled by fear for her husband and their future together. Her only certainty was that she loved him and wanted to spend her life with him. All other considerations paled in the presence of that knowledge. As they both knew, life didn't offer any guarantees. She didn't know if she herself could even conceive, but without Matthew, finding out didn't hold the same allure.

She cried until a fitful sleep claimed her. She tossed and turned until the phone rang at six o'clock in the morning. Garrett Taylor was on the other end.

"I've found Matthew. He's at Our Lady of Mercy Hospital in the Bronx."

Nina brushed the hair from her face and the remnants of tears from her eyes.

"How is he? What was he doing up there in the first place?"

"I'm afraid I don't know the answer to either question. If you give me half an hour I'll pick you up and take you there."

"It's a deal." She thanked Garrett and hung up. In fifteen minutes she was dressed and waiting for Garrett in the lobby of her apartment building, alternately filled with hope that Matthew was okay and filled with dread that he wasn't.

Nineteen

Nina sat beside Garrett in his Navigator as he drove to the hospital, her hands gripped together in her lap. As they stopped at a red light, Garrett's big hand covered both of hers. "Don't worry. I heard back from my friend. Matt's okay. He suffered a concussion and a couple of cracked ribs but other than that he's all right."

Nina closed her eyes and exhaled the breath she'd been holding since Garrett first called her. "Thank God." Despite her relief, anger welled up in her. "What is wrong with you men and your motor-cycles?"

"It wasn't the bike. According to a bystander who came to help him, he was bumped by a van full of kids. He went down but he was all right. But the bump hadn't been an accident. They probably saw the MD plates and thought he had money. Four dubious specimens of humanity piled out of the van. One of them rode off on the bike while the others robbed him of everything else of value on him. All in broad daylight."

"If that's true, how did he end up in the hospital?"

"Do you honestly think your husband simply lay there while these punks waylaid him? Apparently it took all three of them and a tire iron to take him out."

She glanced over at Garrett, incredulous. Only a man would see that as an accomplishment. "You mean he could have come out of this unharmed if he'd let them have their way?"

"Well, if you put it that way . . ."

Nina snorted. "How did you find him anyway? I didn't know you were looking."

"When you didn't call back, I got worried. I know Matt. He's not the type to run off somewhere without telling anyone. I called around a few places, but didn't find out anything. Since they'd taken his wallet, he came in as a JD, John Doe. And since there was a major pileup on the New England Thruway, a bus, a tractor trailer, and a passenger car got into it, finding out that the identity of an unconscious and uncomplaining patient wasn't high on the hospital's list of priorities."

"I suppose not."

Garrett patted her hand. "As I said, don't worry. He's fine."

Nina pressed her lips together. But the question of the hour remained. Were they?

* * *

Matthew had spent the night drifting between consciousness and slumber. Of the two he preferred sleep. In slumber there was no pain, and Nina was there, her gentle fingers caressing him, her tender smile warming him.

He could swear he was awake now, but Nina was here. And she was crying. His right arm didn't seem to work, so he lifted his left to brush the tears from her face. "Shh, sweetheart," he soothed. "Don't cry."

"I can't help it. Why didn't you just let them have the bike?"

His head cleared, and he remembered being forced off the road and bits of what happened after. "I don't give up what's mine without a fight." And that included her. He took her hand and rubbed her knuckles with his thumb. "I'm sorry, Nina. I'm sorry I worried you needlessly. I'm sorry I've been an ass about so many things."

She stared down at him with a confused expression in her eyes. "What are you talking about?"

He didn't know where to start, so he picked the beginning. "Do you remember when you said you couldn't imagine my mother turning her nose up at a sick child?"

"Of course."

"That's because she didn't. I had another sister, Claire. She came along three years after I did, and was born with a congenital heart defect, much like the baby on the island. These days, they've perfected ~~~ect so many problems, but in those was prayer. She died when I

"I'm so sorry, Matthew. That must have been so hard for you. You were so young."

"It was. But it was understandably worse for my parents. Looking back on it, I think Claire's death nearly cost them their marriage. Whenever something happens to a child, those responsible for that child always blame themselves, not just parents. Sometimes older brothers."

"You were a child, Matthew. What could you have done?"

"Nothing, but that didn't stop me from feeling powerless. I feel that way sometimes as a doctor, but in a way it's medicine that's failed, not me. Sometimes there's just nothing possible for humans to do.

"That's hard to take as a physician, but as a parent? I didn't want to ever discover what it would be like as a parent. I made a mistake, Nina. I was afraid, pure and simple, and fear is no basis on which to make life-altering decisions."

"What changed your mind?"

"Remembering that as tragic as her death was, I wouldn't have given up knowing Claire for one moment. Remembering that for every kid that comes in either seriously ill or injured, there are ten more who just have a bean stuck up their nose. There's good and there's bad, and I'd only focused on the bad for a while."

He rubbed his hand up her arm. "I'm willing to take the chance that things will turn out all right for us." He inhaled and let out a heavy breath. "I hear they have a urologist that specializes in reversing vasectomies."

Surprisingly, she laughed. "If you could see how green you look right now you wouldn't expect me to take that offer seriously."

"I am serious, Nina. I know how much having children means to you. Do you think I could be happy depriving you of that?"

"Having children, yes. Bearing them, no. Being a mother has nothing to do with how many stretch marks you have. Besides, I don't want you fooling around with perfectly good equipment and messing it up. There's something I'd never forgive you for."

"Then what do you want?"

"A little boy who needs a loving home and an operation, both of which we can provide."

"Mateo."

She nodded.

"I had a feeling. I already spoke to Aristotle and Verity this morning, as well as an attorney. She doesn't think we should have any problem bringing him to the States."

She threw herself on him and hugged him. He didn't mind, though the pain in his ribs trebled and he could barely breathe. She seemed to realize that, as she pulled back almost immediately, patting him as if to make sure she hadn't crushed anything. "Thank you, Matthew."

"No, baby. I'm the one who should be thanking you. I was walking around with blinders on and would never have known it if it weren't for you."

"So instead you've got your head in a bandage and your arm in a sling. I told you, this macho crap is out."

"I'll remember that the next time I get the urge to hit someone's blunt metal object with my head."

She groaned, an exasperated sound. "What am I going to do with you, Matthew Peterson?"

"Spring me from this joint and we'll figure it out." With a hand at her nape he pulled her mouth down to his for a kiss that held the promise of tomorrow.

Epilogue

Standing at the front of the church, Matthew shoved his hands in his pockets and rocked back on his heels, his eyes scanning the entryway for any sign of Nina. It had been her idea to renew their vows on their one-year anniversary. So where the hell was she? Not even her grandmother, in whose home she'd spent the previous night, knew where she'd disappeared to.

His gaze slid to the crowded front pews of the church. The first time they got married, the guests had separated along traditional family seating. Today, they were seated however they pleased and it pleased him that the two families blended together so well.

And sandwiched between his mother and Nina's grandmother was the group he referred to as the peanut gallery. In the past year, they'd either adopted or were in the process of adopting four children. Mateo, his namesake, had been the first. He was eighteen months old now and finally starting to walk. So far, his treatment had provided a better outcome than any of them had expected.

The second, a girl, tall for her six years and athletic, had been born with a facial deformity that needed correction. Matthew had talked Garrett's friend Robert Delaney into waiving his fee as a plastic surgeon to complete the first of the operations she would need.

Last there were the twins, who were physically perfect but scarred emotionally from neglect. Child Protective Services had rescued them from the filthy vermin-infested apartment where their alcoholic mother had abandoned them.

Not to mention all the other children they had become unofficial godparents for, the ones helped by the Claire Hairston Foundation that he and Nina had begun but his mother now administered. Suddenly spending money on the same things didn't seem like such a bad idea after all.

Now they lived on a twenty-acre spread with horses, dogs, cats, and a menagerie of rodents, most of which they intended to house. Life was better than he had ever anticipated it to be. He'd have nothing to complain about if his wife could manage to show up to their wedding.

As his gaze traveled to the entryway of the church, Nina rushed in, unmindful of the fact that she'd caught everyone but him unaware. The guests rushed to stand while the organist scrambled to play the wedding march. The poor woman must have placed her hands on the wrong keys and treated all assembled to a hasty, discordant rendition of "Here Comes the Bride."

"Matthew, we have to talk," Nina said when she reached him.

He scanned her appearance. She wore an off-white satin dress that clung becomingly to her curves, but the flowers in her hair had gone askew and her cheeks were tinged with color. She looked as if she'd sprinted halfway here rather than just down the aisle. "Now?"

She nodded. "I got a call from Missy Malone at ACS this morning. There was a couple who were supposed to adopt a baby boy born a week ago at Einstein Hospital, but they backed out when they found out the baby wasn't perfect. The mother lied to them and told them she'd gotten off drugs or maybe she started using again, I don't know. But he was born with cocaine in his bloodstream."

Which could cause all sorts of neurological or learning disabilities, not to mention forcing a newborn to undergo withdrawal in the first few hours of life. "Where is he?"

Nina turned her head toward the back of the church. He hadn't noticed another woman come into the church, a woman who held a bundle that could only be a baby. He turned back to Nina, who looked up at him with a familiar expectant look in her eyes.

"He's ours if we want him. Other than that, Missy has to take him to be put in a foster home. I know we decided no more children, but just one more, Matthew. Please, just one more."

That's the same thing she'd said when she brought home Liana. And when she'd found Dex. And when she learned he had a sister. He doubted this would be the last time, either.

But he saw the love shining in her eyes and knew both her heart and his could easily accommodate another child. He sighed and let his shoulders droop in a dramatic, put-upon expression. "I'm going to need another million just to put all these folks through school."

It took a moment for his words to sink in, but when they did, she threw her arms around his neck and hugged him fiercely. "I love you, Matthew," she whispered against his ear.

His arms closed around her, squeezing her tightly. "I love you, too, baby, but the natives are getting restless. We promised them a wedding and some dinner, and so far all we've given them is a show."

She grinned up at him. "Then what are we waiting for?"

"Damned if I know," he teased back. He took her hand and faced the priest. But he didn't need any man, robed or otherwise, to bless their union. Nina had already blessed him with her love and her courage. Everything else was gravy.

Later that night, Matthew settled under the covers of the king-size bed in the hotel room they'd rented for the night. In the morning they were set to catch a plane back to Milagro Island. Nina had claimed to want to see Aristotle and Verity again, but he suspected their big red bed was actually what she wanted to revisit. He hadn't succeeded very well in taming the tigress, but she was his tigress, so he wasn't complaining.

The bathroom door opened and she stepped out wearing a skimpy white nightie and a pair of slippers with fuzzy poofs on the front. "You like?" she asked.

He laughed low in his throat. He didn't know why she wasted good money buying lingerie that lasted two seconds before he had her out of it. "Come here," he said, beckoning her forward with a curl of his finger.

She did as he asked and once he had her in his arms on the bed, he claimed her mouth for a lingering kiss. He pulled back and studied her face, her smiling mouth, and her exotic hazel eyes. "We're not going anywhere tomorrow, are we?"

She shook her head. "How can we go away with a new baby in the house?" She touched her fingertips to his cheek. "You're not sorry, are you?"

"Of course not. I'm looking forward to getting to know our latest edition." He tickled her side until she squirmed. "But you get the first week of changing dirty diapers."

"We have one night at least."

He knew she offered up their one night of escape from a house full of children as a consolation for their lost trip. But he chose to put another spin on her words. "No, baby," he said, "we have a lifetime."

Dear Readers,

I truly enjoyed writing Nina and Matt's story. I hope those of you who wrote to me asking for their story like the results. And just so you know, I have a story brewing for Nelson and Francesca, so the Thorne/Ward series isn't quite over yet!

As always, I would love to hear from you. You can contact me at deirdresavoy@verizon.net or at P.O. Box 233, Bronx, NY 10469. Or stop by my Web site at www.dsavoy.com.

All the best,
Dee Savoy

ABOUT THE AUTHOR

Native New Yorker Deirdre Savoy spent summers on Martha's Vineyard, where, as a teenager, she started writing romances. The island proved to be the perfect setting for her first novel, *Spellbound,* published by BET/Arabesque Books in 1999. She earned the first Rising Star Author of Romance in Color and was voted their Best New Author of 1999. Deirdre also won the first annual Emma award for Favorite New Author.

Deirdre's second book, *Always,* was published in October 2000, *Always* was a February 2001 selection for the Black Expressions Book Club. *Once and Again,* the sequel to *Always,* was published in May 2001 and was also selected by Black Expressions. *Midnight Magic,* the third book in the Thorne family saga, was a 2001 Holiday release.

Deirdre's fifth book, *Holding Out for a Hero,* published in September 2002, featured fictional hero NYPD detective Adam Wexler. Real-life firefighter Paul Haney, the winner of the 2001 Arabesque Man Contest, is on the cover.

In 2003, Deirdre's first hardcover and first anthology, *To Mom, with Love,* was published, along with her sixth novel, *Could It Be Magic?*

In her other life, Deirdre is a kindergarten teacher in New York City. She lives in Bronx, New York, with her husband of ten-plus years and their two children.